The Elizabethan Theatre VI

The Elizabethan Theatre VI

Papers given at the Sixth International
Conference on Elizabethan Theatre held at the
University of Waterloo, Ontario, in July 1975

Edited and with an introduction by
G. R. HIBBARD
Department of English,
University of Waterloo

Published in collaboration with the
University of Waterloo

Archon

Illustrations for "A Reconstruction of the Fortune
Playhouse: Part I" © Richard Hosley 1978

Illustrations for "The Presentation of Plays at Second Paul's:
The Early Phase (1599-1602)" © W. R. Gair

© The Macmillan Company of Canada Limited

Published in Canada by
the Macmillan Company of Canada Limited
and simultaneously published in the United States
of America as an Archon Book by
The Shoe String Press, Inc., Hamden, Connecticut.

Printed in Canada

Library of Congress Cataloging in Publication Data

International Conference on Elizabethan Theatre, 6th,
University of Waterloo, 1975.
The Elizabethan theatre VI.

Includes bibliographical references and index.
1. Theater—England—History—Congresses.
2. English drama—Early modern and Elizabethan,
1500-1600—Congresses. I. Hibbard, George Richard.
II. Title.

PN2589.I5 1975   792'.0941   77-7123
ISBN 0-208-01636-8

This book has been published with the help of a grant from
the Humanities Research Council of Canada, using funds
provided by the Canada Council.

Acknowledgments

Like its predecessors, the Sixth International Conference on Elizabethan Theatre, held at the University of Waterloo in July 1975, owed much both to public support and to private effort. Its major debts were to the Canada Council, the Ministry of Education for Ontario, working through its Department for Cultural Exchanges, and the University of Waterloo itself. The generous financial assistance they gave provided the basis for the entire undertaking, enabling the conference to bring together a strong team of speakers, culled from Great Britain, the United States, and Canada. And, after the conference was over, the Humanities Research Council of Canada supplied the subvention needed for the publication of the papers read at the conference. To all these bodies I express my most sincere thanks.

Warren U. Ober, Chairman of the Department of English at Waterloo, and J. S. Minas, the Dean of Arts, were always to be relied on for solid unobtrusive help with the preparations for the conference; and four willing students, Pam Constable, Laurel Lee Larocque, Brian Rahn, and Julia Schneider, took care of the daily business while it was in session. Once again Mrs. Diane Mew, then of the Macmillan Company of Canada, demonstrated her personal concern for the conference by attending all its meetings. *Music Four* delighted delegates with an admirable programme of Renaissance music and dances; and the Stratford Festival Theatre, perhaps without realizing that it was doing so, offered such a variety of performances that members of the conference were almost spoilt for choice.

The index was compiled by Theresa Dedyna.

G. R. H.

Contents

Introduction

John Marston was born in 1576; Cyril Tourneur and John Webster somewhere about the same time, the date usually accepted for both being *c.*1575. It therefore seemed appropriate that a conference on Elizabethan theatre, held in the summer of 1975, should focus much of its attention on the work of these three playwrights, especially as there are connections between them. Webster, we know, was responsible for some of "the Additions", most probably the Induction, made to Marston's *The Malcontent* when that play was taken over by the King's Men; and the author of *The Revenger's Tragedy*, whether Tourneur or someone else, appears to have been familiar not only with *The Malcontent* but also with two other plays of Marston's, *Antonio's Revenge* and *The Fawn*. Moreover, all three dramatists are of particular interest to students of the theatre: Marston because he wrote for the children's companies and studded his plays with some of the most elaborate and detailed stage directions that we have from the early seventeenth century; Webster because he underlines, with considerable bitterness, some of the shortcomings of the unroofed public playhouses, putting down the failure of *The White Devil*, when it was first performed, to the fact that "it was acted in so dull a time of Winter, presented in so open and blacke a Theater"; and Tourneur because of his brilliant exploitation of theatricality for serious ends.

The years 1599 and 1600 were of crucial importance for the theatre and the development of the drama. Two new theatres were erected and opened: the Globe, home of Shakespeare's company, in 1599, and the Fortune, home of their great rivals, the Admiral's Men, in 1600. At the same time two of the boys' companies were revived: the Children of Paul's in 1599, and the Children of the

Chapel in 1600. It is with different aspects of these matters that the first two papers in the present volume are concerned. The contract for the building of the Fortune, drawn up on January 8, 1600, between Philip Henslowe and Peter Streete, is the most valuable documentary evidence we have about the physical structure of any Elizabethan playhouse. But, while it tells us much, it also leaves much tantalizingly unclear, because the "plot" of the new building, frequently referred to in the contract, has not survived, and because many of the details are covered by the repeated phrase "like vnto the Stadge of the . . . Plaie howse called the Globe". Statements of this nature would have been perfectly intelligible to Peter Streete, who had been responsible for the erection of the newly completed Globe, but they leave the student of theatre architecture in the dark. Consequently, although the contract has been carefully examined on many occasions, there is still room for fresh interpretations of what exactly is being called for in it. Deploying his wide knowledge of the Elizabethan theatre in general and of building techniques in use at the time, Richard Hosley comes up with some novel suggestions about such matters as the depth of the stage, the height of the tiring-house, and the number and size of the bays into which the covered part of the auditorium was divided.

W. R. Gair's paper, "The Presentation of Plays at Second Paul's: The Early Phase (1599-1602)", is, both in matter and in method, a complement to Richard Hosley's. Beginning with an account of the setting-up of the second Paul's playhouse in 1599, he goes on to demonstrate that *Antonio and Mellida* and *Antonio's Revenge* are deliberately designed "to exploit all the special qualities of an indoor theatre" and to exhibit and advertize the innovations in technique that the composition of the company made possible. Then, using details from the plays known to have been performed by the boys as his evidence, he deduces from them the approximate size of the stage. Finally, he offers a most impressive argument to show that the site of the "howse neere St. Paules Church", in which the boys played, was, in fact, within the precinct of the Chapter House, so that their theatre "was at once part of and distinct from the cathedral fabric" and very much "a private house", in the sense that it was actually owned by a certain Mr. Haydon.

John Marston, who was so closely associated with the Children of Paul's, had begun his career as a writer with the publication, in 1598, of his erotic poem *The Metamorphosis of Pigmalions Image*, designed, he asserted, to satirize the Ovidian narrative so fashionable at the time and to take in those who looked to poetry for sexual titillation. Few then and few since have been prepared to take him at his word. The poem raises in an acute form the central issue posed by his work as a whole: how seriously do his professions of seriousness deserve to be taken? The answer, in so far as his plays are concerned, is likely to depend on whether one reads them as dramatic poems or as poetic dramas. William Babula, adopting the first of these approaches, accepts Marston's claim that *Antonio's Revenge* is intended to show "what men were, and are . . . what men must be." It portrays, he thinks, a world that is corrupt beyond all cure, and therefore not susceptible to the reforming efforts of the satirist. *The Malcontent*, on the other hand, he goes on to argue, presents a world that is indeed corrupt but not irredeemably so, with the result that Malevole is able to combine the roles of the avenger and the satirist in a play which is meant to be "educative", in the exemplary sense of that word.

Linking *The Malcontent* to *The Revenger's Tragedy*, R. A. Foakes, who has seen modern revivals of both plays in the professional theatre, takes the opposite line to William Babula's. For him, *The Revenger's Tragedy* is at one and the same time farcical and serious, amusing in its ironies yet disturbing in the challenges it offers to the moral complacencies of its audiences. By comparison with it *The Malcontent* emerges as something far less serious and much more concerned with the "cross-capers" that play such a large part in it. Marston has, of course, something to say about life, and what he has to say is not negligible, but it is confined to the dialogue and receives no support or validation from the action.

This observation provides a fortuitously neat transition to Neil Carson's paper on the early Webster who collaborated with Dekker in writing plays for the Children of Paul's. Carson thinks that the whole tendency of the drama up to 1599, or thereabouts, was towards greater and greater illusionism. The re-emergence of the boys' companies, however, reversed this trend, because those who wrote for them were acutely conscious that the boys were not capable of encompassing the emotional range that adult actors could. The playwrights therefore sought to emphasize the theatrical element in their work at the expense of the hitherto dominant illusionist element. But it was no easy matter for men such as Heywood and Dekker, strongly committed to illusionism, to do this. Consequently a play such as *Westward Ho*, "written during a period of aesthetic uncertainty", reveals "certain confusions of style". Some speeches in it are meant "to bewitch the audience", others are meant "to evoke their laughter or censure". Beginning his career in this uneasy atmosphere, Carson argues, Webster never escaped completely from it; the "tension between naive and self-conscious dramaturgy" persists into his mature work.

The relationship between the playwright and his audience, a subject touched on by both Foakes and Carson, is the explicit theme of M. C. Bradbrook's wide-ranging paper, "Shakespeare and the Multiple Theatres of Jacobean London". After surveying the various kinds of playing places that existed all over the country in the late sixteenth century, Professor Bradbrook points out that with the accession of James provincial progresses and plays declined, the dominance of the London theatres became absolute, and the Tudor myth was replaced by the "far less potent one of Troynovant". Implicit in this comment is a healthily sceptical attitude, soon developed in more detail, towards the tendency in some circles today to regard Shakespeare's later plays as "reflecting themes of the masque and of the court entertainment". On the contrary, Professor Bradbrook contends, the playwrights catering for the common stage, struck by the sharp contrast between court masques and court realities, made the masque a subject for irony in their plays. Far from being coterie works, Shakespeare's romances are written in "an open form", making an appeal to every kind of audience. She concludes by making some brief but incisive comments about some modern revivals and reinterpretations.

One such revival, the production of *The Revenger's Tragedy* by the Royal Shakespeare Company in 1966, is the subject of the paper by Stanley Wells. Seeking "to give an objective account of some features of the production, and of its reception", Dr. Wells draws on his own memory, on the promptbooks used, and on the numerous reviews that appeared in the press. The result is a fascinating study of attitudes both within the theatre and outside it. The Royal Shakespeare Company was not content to let the play stand on its own feet. Instead, John Barton wrote some extensive additions to it, given in an appendix to the paper, designed "to clarify the action"; there was extensive rearrangement of scenes and some were omitted altogether. Nevertheless, the play survived, largely through the acting ability of Ian Richardson and Alan Howard, playing Vindice and Lussurioso respectively, and in spite of notices in the popular press which revealed an almost total lack of understanding as to what it was all about.

Professor D. F. Rowan was prevented by illness from completing the paper he was preparing for the conference. In lieu of it the editor has included the text of a public lecture he himself gave at University College in the University of Toronto in the fall of 1975.

G. R. Hibbard
Department of English
University of Waterloo

A Reconstruction of the Fortune Playhouse: Part I

RICHARD HOSLEY

In this, the first part of a two-part essay, I examine some basic questions which have arisen in an attempt to reconstruct the first Fortune playhouse: depth of stage, height of tiring-house storeys, number and size of bays of the playhouse frame, location of yard entrances, and location of staircases. In Part II, to appear in Volume VII of *The Elizabethan Theatre*, I deal with remaining aspects of the reconstruction, among them seating and sightlines, the stage super-structure, and the design of the tiring-house facade.

The first Fortune was built by Philip Henslowe and Edward Alleyn during the spring and summer of 1600.[1] The site lay just outside Cripplegate between Golding or Golden Lane and White-cross Street, near the bars of the City of London and in the county of Middlesex. The parcel of land on which the playhouse stood was described in 1622 as measuring 130 ft. from east to west and 131 ft. 8 in. from north to south.[2] Unlike the majority of public playhouses, which were round buildings, the Fortune, like the Red Bull after it (*JCS*, VI, 215-16), was built to a ground plan in the shape of a square. The builder was Peter Streete, Carpenter, who appears to

1. Good general accounts of the Fortune playhouse are provided by Joseph Quincy Adams, *Shakespearean Playhouses* (Boston, 1917); E. K. Chambers, *The Elizabethan Stage (ES)*, Vol. II (Oxford, 1923); and G. E. Bentley, *The Jacobean and Caroline Stage (JCS)*, Vol. VI (Oxford, 1968). Contemporary documents relating to the Fortune are printed by Chambers, *Elizabethan Stage*, Vol. IV.
2. W. W. Greg (ed.), *Henslowe Papers (HP)* (London, 1907), p. 29. I am in some doubt about Glynne Wickham's suggestion that the playhouse was built in a courtyard; *Early English Stages*, Vol. II, Pt. 2 (London, 1972), pp. 111-13.

have been also the builder of the first Globe in 1599. Streete's contract with Henslowe and Alleyn, dated January 8, 1600, is preserved among Alleyn's papers at Dulwich College.[3] According to the contract, Henslowe and Alleyn agree to pay Streete £440 for materials and labour. (In his *Diary* Henslowe records that the total cost of the playhouse, presumably including the expenses of painting, for which Streete was not responsible, came to £520; *HD*, p. 302.) For his part, Streete undertakes to complete the work by July 25, 1600, "beinge not by anie aucthoritie Restrayned". The escape clause indicates the possibility of government prohibition of the playhouse, and so too does a warrant of January 12 from Alleyn's patron the Earl of Nottingham, Lord Admiral, to the Middlesex Justices of the Peace enjoining them to permit Alleyn to proceed with construction (*ES*, IV, 326). (One of Nottingham's arguments is that Alleyn's company of players, the Lord Admiral's Men, need a new playhouse because of the "dangerous decaye" of their present house, the Rose, on Bankside.) The possibility of opposition was soon realized, for on March 9 the Privy Council ordered the Middlesex Justices to prevent or inhibit building of the playhouse (*ES*, IV, 326). However, on April 8 the Privy Council again wrote to the Justices, this time licensing construction of the Fortune (*ES*, IV, 328); and on June 22 the council formally confirmed their licence, giving reasons for it as well (*ES*, IV, 329).

In the meantime work had been going forward, Henslowe on May 8 recording a payment on Streete's behalf "to the laberers at the eand of the fowndations" (*HD*, p. 314). Henslowe's records of expenditures for construction break off shortly after a payment dated June 10, but since he was taking meals regularly with Streete until August 8 (*HD*, p. 193), it seems likely that Streete's work was not completed until mid-August or later. Allowing time for painting after the end of construction, we may suppose that the Fortune probably opened in September of 1600. In 1601 there was a house, recently built by Alleyn, adjoining the south side of the playhouse (*HP*, p. 26); and in 1618 we hear of a messuage or tenement called the Taphouse which adjoined the playhouse (*HP*, p. 28). The first Fortune was destroyed by fire on December 9, 1621. According to John Chamberlain, who called it "the fayrest play-house in this towne", "It was quite burnt downe in two howres, and all their apparell and play-bookes lost, wherby those poore companions are

---

3. Printed in R. A. Foakes and R. T. Rickert (eds.), *Henslowe's Diary (HD)* (Cambridge, 1961), pp. 307-10.

quite undone" (*ES*, II, 442). Two years later the second Fortune, "a large round brick building",[4] was erected on the site of the first.

The Fortune contract gives dimensions of the "fframe" and "Stadge" of the first Fortune but tells us little about the "Tyreinge howse", the "shadowe or cover over the saide Stadge", or the "Stairecases". For these elements, therefore, we must rely on documents relating to other playhouses, chiefly the De Witt drawing of the Swan playhouse (*c.* 1596) and Hollar's depiction of the second Globe and the Hope both in his "Long Bird's-Eye View of London" (1647) and in the preliminary pen-and-pencil sketch for that engraving (*c.* 1640).[5] The builder's contract for the Hope (1613) also provides useful analogues for elements of the playhouse frame (*HP*, pp. 19-22).

There have been four noteworthy reconstructions of the Fortune playhouse: by Gottfried Semper in collaboration with Ludwig Tieck (1836),[6] by Walter H. Godfrey in collaboration with William Archer (1907),[7] by A. Forestier (1911),[8] and by C. Walter Hodges (1953).[9] The first two are historically significant, Semper's because it is the earliest reconstruction of any Elizabethan playhouse, and Godfrey's because it has had considerable influence on twentieth-century opinion about the Elizabethan playhouse in general. Forestier's reconstruction has some original features but is largely derivative from Godfrey's. Because of numerous assumptions that are no longer tenable, none of the three early reconstructions has been of much use in the present inquiry. The reconstruction by Hodges, on the other hand, has been of great help, not least in those instances where I have felt constrained to depart from it; and in such instances I have endeavoured to make clear the reason for my disagreement.

The Fortune contract provides that the playhouse frame shall be "sett square" and that it shall measure 80 ft. each way on the outside and 55 ft. each way on the inside (Fig. 1). The contract also specifies that the frame shall be 12 ft. 6 in. deep in the first storey, and this dimension is confirmed by the fact that the depth of the frame must

4. Joseph Wright, *Historia Histrionica* (1699); quoted in Chambers, *Elizabethan Stage*, Vol. IV, p. 372.
5. Reproductions in C. Walter Hodges, *The Globe Restored* (London, 1968; originally published in 1953).
6. Drawings in Wolf Grafen von Baudissin, *Ben Jonson und seine Schule* (Leipzig, 1836).
7. Godfrey, "An Elizabethan Theatre", *Architectural Review*, Vol. XXIII (1908); Archer, "The Fortune Theatre, 1600", *Shakespeare Jahrbuch*, Vol. XLIV (1908).
8. "The Fortune: A Reconstruction", *Illustrated London News* (August 12, 1911).
9. Reconstruction drawing in *The Globe Restored*, p. 151.

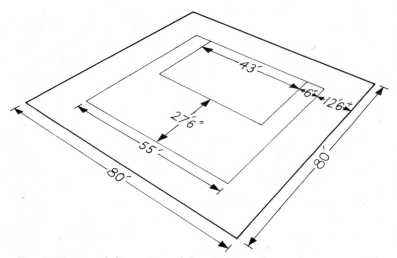

Fig. 1. Horizontal dimensions of the playhouse frame, the stage, and the yard, as stated or implied in the Fortune Contract.

be half the difference between the outer and inner dimensions of the frame (80 and 55 ft.). This confirmation of the specified depth of the frame suggests that the author of the contract included in his unqualified horizontal dimensions the thickness of vertical timbers at each side of the unit measured—that is to say, he gave unqualified horizontal dimensions as external rather than internal measurements.

The contract states that the stage shall be 43 ft. wide and that it shall "extende to the middle of the yarde". Practically all investigators of the Elizabethan playhouse conclude that the Fortune stage was therefore 27 ft. 6 in. deep, but, as I shall suggest below, this does not necessarily follow. It does follow, certainly, that the yard was 27 ft. 6 in. deep in front of the stage and 6 ft. wide on either side of it (Fig. 1).

The contract calls for three storeys in the playhouse frame, the first to measure 12 ft. in height, the second 11 ft., the third 9 ft. (Fig. 2). (The same height of first storey is apparently called for in

4

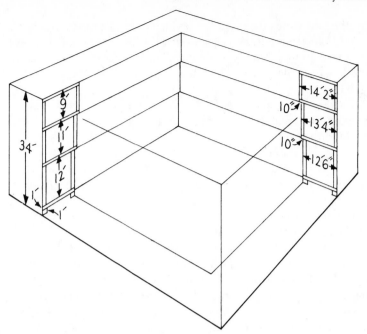

Fig. 2. Vertical and horizontal dimensions of the playhouse frame, as stated or implied in the Fortune Contract.

the Hope contract, which requires that the "inner principall postes of the first storie" of the frame of that playhouse be "twelve footes in height".) Since the author of the Fortune contract appears to have given unqualified horizontal dimensions as "from outside to outside", we may suppose that he also gave unqualified vertical dimensions as from one floor to the floor next above, including in his measurements the thickness of horizontal timbers lying beneath the upper of the two floors in question. This conventional method of measuring "from floor to floor" necessarily leaves out of account both the thickness of the floor of the first storey and the height of the horizontal timbers lying beneath that floor — groundsills resting upon the foundation, and binding-joists let into the groundsills at the same elevation. If, in view of recorded fifteenth-century groundsills measuring 10 in. and 12 in. in height,[10] we assume a height of 11 in. for the Fortune groundsills and a thickness of 1 in. for the floorboards lying upon the joists, we arrive at a height of 1 ft.

10. L. F. Salzman, *Building in England down to 1540* (Oxford, 1952), pp. 516, 542.

for the first-storey floor and the underpinnings of the frame (Fig. 2). In addition, the contract requires that the foundation stand at least 1 ft. above ground. Taking this dimension as exactly 1 ft., we find that the height of the frame is 34 ft. above ground (1 + 1 + 12 + 11 + 9 = 34).

The Fortune frame was 12 ft. 6 in. deep in the first storey, but greater than that in the middle and top storeys because of the requirement of the contract that there be a 10-in. "Juttey for-wardes" in "either" of the two upper storeys. Here the word "either" can mean "one or other of the two", in which case we are dealing with an overhang in one upper storey only—presumably the middle storey, as in Godfrey's reconstruction, although Semper preferred the top; or it can mean "each of the two", in which case the requirement indicates an overhang in both of the upper storeys, as in the reconstructions by Forestier and Hodges. On balance I consider it unlikely that the first arrangement can have been the one intended, for if it were the signers of the contract, knowing which of the two upper storeys they wished to contain the single overhang, would presumably have avoided ambiguity by specifying it. In the present reconstruction I have therefore followed Forestier and Hodges in interpreting the requirement as calling for two over-hangs. Thus the middle storey of the frame would have been 13 ft. 4 in. deep, the top storey 14 ft. 2 in. (Fig. 2).

I return to the depth of the stage. The author of the Fortune contract specifies that the stage is to "extende to the middle of the yarde". This is clear enough, and yet it also seems to be a curiously oblique way of putting the matter. One would expect the author to have said simply and directly that the stage should be 27 ft. 6 in. deep, which would of course be the case if the tiring-house, like the frame, were 12 ft. 6 in. deep. Alternatively, then, let us suppose that the depth of the tiring-house was to be greater than 12 ft. 6 in., and also that the author of the contract knew this but not exactly how much greater. In this case, not knowing the exact depth of the tiring-house, he wouldn't have known the exact depth of the stage; and thus it becomes clear that his specification is not vague or circumlocutory but an efficient way of indicating what he wanted. That is to say, the specification provides that the depth of the stage shall be as great as possible, depending on the distance available between the tiring-house facade and the middle of the yard, while at the same time it guards against the undesirable possibility of per-mitting the stage to extend beyond the middle of the yard. The efficiency of the phrasing can be appreciated if we imagine that the author of the contract had specified, instead, a particular depth of stage which turned out, in construction, to be not exactly the same as the distance available between the tiring-house facade and the middle of the yard. In this case the particularity of the specification would have caused the stage either to be shallower than need be if the specified dimension were too small (since then the stage would not have extended so far as the middle of the yard), or to extend beyond the middle of the yard if the specified dimension were too large. In order to clarify this complex architectural situation, Henslowe and Alleyn provided Streete with a "Plott" or ground plan, mentioned in the contract, which indicated how the stage was to be "placed and sett" in relation to its adjoining structure the tiring-house. Since this plan has not survived, we must attempt to recover its information by analysis.

The depth of the stage depends on the distance of the tiring-house facade from the middle of the yard, and that distance in turn depends on the relationship of the tiring-house facade to the three faces of the frame resulting from the overhangs of its two upper storeys. If the tiring-house structure had overhangs corresponding to those of the frame, the resulting three planes of the tiring-house facade would join neatly, on either side of the tiring-house, with the three faces of the frame, the first storey of the tiring-house would be 12 ft. 6 in. deep, and the stage would be, as commonly supposed, 27 ft. 6 in. deep (Fig. 3-A). However, the Swan drawing, our only pictorial evidence for a public-theatre tiring-house, records a tiring-house facade in a single plane—that is, without an overhang. In the present reconstruction I have therefore supposed that the facade of the Fortune tiring-house was in a single plane.

With which of the three faces of the frame did the tiring-house facade meet? 1) If it met with the face of the first storey of the frame, the tiring-house structure would be 12 ft. 6 in. deep throughout its three storeys, and the stage would again be 27 ft. 6 in. deep (Fig. 3-B). In this case the tiring-house, because of the overhangs of the frame, would be recessed 10 in. within the frame at the elevation of the middle storey of the frame and 20 in. at the elevation of the top storey. 2) If the tiring-house facade met with the face of the middle storey of the frame, the tiring-house structure would be 13 ft. 4 in. deep throughout its three storeys, and the stage would be reduced to a depth of 26 ft. 8 in. (situation not illustrated). In this case the tiring-house, because of the overhangs of the frame, would project

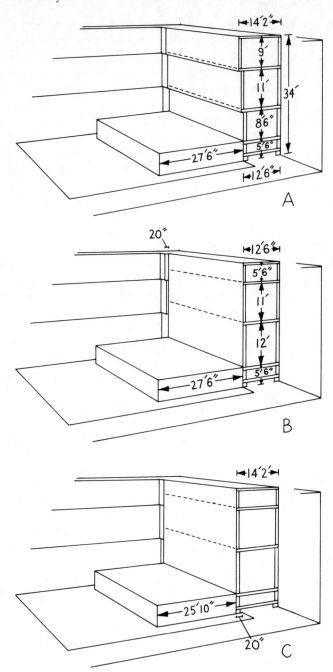

10 in. from the frame at the elevation of the first storey of the frame and be recessed 10 in. within the frame at the elevation of the top storey. 3) If the tiring-house facade met with the face of the top storey of the frame, the tiring-house structure would be 14 ft. 2 in. deep throughout its three storeys, and the stage would be reduced to a depth of 25 ft. 10 in. (Fig. 3-C). In this case the tiring-house, again because of the overhangs of the frame, would project 20 in. from the frame at the elevation of the first storey of the frame and 10 in. at the elevation of the middle storey.

At this point further appeal to the evidence of the Swan drawing seems appropriate. That document shows a tiring-house which clearly projects from the surrounding circle of the playhouse frame. In the present reconstruction I have therefore accepted the third interpretation, namely that the facade of the Fortune tiring-house met with the face of the top storey of the playhouse frame; that the tiring-house, being 14 ft. 2 in. deep, projected 20 in. from the frame at the elevation of the first storey of the frame; and that the Fortune stage, since it was to "extende to the middle of the yarde", was 25 ft. 10 in. deep (Fig. 3-C).

One of the disadvantages of an overhang in the second storey of the tiring-house (Fig. 3-A), as in Richard Southern's reconstruction of a round Elizabethan playhouse,[11] is that it forces the first storey to be only 8 ft. 6 in. high, since the first-storey floor of the tiring-house must be set at the same elevation as that of the stage, which, following Hodges, I take to have been 5 ft. 6 in. above ground. Hodges, although not using an overhang, also accepts a height of 8 ft. 6 in. for the first storey of the Fortune tiring-house. This height, while technically feasible in the sense that it would have provided

11. "On Reconstructing a Practicable Elizabethan Public Playhouse", *Shakespeare Survey 12* (1959), p. 27.

Fig. 3. *(Opposite page)* Depths of the stage and tiring-house; heights of the tiring-house storeys. (A) Tiring-house facade in three planes meeting with the three faces of the frame; first storey of the tiring-house 8 ft. 6 in. high. (B) Tiring-house facade in a single plane meeting with the face of the first storey of the frame; first storey of the tiring-house 12 ft. high. (C) Tiring-house facade in a single plane meeting with the face of the top storey of the frame; first storey of the tiring-house 12 ft. high.

adequate head-room, strikes me as inappropriately low in view of the requirement of the Fortune contract that the first storey of the frame be 12 ft. high (for one thing, it would have limited the height of the tiring-house doors to about 7 ft. 6 in.); and making the height of the second storey of the tiring-house greater in relation to the height of the first (11 ft. above 8 ft. 6 in.) seems at variance with the principle of architectural design evident in the requirement of the contract that the height of the second storey of the frame be less in relation to the height of the first (11 ft. above 12 ft.).

The problem lies in the assumption that the second-storey floor of the tiring-house lay at the same elevation as the second-storey floor of the frame. Admittedly it is a sound principle of design, and also a desirable practicality, to line up the corresponding floors of two integrated structures. However, since there is already, inevitably, a differential (3 ft. 6 in.) between the first-storey floor of the tiring-house (5 ft. 6 in. above ground) and the first-storey floor of the frame (2 ft. above ground), the principle in question has already been violated. Moreover, it seems unlikely that the two middle-storey floors would have been set at the same elevation as a practical measure in order to avoid the need of connecting them by stairs since there could hardly have been much, if any, traffic between the second storey of the tiring-house and the middle gallery of the playhouse frame. There seems to be nothing in the evidence or in the nature of things to forbid our treating the tiring-house and the playhouse frame, as indeed the contract seems to do, as separate, although integrated, structures conforming each to its own generic nature; and thus nothing to forbid our setting all three of the corresponding floors of the two structures at different elevations. (Hodges, p. 150, with characteristic flexibility, adopts precisely this line of approach in his reconstruction of a round playhouse based on the Swan drawing.) In the present reconstruction I have therefore made the heights of the first and second storeys of the tiring-house 12 ft. and 11 ft., respectively, on the analogy of the heights of the first two storeys of the frame as given in the Fortune contract.

Assuming heights of 12 ft. and 11 ft. for the first two storeys of the tiring-house structure results in a top storey only 5 ft. 6 in. high (Fig. 3-C). This awkwardly low height could, in theory, be improved on by borrowing, say, one foot from each of the two lower storeys, so as to give the three storeys of the tiring-house heights of 11 ft., 10 ft., and 7 ft. 6 in. respectively. In practice, however, such an expedient is discouraged by the consideration that, as I shall suggest in Part II of this essay apropos of the stage superstructure, the height of the top storey of the tiring-house cannot well be greater than 5 ft. 6 in., if, as seems desirable, its floor is to be set at the same elevation as the floor of the stage cover. And there are other considerations which, when the construction of the top storey of the tiring-house is fully analysed, make a height of 5 ft. 6 in. less impractical than at first glance appears.

A basic question about the frame of the Fortune playhouse is the number of bays in which it was constructed. Hodges divides the 55-ft.-10-in. length of the frame running along each side of the yard into four bays, each measuring 13 ft. 11½ in. on centres of the defining principal posts (Fig. 4). (The length of the range of bays is here given as 55 ft. 10 in., rather than 55 ft., because of the need to take measurements from, and to, the centres of the first and last posts of the range, these presumably being, as at the Hope in accordance with the builder's contract for that playhouse, 10 in. square.) Thus Hodges postulates a frame constructed in twenty bays, including the four at the corners. In the present reconstruction I have divided the 55-ft.-10-in. length of the frame running along each side of the yard into five bays, each measuring 11 ft. 2 in. on centres of the defining posts (Fig. 5). Thus I suppose a frame constructed in twenty-four bays, including the four at the corners. The two different arrangements seem to depend on different approaches to the reconstruction of round playhouses. The larger bay preferred by Hodges (Fig. 6-A) is consistent with the larger size of bay resulting from his use in *The Globe Restored* of a sixteen-sided ground plan in a reconstruction of the round first Globe measuring 80 ft. in diameter (Fig. 6-B),[12] whereas the smaller bay that I have preferred (Fig. 6-C) is consistent with the smaller size of bay resulting from my use of a twenty-four-sided ground plan in a reconstruction of the round Swan measuring 96 ft. in diameter (Fig. 6-D).[13]

The author of the Fortune contract tells us nothing about the entrances to the playhouse.[14] However, useful information is preserved in Agnes Henslowe's assignment in 1616 of Henslowe's lease of 1601 of Alleyn's moiety of the Fortune property, for this lease

12. In *Shakespeare's Second Globe* (London, 1973), Hodges proposes a round frame built to a sixteen-sided ground plan measuring 92 ft. in diameter. In this reconstruction the dimensions of an individual bay of the frame are of course even greater.
13. "The Swan Playhouse, 1595", in *The Revels History of Drama in English*, Vol. III (London, 1975).
14. His silence in so important a matter is surprising; in note 17 below I suggest a possible explanation for it.

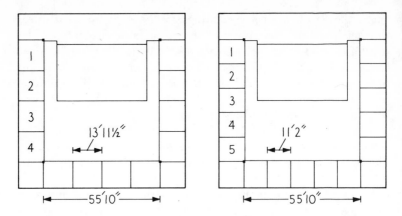

Fig. 4. Frame constructed in 20 bays, four in the range of bays running along each side of the yard.

Fig. 5. Frame constructed in 24 bays, five in the range of bays running along each side of the yard.

mentions two doors on the south side of the playhouse:

> ... wth a competent waye the Breadth of a Carte waye at the least on the south side aforesaid of the said house from one doore of the said house to an other to be used in Common by and betweene the said parties theire executors & assignes wth free ingresse egresse and regresse into and from the said house by the waye and wayes thereunto nowe used and accustomed In so large & ample manner & forme as the said Edward Alleyn then had or enjoyed the same waye or wayes. . . . (*HP*, p. 26)

These two "doors" of the playhouse, connected by a "way" running along its south side, may have given access to the yard, to the galleries, or to both the yard and the galleries. For the moment I shall assume that they gave access to the yard and only to the yard.

If both entrances to the yard were located in one of the four sides of the playhouse frame, it seems likely, on the assumption of a symmetrical arrangement, that the side in question would have been either the side of the frame at the rear of the stage or the side in front of the stage. Hodges has proposed the first arrangement, which would place the stage in the southern half of the yard (Fig. 7); I am now proposing the second, which would place the stage in the northern half (Fig. 8).

Hodges suggests, with a query, that the yard entrances at the

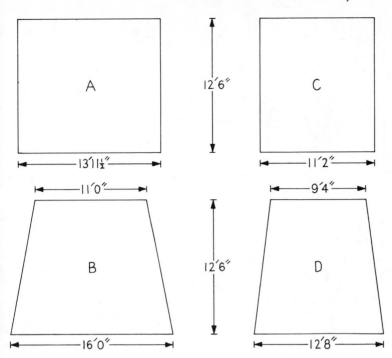

Fig. 6. Dimensions of variously sized and shaped bays of the frame. (A) in a reconstruction of the Fortune with a frame constructed in 20 bays. (B) In a reconstruction of a 16-sided round playhouse measuring 80 ft. in diameter. (C) In a reconstruction of the Fortune with a frame constructed in 24 bays. (D) In a reconstruction of a 24-sided round playhouse measuring 96 ft. in diameter.

Fortune lay on either side of the tiring-house, spectators passing through the frame at those points and along the 6-ft.-wide "gang-ways" (as he calls them) lying on either side of the stage (Fig. 7).[15] This location would have had the advantage of making good use of the 6-ft.-wide areas of the yard lying between the sides of the stage and the frame. However, although the system would undoubtedly be effective in evacuating a filled yard, I doubt that it would work well in filling an empty one, for the reason that, as I suggest in the diagram, first-come spectators would naturally take up the most desirable positions around the front and sides of the stage; and those that stood along the sides of the stage would have clogged the gangways long before the yard was even half-filled, such spectators

15. In *The Globe Restored*, pp. 10, 151.

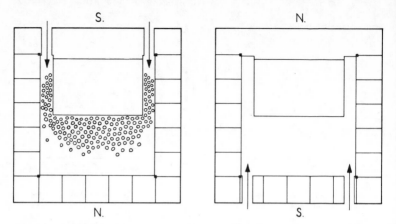

Fig. 7. Yard entrances located in side of frame lying at rear of stage; stage in southern half of yard.

Fig. 8. Yard entrances located in side of frame lying in front of stage; stage in northern half of yard.

presumably being reluctant to yield place to later-arriving spectators since in so doing they would have had to move on to the as-yet-unfilled parts of the yard and thus to surrender their relatively choice stands along the sides of the stage. I therefore assume that the entrances to the yard were located elsewhere, interpreting the narrow sections of the yard on either side of the stage not as gangways but simply as shallow side-stage standing-areas.

If the entrances to the yard were not located in the side of the playhouse frame at the rear of the stage, they were presumably located in the side of the frame in front of the stage. More specifically, I suggest that the yard entrances were located in the two end-bays of the range of five bays facing the stage (Fig. 8). This location would have had the advantage of permitting spectators, upon passing through the frame, to debouch into those parts of the yard, the corners opposite the front of the stage, which would fill up last with spectators standing in the yard. Thus spectators arriving early who took up positions around the front and sides of the stage would have been well out of the traffic-flow of those arriving later.

The author of the Fortune contract several times mentions stairs or staircases of the frame; these of course would have led to the galleries. The "steares", apparently referred to as "withoute", are to be similar to the stairs of the first Globe. The "stearecases of the saide fframe" are to be "placed and sett" as indicated in a "Plott" or ground plan which has not survived. The "stearecases", like the

14

frame and the stage, are to be "covered with Tyle". And the "Staire-cases", like the frame, are to be "sufficyently enclosed withoute with lathe lyme and haire". It should be noted in passing that the term "staircase" seems here to be used not in the usual modern sense of a flight of stairs but in the original sense of "The inclosure of a pair of Stairs, whether it be with Walls, or with Walls and Railes and Bannisters, etc." (Moxon, 1679; quoted in *OED*). The number of staircases is not specified; presumably there were two, as at the Hope, the Swan, and the second Globe.

Hodges puts the gallery staircases at the Fortune inside the playhouse frame, one in each of the angles of the frame on either side of the tiring-house. In so locating them, however, he neglects the implication of the contract that the staircases, since they are to be, like the frame, "covered with Tyle", have roofs distinct from the roof of the frame. Thus they would have been outside the frame, though of course adjoining to it. Accordingly, I suggest that the Fortune staircases were generally similar to the external staircases which Hollar attributes to the second Globe and the Hope in his "Long Bird's-Eye View of London" and in the preliminary sketch for that engraving—that is to say, tall, narrow, gabled structures projecting from the outer wall of the playhouse frame. Specific details of the staircases are treated in Part II of the present essay.

The location of the staircases in relation to the frame was specified in the lost "Plott" or ground plan accompanying the Fortune contract, for the reason, presumably, that it was impractical to convey this information by verbal stipulation or by reference to the Globe. In the absence of this plan I suggest that the staircases were located at the same points on the playhouse frame as the entrances to the yard—or, more specifically, that each of the staircases butted up against an end-bay of the range of five bays facing the stage (Fig. 9). Thus the two playhouse doors mentioned in the Henslowe-Alleyn lease of 1601 would have been the only general entrances to the playhouse.[16] As such, they would have given access to both the galleries and the yard, gallery spectators mounting the stairs to one or another of the galleries immediately after entering the staircase (Fig. 9-A) but yard spectators passing through the foot of the stair-

16. Two general entrances may be involved in the report of "two narrow doors" at the first Globe in 1613 (Chambers, *Elizabethan Stage*, Vol. II, p. 420) and of "both gates" at the second Fortune in 1643 (*Jacobean and Caroline Stage*, VI, 174). The interpretation assumes that in each instance there was also, at the rear of the playhouse, a special third door giving access to the tiring-house and to the lords' rooms over the stage.

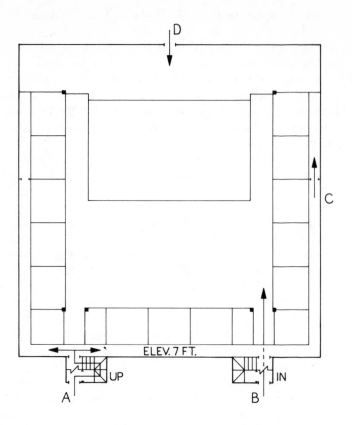

Fig. 9. Two entrances each giving access to both galleries and yard. (A) Access to galleries by way of stairs. (B) Access to yard by way of ground-level passageway through frame. (C) Door giving access to gentlemen's rooms. (D) Door giving access to tiring-house and (by way of tiring-house stairs) lord's rooms over the stage.

case in order to enter the ground-level passageway leading through the frame to the yard (Fig. 9-B).[17]

This location of the staircases, about 55° apart on the outside of

17. If entrances to the yard were customarily located in the staircases of Elizabethan playhouses, we should have an explanation of the failure of the author of the Fortune contract to indicate the location of either yard or general entrances: he would not have needed to locate such entrances since he would already have done so in specifying the location of the staircases in the "Plott" or ground plan supplementary to the contract.

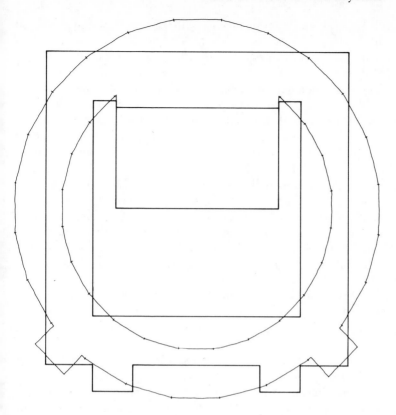

Fig. 10. Location of staircases in present reconstruction of the Fortune compared with location of staircases in a 24-sided Second Globe measuring 96 ft. in diameter.

the frame of the square Fortune, may be compared with the location of staircases about 90° apart on the outside of the round second Globe as pictured by Hollar in the "Long Bird's-Eye View of London" and in the preliminary sketch for that view. Superimposed ground plans of the two playhouses are given in Fig. 10, where the round playhouse is represented as a twenty-four-sided building measuring 96 ft. in diameter.

The hypothesis that each of the exterior doors mentioned in the Henslowe-Alleyn lease of 1601 gave access to both the yard and the galleries is supported by Thomas Platter's well-known description of the progressive gathering of admission fees at a Bankside playhouse in 1599 (presumably the Globe): "For he who remains standing below pays only one English penny, but if he wants to sit he is let in at another door, where he pays a further penny. . . ."[18] So far as I know, this statement has always been interpreted as implying that both yard and gallery spectators paid a penny for entrance at the same exterior door, the gallery spectators then paying "a further penny" at "another door" which stood beyond the first and could, of course, be reached only by passing through it. The interpretation is enforced by Platter's choice of language for the second payment, for an entrance leading only to the galleries would have required payment not of "a further penny" but of twopence at one shot. The proposed arrangement at the Fortune (Fig. 9) is consistent with Platter's evidence if we suppose that within the staircase there was "another door", either at the foot of the first flight of stairs or at the first-landing entrance to the playhouse frame, where the second penny could have been gathered.

The proposed arrangement of staircases assumes that a spectator reached the first gallery in the following manner (Fig. 9-A). He would enter a staircase by an exterior door at ground level and ascend the stairs to the first landing, at the same elevation (7 ft. above ground) as that of a raised passageway running round the rear of the first gallery behind the "rooms" containing degrees for seating. The spectator would then pass, through a door in the outer wall of the playhouse frame, from landing to passageway, turning to right or left after entering the frame so as to proceed along the passageway to the room of his choice. (Presumably the further operation of the system, at the levels of the middle and top galleries, was essentially the same, spectators in all three galleries paying the same admission fee of twopence for entrance to the galleries.) It should be noticed that, since the first-gallery passageway is at an elevation of 7 ft. above ground, the passageway for yard spectators, running through the frame at ground level, passes under the gallery passageway with some 6 ft. 2 in. of head-room beneath the joists. The relationship of the two passageways is illustrated in Fig. 9-B.

Platter's account of the gallery spectator's progress continues: ". . . but if [having paid a second penny] he desires to sit on cushions in the pleasantest place, where he not only sees everything well but can also be seen, then he pays at a further door another English

18. Translation by Ernest Schanzer, in "Thomas Platter's Observations on the Elizabethan Stage", *Notes and Queries*, C CI (1956), 466.

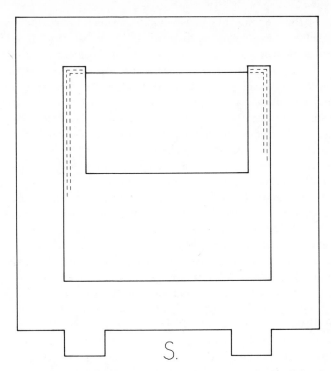

Fig. 11. Diagram containing the information on location of stage and staircases presumably included in the lost "Plott" or ground plan supplementary to the Fortune Contract.

penny." I assume that Platter here refers to the gentlemen's rooms on either side of the stage, since they, unlike the lords' rooms in the second storey of the tiring-house, could readily have been reached by way of the postulated paying stations at the first and second doors of the staircase, the spectator paying his third penny at a door in the gallery passageway giving access to the gentlemen's rooms (Fig. 9-C). Presumably spectators intending to sit in the lord's rooms entered the playhouse through the players' door at the rear of the tiring-house (Fig. 9-D), ascending to the rooms over the stage by way of the tiring-house stairs. Since a gatherer would have had to be stationed at each of the passageway doors giving access to the gentlemen's rooms, and still another at the tiring-house door, the total number of gatherers required, including two in each staircase, is seven.

In this essay I have suggested "locations" for the stage and staircases of the Fortune playhouse—matters which, since they could not readily be made clear in the contract by verbal stipulation or by reference to the Globe, were made the subject of a "Plott" or ground plan supplementary to the contract but not now extant: "... which Stadge shalbe placed and sett As alsoe the stearecases of the saide fframe in such sorte as is prefigured in a Plott thereof drawen". The supplementing of a contract by a plan was not, incidentally, an uncommon practice; Salzman prints contracts in which the sup- plementary plan is variously called a "portatur", a "platt", and a "trasyng".[19] Since the concept of location has significance only by virtue of an accompanying reference point, in "locating" the stage I have sought to establish the relationship of the stage to its adjoining structure the tiring-house; and, in locating the staircases, to estab- lish the relationship of the staircases to their adjoining structure the playhouse frame. In each case, since there is no other adjoining structure, no other reference point is available. The proposed loca- tions are illustrated once again in Fig. 11, which, I suggest, contains the essential information that was presumably communicated in the lost ground plan: the stage is "placed and sett" in relation to the tiring-house, the facade of which is in turn related to the three interior faces of the playhouse frame; and the staircases are placed in relation to the frame. With hardly more than a glance at some such plan as that given in this illustration, Peter Streete, knowing from the contract that there were to be two 10-in. overhangs in the frame and that the stage was to extend to the middle of the yard, would have known exactly where and how to place the stage and staircases of the Fortune playhouse.

---

19. In *Building in England*, pp. 518, 573, 583.

The Presentation of Plays
at Second Paul's:
The Early Phase (1599-1602)

REAVLEY GAIR

In the summer of 1599 William Stanley, Sixth Earl of Derby, was "busy penning comedies for the common players",[1] but he may have had an unpleasant experience with the reaction of the professional theatre to his work. Certainly John Marston, who had written "privately" for lawyers,[2] had a short-lived professional association with Henslowe in September of this year, when he was advanced £2 "in earneste of a Boocke".[3] Both Stanley and Marston were resident in the Inns of Court in the late 1590s, the former in Lincoln's Inn, the latter in the Middle Temple. Fortunes for both changed quickly; Marston's father died in the fall and left him a substantial inheritance and, by early November, Stanley had "put up the playes of the children in Pawles to his great paines and charge".[4]

Stanley and Marston would probably have found a sympathetic friend at Paul's in Ambrose Goulding who had become curate of St. Gregory's in about 1585 and then, in 1596, had also acquired a curacy in Sargeant's Inn.[5] In 1598 it was reported that Goulding and

1. *Calendar of State Papers, Domestic, Elizabeth*, 1598-1601, 227. None of Stanley's plays is extant.
2. P. J. Finkelpearl, "John Marston's *Histrio-Mastix* as an Inns of Court Play: A Hypothesis", *Huntington Library Quarterly*, 29 (1966) 223-34 (*passim*).
3. *Diary*, ed. W. W. Greg (London, 1904), I.112.
4. *Historical Manuscripts Commission, Lord de l'Isle and Dudley*, II. 415. Rowland Whyte to Sir Robert Sidney.
5. St. Paul's Cathedral Library MS A. 53/17/f.17ᵛ: subsequent references are given in the text by "P" and a folio number.

his friend Hugh Andrews "doe table; and lodge, and entertaine gentlemen, and captaines by meanes where of, the colledge [of the Minor Canons] gates are often kept open all night. . ." (P. f.6). Apart from these two "gallants", there were others at Paul's with a liking for drama:

> In January 1597 certaine weomen would have a maske to make themselves famous Robert Parkers wife the bellringer Edward Smythes wife Edward Owens wife And ii of Mr. Sleggs daughters Marie and Honor [all residents of the Cathedral precincts]. Theise daunced at Sleggs till aboute xii of the clocke in the nyghte and then came downe and daunced in the College garden with their minstrells and in the end went to the College gates which being locked accordinge to order theise maskers breake open most audaciouslie. . . . (G.f.52ᵛ)[6]

Stanley's "paines" may have been great in the revival at Paul's, but his "charges" were perhaps not so substantial, for there were "in longe Chaple . . . lyinge ould furr pooles and other ould lumber which was laid there After the mendinge of the Churche when it was burned" (G.f.47). It would certainly be well-seasoned, for it was on Wednesday, June 4, 1561

> Between four and five of the clock, [that] a smoke was espied by divers to break out under the bowl of the . . . shaft of Paul's . . . and suddenly . . . flame brake forth in a circle, like a garland, round about the broche [i.e. spire], . . .and increased in such wise that, within a quarter of an hour, or little more, the Cross and the Eagle on the top fell down upon the South cross Ile.[7]

In 1598 Bishop Bancroft was informed that "Mr Gyles mr of Quoiristers hath the possession of the great vaulte under the south side of the churche which he useth to laie in wood and other old lumber" (G.f.55). Thus there were materials and storage space readily at hand and St. Faith's Chapel, in the cathedral crypt, was "in the possession of . . . a ioyner who useth the same for his dwellinge house and for his shopp to worke in. . ." (G.f.55) and the "green yard" outside the church was used as a store for timber and boards (G.f.55-55ᵛ).

---

6. Guildhall Library MS 9537/9, "The Visitation Book of Bishop Bancroft": subsequent references are given in the text by "G" and a folio number.
7. *The True Report of the burning of the Steeple and Church of Paul's in London, 1561*, ed. Arber, *An English Garner* (London, 1896) VIII, 112.

One of the first plays—perhaps the very first, since it introduces its actors, its author, and possibly its patron to the audience— produced at second Paul's, was *Antonio and Mellida*. There is every reason to presume that it was first performed before the end of 1599. It begins with a non-dramatic illusion, as if it is still in rehearsal; eight boys enter *"with parts in their hands: having cloakes cast over their apparrell"* (3-4).[8] They then proceed to discuss the difficulties they have encountered in preparing the play for performance; they know their words, but are unsure about dramatic technique; they must double some parts (the same boy plays Alberto and Andrugio) and each coaches the other in his role. They reach the conclusion that they have so much to offer that one play is insufficient, so a sequel is promised, provided that this first play finds "gracious acceptance" (151-2).

The effect of this Induction, played without properties, costume, or scenic effect, is at once apologetic (with an implied request for the tolerance of inexperience) and invitational (soliciting response from the audience in guiding the future development of this theatrical enterprise). Marston is genuinely inviting audience reaction and promising, where necessary, to adapt his style to conform to this criticism; as the Epilogue insists, "What imperfection you have seene in us, leave with us, and weele amend it (1985-6). . . . You shall not be more ready to embrace any thing commendable, then we will endeavour to amend all things reproveable" (1987-9). This was an invitation which some members of the audience were only too willing to accept.

After a Prologue, almost unctuous in its flattery of the audience, "this fair troop" (158), "Select, and most respected Auditours" (159), "your authentick censure" (165), "attentive eares" (170), "your health of wit" (172), "your fertile spirits" (174), "such eares" (175), "most ingenious" (176)—the first act opens with a military parade of the principals in the company (219-23), and then proceeds to demonstrate to the audience the acting areas available to the players. Three Ladies enter "above" (291), while "below" Galeatzo enters with attendants at one door (292-3) and Piero enters at the other door (293). There are now three ladies above, and below there is a total of ten named characters (one of whom, Antonio disguised as an Amazon, is invisible to the others) and an unspecified number of

8. All quotations from *Antonio and Mellida*, or *A&M* are taken from the Malone Society Reprint of 1921.

attendants: the Paul's company is thus displayed in pageant form at the earliest possible point in the action, and the audience has been shown both the upper and lower acting areas in use. The three ladies now proceed to watch from above and comment upon a mime which takes place on the main stage: this, as Dieter Mehl has pointed out, is a new development of the convention of eavesdropping.[9] Having shown off his company and its theatrical facilities, Marston at once displays his own dramatic innovations both in action and dialogue. The audience must surely have been aware by the end of the first act that Marston was offering a linguistic feast for their "attentive ears", because he creates, or uses for the first time on stage, a new word on the average every fourteen lines — including terms like "acceptance" (152), "juiceless" (40-1), "strenuous" (41), "impregnably" (114), "abstruse" (166), "abhorred" (183), "canon proofe" (300), "glibbery" (305), and "monkish" [i.e. monkeyish] (334).[10] In the second act, in case these "select auditors" had been rather slow in noticing his verbal invention, Marston deliberately draws attention to it, when Balurdo savours one of these new-coined words; "my legge is not altogether unpropitiously shap't. There's a word: unpropitiously? I thinke I shall speake unpropitiously as well as any courtier in *Italy*" (584-7).

In the three central acts of the play Marston offers us more intimate glimpses both of himself and the boys. Dildo, who is "diminutive" (471), Catzo "a glibbery urchin" (475-6), and Castilio who, while "a most sweete youth" (960), is also a "minnikin" (970) are introduced to us as the younger and shorter members of the company in contrast to Flavia, Balurdo, and the other older boys who take the major parts. We find that Balurdo, Catzo, and Lucio are soloists, Castilio sings "fantastically" (528-9), Rossaline dances, or rather runs, a "Caranto pase" (529) and, while Antonio is lamenting his supposed loss of Mellida, an effect peculiar to choristers is created. Marston directs, *"The boy runnes a note, Antonio breakes it"* (1408) — the sudden rupturing of a held tone, perhaps a high C, to act as an emotional shock to reinforce Antonio's lamentation.

We are not allowed to forget the personality of the author either, for Antonio and Mellida exchange lovers' confidences in Italian (for

9. D. Mehl, *The Elizabethan Dumb Show* (1965), p. 124.
10. The assertion that these are used for the first time is made with the caution that, based as it is upon the *OED* which is far from complete, it cannot pretend to statistical accuracy.

some twenty lines) and while the page apologizes for this "confusion of Babell" (1474), the author's excuse is that "some private respect may abate the edge of the keener censure" (1482-3). Marston is speaking directly to those in the audience who know him and reminding them of his origins: his mother was Marie Guarsi, daughter of an Italian surgeon.

Marston goes on to exploit all the special qualities of an enclosed theatre. Act I takes place in daylight; Act II occurs in early evening, when torches are needed (528); Act III is at dawn; and Acts IV and V progress during the morning of that day: sufficient lighting changes to keep the tireman, who seems to have been responsible for the trimming of candles at Paul's, very busy.[11] The "above" is again used when Mellida speaks to Antonio and then quickly descends to the main stage when she hears a number of people ascending the stairs: these stairs (1145) were, apparently, invisible to the audience. Mime plays a part too: while Piero is recounting the supposed drowning of Antonio, Mellida is forcibly taken to dance by her two parentally approved, but personally rejected suitors, Galeatzo and Matzagente (646-8) — the visual dance reinforces the emotional irony. So too the audience is not allowed to forget the experimental and provisional nature of the play, for Balurdo and Rossaline are shown practising expressions and gestures suitable for different moods, and it is stressed that the short period now available for their performances, the limited plot of the play, and their restricted acting area prevent a full display of their talents (1069-72): surely a blatant example of advertizing?

It is in the final act that the personal element, both authorial and dramaturgical, culminates. A Painter enters with two pictures and Balurdo describes them;

... whose picture is this? *Anno Domini 1599*. Beleeve mee, master *Anno Domini* was of a good settled age when you lymn'd him. 1599. yeares old? Lets see the other. *Etatis suae 24*. Bir Ladie he is somewhat younger. Belike master *Etatis suae* was *Anno Dominies* sonne. (1589-94)

It has been agreed by most critics that the second of these portraits

---

11. I am suggesting that Marston used changes of lighting at Paul's (i.e. the tireman lit or put out candles during the entr'acte music) although there are no supporting stage directions: there is, however, a great deal of internal evidence in Marston's plays to suggest that he did this. A.R., in particular, stresses in each act the change of time and light from the preceding act.

is of Marston, who was in his twenty-fourth year in 1599. I suggest that the first portrait which is "of a good settled age", and thus somewhat older than the twenty-four-year-old Marston, is Stanley, who was about thirty-eight in 1599. If I am correct in this identification, the audience at Paul's would now have no doubt at all about the identity of both the author of the play and the patron of the theatre.

A golden harp is now offered as a prize in a singing contest; there are three competitors and Balurdo is not only the winner, but is also clearly established as the leading choir soloist, since he declares that he reached a note above upper E in the treble (1812): the play suggests that he and Flavia are about fourteen (1823-4). Apart from soloists, then, the company can boast a harpist and a painter, who later took the part of Earle Lasinberg in *The Wisdome of Doctor Dodypoll*, for after a curtain is drawn he is discovered "*(like a Painter)* painting Lucilia, *who sits working on a piece of Cushion worke*" (1-3). [12] The boys are, however, unable to display their dancing abilities as there is not enough room for a dance by three of them (1769), when there are eight other characters and a harp on the stage. The play concludes with a daring spectacle, the resurrection of Antonio. The Epilogue repeats the humble tone of the Prologue in its obsequious desire for support both for the company and the author.

The overall impression created by this presentation is distinctly one of direct personal involvement by the author in the company. Marston consciously exploits talents peculiar not merely to choirboys in general, but to this particular group of Paul's boys; he displays an ardent desire to be accepted into the select milieu represented by the audience, and he gives us a clear impression that this is an introductory play, which seeks to make both the company (as individuals and as actors) and the author personally known to the audience. Finally it is clear that help, critical and perhaps financial—to enlarge their facilities—is being solicited on behalf of the company as a whole.

Marston seems to have had a group of boys who were well disciplined to deal with, for Thomas Gyles appears to have been a conscientious master as far as training was concerned; in 1598 the boys were described as being

12. All quotations from *Dr. Dodypoll* are from the Malone Society Reprint of 1964.

well instructed and fitt for their places and they doe diligentlie keepe theire accustomed howers in repayringe unto divine service, they come to the Churche in decent order, but they have not theire gownes lyned as in former tymes were used theire surplice are most Comenlie uncleane, and theire apparell not in suche sorte as decencie becometh as we are informed they have sufficient allowance of meate and drinke. (G.f.56ᵛ)

The costumes were, one trusts, better kept by the theatre than the surplices by the master.

At least one member of the Paul's audience responded constructively to Marston's appeal for involvement: William Percy proceeded to create his own plays in versions specially modified for performance by Paul's.[13] Most of the spectators, however, seem to have responded negatively. Marston's next play is disillusioned; Planet, who, if not the author's mouthpiece, is certainly a supporter of Paul's, says:

> ... I do hate these bumbaste wits,
> That are puft up with arrogant conceit
> Of their owne worth, as if *Omnipotence*
> Had hoysed them to such unequald height,
> That they survaide our spirits with an eye
> Only create to censure from above,
> When good soules they do nothing but reprove. (IV, H)[14]

Jack Drum's Entertainment is a defence by Marston against his detractors: the extent of the adverse criticism that *Antonio and Mellida* received may be gauged by the fact that this reply exists at all.

It begins in the same way as *Antonio and Mellida* with a non-dramatic illusion. The Tireman is sent on to apologize to the audience that the play will not take place; a degree worse than the rehearsal which began the former play. But then, as before, one of the children explains that the author is restraining them because he does not consider either the play or the actors good enough for this

13. There are three extant manuscripts of these plays: two owned by the Duke of Northumberland in Alnwick Castle, 508 (mainly fair copy) and 509; the other, perhaps a presentation copy, is in the Huntington Library (San Marino), HN 4. My quotations are identified only by the MS number since all three manuscripts are unfolioed.
14. All quotations from *Jack Drum's Entertainment*, or *J.D. Ent.*, are taken from the Tudor facsimile of 1912.

"generous presence" (A2), this "choice selected influence" (A2), and the boy concludes with the avowal

> Weele studie till our cheekes looke wan with care,
> That you our pleasures, we your loves may share. (A2ᵛ)

Marston evidently felt that his best hope of surviving the attacks of his critics lay in securing the support of this audience to whom he had been at such pains to make himself known. He takes no theoretical stand to justify his dramatic form, rather he argues that his whole dramatic purpose is merely to amuse and entertain. This is probably the reason why this play has little plot and indeed the whole first act, apart from a general attack on his detractors, is remarkable only for a display of morris dancing: did Marston try to win friends by going to the expense of hiring a morris troupe who normally performed on Higate Green (A3ᵛ)?

One of the aspects of *Antonio and Mellida* which seems to have been criticized was its verbal display, for by the.end of the first act of *Jack Drum's Entertainment,* the frequency of his coinages has dropped by two-thirds, to an average of one in thirty-seven lines, but—as in *Antonio and Mellida*—several of the words are still with us, "barmy" (A3), "squeas'd" (A4ᵛ), "slopt" (B), and "feathry" (B3ᵛ). Some of his dramatic effects, however, had been praised, for Marston re-uses two of them in a new combination. While Mamon is singing the song "Lantara" Pasquil, who is supposed to be dead, "riseth and striketh him" (D2): a replay of both the interruption of the held tone and the resurrection scene in *Antonio and Mellida*. The use of the "above" also seems to have been a success, for two parts of scenes take place at a "casement" (C3ᵛ). The upper level of the Paul's stage had a "window" (D2) which could represent the upper storey of a house (G3): it was presumably distinct from the upper acting area used for the three ladies in *Antonio and Mellida*, for the "casement" could be shut to effect an exit (C3ᵛ). The manipulation of light and dark to suggest day and night scenes had not, apparently, been particularly noted for it is no longer exploited except when Flawne enters with a candle (C3) to indicate the time of day.

In this play Marston is less concerned with innovation—but he still complains about the smallness of the stage (H4) despite the fact that, with ten actors on it, it was possible to dance a galliard—than with self-congratulation: he gloats about the select, though small, audience at the Paul's house. As Planet remarks,

> ... I like the Audience that frequenteth there
> With much applause: A man shall not be choakte
> With the stench of Garlicke, nor be pasted
> To the barmy Jacket of a Beer-brewer. (H3ᵛ)

The spectators were not tightly packed either because the seats were further apart than in the public theatre, or because there were not many of them: but the new "moderne wit" Mellidus (F4) finds the few preferable to the many. One other element which he does not change is the frequency of the songs during the performance; there are eight in both of these plays and both end with a call for an instrumental performance. Marston was well aware that music and song were one of the most important assets of the children, particularly noted by visitors, as the Duke of Stettin-Pomerania reported:

> For a whole hour before [the beginning of the play] a delightful performance of musicam instrumentalem is given on organs, lutes, pandores, mandolines, violins, and flutes; and a boy's singing cum voce tremula. ...[15]

During this early phase of the revival at Paul's they averaged over seven songs to a play.

Apparently confident that his retort in *Jack Drum's Entertainment* would silence his critics, Marston now produced for his supporters a sequel to *Antonio and Mellida* to fulfil the dramaturgic promises he had made in that play: *Antonio's Revenge* disproves the rule about sequels, for it is better than its original.[16] In it, all the "modern" devices of the Paul's company reach their apotheosis.

At the burial of Feliche, son of Pandulpho, who has been murdered by Piero, Antonio asks the page to "sing a dirge" (IV.v.65) but Pandulpho, deliberately misunderstanding him, replies on Feliche's behalf

15. *Diary*, September 28, 1602 (*Transactions of the Royal Historical Society, New Series*, 6, 1892).
16. All quotations from *Antonio's Revenge*, or *A.R.*, are taken from my edition for the Revels series. A more elaborate discussion of the various features of *A.R.* will be found in the introduction to this edition, as well as a full analysis of the problem of dating both it and *A&M*.

> No; no song; t'will be vile out of tune.
> Indeed he's hoarse; the poor boy's voice is cracked. (66-7)

The interruption occurs here before the song is begun, and we are also perhaps expected to be aware that the boy who played Feliche a year and a half previously – he appears in *Antonio's Revenge* only as a corpse, but is important in *Antonio and Mellida* – is now "cracked" of voice; he is no longer a boy, but a man. So too in place of the sudden resurrection we have not one, but several reappearances of the dead in the person, or rather the ghost, of Andrugio who takes a dominant part in the structure of the plot.

Artificial light is exploited: each act, except the fourth, begins with a scene in torchlight; the fourth act has all its scenes in daylight, but it follows an act with all its scenes in semi-darkness. Time is strictly regulated into exactly two days and the place never varies from the Venetian court. Extensive use is made of mime to create visual dramatic irony and, as in *Dr. Dodypoll*, Marston exploits the surprise effect of the sudden drawing of curtains. This is used to reveal (probably above) not Mellida, as Antonio expects, but the *"body of FELICHE, stabbed thick with wounds"* (i.iii.298.1-2) and then, "below", the curtains of a bed are drawn to display to Maria the *"Ghost of ANDRUGIO"* (iii.iv.62.1-2). So too Marston offers an audacious scene in which Antonio holds up the body of the young Julio, son of Piero, whom he has just stabbed and allows his blood to drip upon Andrugio's tomb as a sacrificial offering to the god of Vengeance (iii.iii.40ff). During this pagan invocation the ghost of Andrugio is heard groaning under the stage, so we are made aware that Paul's now have a large trap.[17] Not merely is Feliche's body buried in the trap and Marston is at pains to direct "the grave openeth" (iv.v.64.1) – it operates from below – but Balurdo uses it, quite unnecessarily, as a dungeon and climbs out of it onto the stage (v.ii).

It is in the concluding two scenes of the play, however, that Marston unites all his devices into one culminating vocal and spectacular effect. On the main stage the three conspirators against

17. I am suggesting that the second Paul's venture was progressive in the sense that just as the plays were experimental, so the facilities available were gradually improved as the speculation proved popular. This is the reason why I say "now", referring to the trap, in 1601. I can find no evidence to suggest that first Paul's (assuming that Westcott used the same building) had a trap. I suggest that the trap was operated from below because the S.D. seems to so indicate.

Piero dance a measure (v.v.17.1), watched by eight named and five un-named characters; in the recessed "discovery space" is set a table of sweetmeats (v.v.45.1). During the dance the ghost of Andrugio is positioned behind the curtain which covers the upper acting area, located above the discovery space (v.v.17.2-3). [18] At either side of the curtained upper space the musicians are seated behind the "casements". Symbolically Andrugio looks down from heaven upon the hell in which Piero will find himself, a hell in which he suffers not merely the plucking out of his tongue but also the discovery that he has eaten the flesh of his son, prepared for him by the con-spirators. Marston is thus using the resources of his stage to create a visual symbol of fulfilled vengeance. The scene ends with the cur-tains being drawn across both upper and lower discovery spaces, to effect the removal of the ghost and the body of Piero as well as the banquet table. The play ends with a cantata on the theme "Mellida is dead", sung by five named and three or four un-named characters on stage with the remaining six choristers providing additional vocal accompaniment from behind the scenes—probably "above", with the musicians.

In addition to this final spectacle, Marston makes it clear to us that the boys now have a grating in or near one of the doors (II.iii.122.1), for use as a cell, and they can muster seventeen actors, of whom at least thirteen could take speaking parts. Seventeen players is their probable maximum, for in the penultimate scene when "ANDRUGIO'S *ghost is placed betwixt the music houses*" (v.v.17.2-3) there are sixteen on stage, and the one remaining played the part of Mellida (now dead) and—unlikely though it may seem—doubled with the part of the ghost of Andrugio. Just as in *Antonio and Mellida*, Marston makes a point in this play of feasting us with new words and phrases: the incidence by the end of the first

18. I have placed Andrugio's ghost "above" for the following reasons: symbolically the setting of the conclusion of the play needs him to overlook the action ("Here will I sit, spectator of revenge", v.v.21); he is seated behind a curtain and between the music houses and the musicians were, in all probability, "above" in the upper level of the "houses" (since, if they had been below behind the doors of the lower facade, they would have taken up the space needed by the actors); Andrugio exits when the curtains have been drawn (v.v.82.1) and Piero (now dead) is removed later, together with a banquet table when "The curtains are drawn" (v.vi.36.1)—Piero moved to or was led to this table and was stabbed there while Andrugio's ghost observed (v.v.45*ff*), but Andrugio leaves before the curtains are drawn across Piero's body. Andrugio and Piero must have been in separate curtained spaces: "above" and "below", with Andrugio overseeing the vengeance is the placing demanded by probability and the symbolism of the action.

act is almost back to its original density — a new word every sixteen lines. Balurdo emphasizes this verbal invention in every act, save the second.

Tragedy would hardly suggest itself as the most suitable context for the use of the non-dramatic illusion device of which Marston was so fond, but it does occur in *Antonio's Revenge*. Balurdo enters hurriedly in answer to Piero's summons in the first scene of the second act and apologizes for his tardiness, by blaming the tireman. Marston directs, *"Enter BALURDO with a beard half off, half on"* (II.i.20.1). Piero says in surprise "What dost thou with a beard?" (II.i.22), and Balurdo explains that it is to cover his "bald wit" (24): the point of the incident, however, is that beards were not used at Paul's. Wigs were, of course, used for the ladies (*A&M*, 1101-2) but both beards and moustaches were felt to be absurd. This point is made clear by Percy in the *Dramatis Personae* to *Arabia Sitiens or Mahomet and his Heaven* where Mahomet is described as "without Moustache if for Pouls" (508) and again in the first scene of the first act occurs the direction, "Here he held him by the Bearde, or clawd him on the face. If for Poules this, Bearde for th'other" (509). Balurdo's appearance was, then, a readily recognizable absurdity, for it directly contravened the practice at Paul's.

What You Will bears the same relation to *Antonio's Revenge* as *Jack Drum's Entertainment* does to *Antonio and Mellida*; it is at once a riposte to critics and an avowal of continued determination despite detractors.[19] *What You Will* begins, as did *Antonio and Mellida* and *Jack Drum's Entertainment*, with what appears to be simply a non-dramatic illusion, but it is also a new method of opening a scene. Three gallants sit talking on the stage after the tireman has lit the candles, which was the signal for the play to begin: up to this point, probably for reasons of economy, the audience had remained in semi-darkness. The conversation of Atticus, Doricus, and Phylomuse (who is an ardent fan of Marston's) involves an attack on the Paul's critics coupled with oblique allusions to Paul's plays: Doricus speaks of *"sineor Snuffe, Mounsieur Mew,* and *Cavaliero Blirt"* (A2), a reference to *Antonio's Revenge* (I.iii.65,66), *Jack Drum's Entertainment* (in which Mounsieur John fo de King plays an important part) and Middleton's *Blurt, Master Constable* (also a Paul's play). They dismiss the objections of the critics on the

19. All quotations from *What You Will*, or *W.Y.W.*, are taken from the Quarto of 1607.

same grounds as those put forward in the Induction to *Jack Drum's Entertainment*, insisting that the whole purpose at Paul's is amusement (for actors and audience), with the implication that "rules of art" (A2ᵛ) do not apply to them. They introduce *What You Will* in a deliberately disparaging way to disarm criticism; it is "a slight toye, lightly composed, to swiftly finisht, ill plotted, worse written, I feare me worst acted" (A3). The gallants then retire inside the curtains—presumably those across the lower discovery space—because, as they point out, the stage is too small to allow spectators to sit on it. This means that at Paul's no one sat on the stage so that, when three gallants were seen on it before the beginning of *What You Will*, it would be immediately recognizable as a departure from previous habit: it would soon be apparent, however, that it was not a new precedent but rather a variation in Marston's non-dramatic illusions.

The next person to appear is the Prologue who, as in *Jack Drum's Entertainment*, vows to expend "industrious sweat" (A3ᵛ) to please these "gentle minds" (A3ᵛ), but on behalf of the author, not the actors. The play proper begins in almost exactly the same way as *Antonio's Revenge*; a defiant gesture after Marston's humiliation in *Poetaster*. *Antonio's Revenge* began with Piero's entry "unbraced", carrying a torch and followed by Strotzo with a "cord" (1.i.0.1-3); *What You Will* begins with Quadratus' entry, preceded by a Page with a torch and followed by Phylus with a lute (1.i.0.1-2), twenty-one lines later Iacomo enters "unbraced". At once we are offered a replay of Marston's successful interruption technique; Phylus sings to the lute and "*is answered, from above a Willow garland is floung downe and the songe ceaseth*" (Bᵛ)—this time the song has been likened to that which brought Eurydice back from the underworld, and it is interrupted by a garland of mourning. The inference is that heaven has answered the complaint.

What You Will is not so much a play as a loose assemblage of dramatic elements and incidents. The only character of note is Iacomo, the lover, but even he refuses to take his dramatic role seriously, as he remarks at one point,

> ... hay for the *French*,
> And so (to make up rime) god night sweete wench. (B2ᵛ)

In a similar way Marston, making allusion to *Poetaster*, dismisses the notion of taking revenge in dramatic form; Quadratus replies contemptuously to Lampatho's threat that he will be revenged, "How pree-thee? in a play?" (F4) Marston refuses either to offer a theoretical justification for his dramatic methods or to take revenge against his detractors by arraigning them on the stage.

The most interesting aspect of the play's presentation is not its content but its devices at the beginning of the acts. Act I, as we have seen, was a defiant echo of *Antonio's Revenge*; Act II recalls the opening of *Dr. Dodypoll* for "*one knockes*; Laverdure *drawes the Curtaines sitting on his bed apparalling himselfe*". Act III presents a dumb show, which takes place while the music is playing, in it Francisco is dressed by Iacomo, Andrea, and Randolpho while Bydet looks on—this represents the incorporation of the anti-dramatic mime of *Antonio and Mellida*, where Balurdo and Rosaline practised faces before mirrors, with the actual exigencies of the plot: the actors at the beginning of the third act of *What You Will* are tiring themselves, as they would normally do during the introductory music, but also are dressing as part of the plot. Finally Act V begins with the drawing of the curtain from the discovery space by a page to reveal four couples at dinner: this is an example of the simple technique of beginning a scene with a discovery, but it is also directly analogous to the raising of the curtain from the proscenium arch, in that it reveals an animated-talking-scene-in-progress which is the play. The dinner party continues while a song is sung to entertain both the diners and the audience, and then the act emerges out of the diners' conversation. Surely Marston and Paul's have by now clearly earned the right to be called an "experimental" theatre? Dramatic technique continued to develop here, even if "plot" became devalued.

As he had done in his previous plays for Paul's, Marston continues to offer intimate glimpses of the organization, structure, and operational pattern of the choristers. He presents in Act II a mock school lesson as a result of which some of the boys are recruited to become actors. Paul's could have recruited from Mulcaster's school, or from the boys taught in St. Gregory's (P.f.35), or those taught in the chapel of St. Catherine (P.f.35) or in that of St. John the Baptist (G.f.54), all of which were used as schoolrooms.[20] One of the

20. The Citizen's wife in *The Knight of the Burning Pestle* assumes that Paul's recruited from Mulcaster (I.ii.26-7), but there were a lot of boys available for John Howe, a verger, complains that Mulcaster "and other schoolemasters nere adioyinge to the Church" (G.f.60) let their boys run wild in the churchyard and break the windows.

schoolboys is rejected as unsuitable "to play the Lady in commedies presented by Children" (D) because "his voice is to smale and his stature to loe" (D), but this is not true, for the boys are recruited in *What You Will* as pages and perform a play within the play, one of them *"attired like a Merchants wife"* (G4ᵛ). To be small and to have a treble voice were not disqualifications in actors at Paul's; there are some "minikins" in *Antonio and Mellida*.

In *What You Will* there is one aspect of his dramatic practice over which Marston completely capitulates to his critics. By the end of the first act of this play only six new words have appeared and four of them are doubtful—"fan'd" (B2ᵛ), "coach'd" (B2ᵛ), "muff'd" (B2ᵛ), and "ladied" (B2ᵛ), which are used as terms to describe the fitting out of a gallant: technically these are new but hardly startling. The incidence of verbal invention has dropped to one in sixty-eight lines, or if the four doubtful words are omitted, to one in over two hundred: in *What You Will* new words occur over ninety per cent less frequently than in the *Antonio* plays. Ironically too Iacomo, with whom the more extravagant language of the play is associated, is tolerated by the other characters as a harmless freak. Does this acknowledge that criticism of his diction came from his "respected auditors" as well as from Jonson?

Our knowledge of the Paul's theatre between late 1599 and early 1602 is based upon these four plays by Marston and upon four other plays: *The Wisdome of Dr. Dodypoll* and *The Maydes Metamorphosis*, both anonymous; Middleton's *Blurt, Master Constable* and Dekker's *Satiromastix* (although the latter play was first performed at the Globe). In addition there is supplementary information in Jonson's *Poetaster* and in the five plays by William Percy (which, whether or not they were actually performed at Paul's, were certainly modified to make them suitable for that house);[21] finally, some extra details come to light in the law suits over Chapman's lost *Old Joiner of Aldgate*. Of these fourteen plays known to have been performed at or designed for Paul's over a two and one-half year period, four (Marston's) were specifically intended to give the audience an intimate knowledge of the workings of this particular company: this is a broad base upon which to rest conclusions about, at least, the interior of the Paul's house.

21. In some cases Percy's modifications for Paul's have past tense marginal notes, e.g. in the Paul's version of *A Country Tragedy*, "The Presenter departing Antonie and Cleopatra tooke their places on either side the altar" (HN 4).

It is possible that Marston was partially responsible for the interior design, since Crispinus confesses to Horace in *Poetaster*,[22]

By PHOEBUS, here's a most neate fine street, is't not?... I am enamour'd of this street.... There's the front of a building now. I studie architecture too: if ever I should build, I'de have a house just of that *prospective*. (III.i.30-5)

As we have seen, the Paul's stage had doors and a casement and part of it, at least, could be described as a house.

The area of the main stage was small, but large enough to hold seventeen actors at one time, provided that they were not wearing wide costumes—as Percy says of his attendant angels in *Arabia Sitiens*, "without cumber of wings, if for Poules" (508): it was not large enough for spectators to sit on it (*W.Y.W.*, Induction). By late 1600 it had a large trap operated from below, long enough and wide enough to use as a grave (*A.R.*, IV.v.64.1); actors could enter from this trap (*A.R.*, v.ii.) which was probably in the middle of the stage ("A Trap doore in Midde of the Stage", Percy, *Aphrodisial, The Properties*, HN4). There were access doors to the stage at either side; adjacent to, or in, one of them was a grating (*A.R.*, II.iii.122.1); in the middle there was a wider door, which was curtained and left open for use as a discovery space (or all three doors could be used for entries) as in *M.M.*, III.ii.0.1-2, "Enter Joculo, Frisco and Mopso at three severall doores").[23] This positioning for the doors is, I suggest, implicit in the *Antonio* plays and Percy, in his list of properties for *Arabia Sitiens*, saw no need to modify his statement—"At one doore Mecha...At Middle doore... Olympus...At furthest doore Amphipolis" (HN4).

The discovery space was curtained at the front and large enough to accommodate a dining table at which eight persons could be seated (*W.Y.W.*, v.i); access could be gained to it from behind and it was probably hung (by 1604, at any rate) with "arras" or curtains which allowed unseen passage (*Bussy D'Ambois*, v.i.185.1-2). It may have had a canopy over it to create the illusion of greater depth,

22. All quotations from *Poetaster* are from the Herford and Simpson edition.
23. According to *The Puritan* (Q.1607, G2ᵛ-G3) one of these doors had an operating lock and keyhole and in *The Phoenix* (Q.1607, H2ᵛ) at least one door had a ring in it. All quotations from *The Maydes Metamorphosis*, or *M.M.*, are from R. W. Bond, *John Lyly* (Oxford, 1892), III.

as Percy describes it "At Middle doore a Canopie with a Tribunal and but a greene cushion for Mahomet to sit on, over him Olympus", (*Arabia Sitiens, The Properties*, HN4).

The "above" appears to have been as wide as the main stage and essentially its design created the effect of three locations, which could be described as "houses" (*J.D.Ent.*, G3); Percy assumes this form in his list of properties for *A Country Tragedy in Vacunium*, "Tremellioes Castell, Affranioes Mannour, Sir Clodioes Desmene" (508). At least one side of the above had a "casement" which could be opened and shut—again in Percy's words "A Trap windowe full hie and aloft... shutt to or [o]pend out" (*Arabia Sitiens, The Properties*, HN4): for the sake of symmetry it is tempting to assume that there was a "casement" at either side, certainly the upper acting area appears to have been in the middle (*A.R.*, v.v.17.2-3). This upper acting area, then, seems to have been above the discovery space on the main stage, and like it, it was curtained (*A.R.*, I.iii.128.1-2) at the front and perhaps also at the back and sides, for this would allow cross-stage access; it was large enough to accommodate at least three players (*A&M*, I.i.98.2). There was a staircase to the "above", invisible to the audience, which did not require more than eight lines to descend (*J.D.Ent.*,C4-C4ᵛ). The musicians, who provided the entr'acte entertainment, were accommodated above at either side of the central acting area: on occasion additional choristers could be placed there to supplement the voices on the stage (*A.R.*, I.iii.133.1n). It was the custom at Paul's to provide music before and after each performance and also at the beginning and end of each act.

Paul's Choir could muster seventeen actors by late 1600, eleven of whom were on the foundation in 1598, the extra six being recruited specially for the plays.[24] The older boys were about fourteen, the youngest perhaps aged ten or less. They did not have an extensive stock of properties; Percy is at pains to provide an alternative form for the masque-like ending of *Arabia Sitiens*, to make it suitable for Paul's;

---

24. We definitely know the names of two of them, John Norwood and Robert Coles; they acted in *A&M* 1278.1: H.N. Hillebrand (*The Child Actors*, Urbana, 1926) lists the choirboys in 1598, p. 111. In addition one of the *Dramatis Personae* in Percy's *Faery Pastoral* is "Saloman, a schoole Boye"—Salmon Pavy was "apprentice to one Peerce" and there was an Alvery Trussell "an apprentice to one Thomas Gyles" [Hillebrand, 161]. Edward Pearce had succeeded Thomas Gyles as Master by August 15, 1600 [Chambers, II.19].

If for Actors, A Huge Globe of Fyre Pendaunt from Roofe of the Howse, withever and anone, a chattring, howling, singing, wayling and laughing betweene, *within or* without the Globe, on either syde, by the Two Angells supposed. If for Powles, A Full Moone onely appearing on face of the stage thourough the cloth and right over the Tribunall, So till the whole companie be departed. (509)

In *Poetaster* Histrio, a common player, informs Lupus that he and his fellow-sharers were sent a letter by a private company which was a request "to hire some of our properties; as a sceptre, and a crowne, for Jove; and a *caduceus* for MERCURY: and a *petasus*"(IV.iv.11-13). Paul's seem to have hired special properties, probably from the Globe, when need arose. They did have an assortment of wigs, costumes, paintings, severed human limbs, a tomb, beds, tables, and chairs. They did not use either false beards or moustaches. At least three of the company were accomplished soloists and the boys could perform a *coranto pace* (*A&M*, II.i.49.1-2), a galliard (*J.D.Ent.*, v), a Spanish pavin (*Blurt*, IV.iii.29), a measure (*Blurt*, I.i), and dance appropriately for a masque (*A.R.*, v.ii.69.1-2). They were assisted by a tireman, who was from time to time pressed into service as an actor, but who was also responsible for trimming the candles and torches during their often complex lighting effects.

The boys performed on Mondays, and apparently also on Sundays, between the hours of 4 and 6 p.m. (when the gates of the church were locked).[25] Even on Sundays in Paul's one could buy beer and ale and gamble in the Minor Canons' buttery (P.f.27), and it was common to smoke during the services (P.f.6). It must have been hard to concentrate on prayer since

people use to passe uppe to the steeple uppon Sundays and holy dayes in tyme of divine service the which people useth to hallow and make a great noyse to the great disturbance of the service of god, and also they use to throw downe stones into the churche uppon those that walke there.... (P.f.5)

In addition there was apparently no cessation of the use of the

25. See C. Sisson, *Lost Plays of Shakespeare's Age* (Cambridge, 1936), p.77 and Percy (HN4) "... The children not to begin before Fowre after Prayers And the gates of Powles shutting at six" printed by Chambers, *Elizabethan Stage*, IV. 369: Flecknoe (*c.* 1660) speaks of Paul's acting plays "on Week-dayes after Vespers" [Chambers, *Elizabethan Stage*, IV. 369]. The boys appear to have acted most days of the week.

cathedral as a major "thoroughfare of all kynd of burden bearinge people as Colliers with sacks of coles porters with basketts of flesh and such like, and also . . . a dailie receptacle for Roges and beggars howsoever diseased" (G.f.59ᵛ).

During this first phase of the revival, Paul's may have subsisted on voluntary donations and the dramatists may have financed their own productions. Even in 1601 the price of a first night at Paul's was only 2d.[26] The boys may have been rewarded for their acting on the basis of their traditional right to demand spur money, a fee required of anyone entering the church wearing spurs, whereby the choristers used to "importune men to give them monye for their spurres without regard either of person or time or place and trouble them in their prayers" (G.f.61ᵛ). In *The Gulls Hornbook* (1609), Dekker advised the gallant who wished to be noticed in the cathedral to "quote Silver into the Boyes handes" (p.20). This may explain why Paul's was expensive, despite the cheap entry; spectators were expected to reward the actors as well as pay a fee to the gatherers.

Perhaps the most difficult question about Paul's, however, yet remains. Where exactly did they perform their plays? A number of locations have been suggested; Chambers put forward the church of St. Gregory (mainly because in the twelfth century it was the choir singing-school), but he also suggested the Chapter or Convocation House (because he believed that the boys used an amphitheatre)[27]: Hillebrand felt that "When we try to fix the place in which the Paul's boys set up their theatre, we meet everywhere with the most baffling mystery" but, eventually, he settled rather vaguely for an unspecified "residence in the northwest part of the south church-yard".[28]

This uncertainty is surprising in view of the fact that there are a number of quite specific statements, in the first decade of the seventeenth century, referring to the Paul's theatre building. We know that the theatre was so much a part of the cathedral that it could be identified with it: plays were described simply as being performed "at Paul's": it was located within the area shut off to public access, when the gates were locked in the evening. At the

26. Percy, *Cuckolds and Cuckqueanes Errants*, I.ii: see also *M.M.*, *Prologue* 13-14.
27. E. K. Chambers, *The Elizabethan Stage*, II. 11 and III. 430 as well as the illustration of the Chapter House in Vol. II.
28. Hillebrand, *The Child Actors*, pp. 112-14. Gyles did have a partial interest in a house built at the southwest end of the Chapter House wall (G.f.55ᵛ), but this house does not square with the contemporary references to the Paul's playhouse with the precision of the house in the shrowdes.

same time the building was not wholly circumscribed by the fabric of the cathedral, for it was described by Burbage, Heminge, and Condell as being "neere St. Paules Church".[29] Furthermore, in 1607-08 it was "in the handes of one Mr. Pierce But then unused for a playe house":[30] while owned by the Master of the Choristers, this playhouse was subject to the control of the Dean and Chapter.[31] Finally, in 1603 Thomas Woodforde had stated under oath that Chapman's *Old Joiner of Aldgate* "was played by the children of powles in a private house of a longe tyme keepte used and accustomede for that purpose".[32]

None of the locations so far suggested satisfy all these contemporary conditions: both St. Gregory's and the buildings in the south churchyard were accessible without going through the main gates of the cathedral, and the Chapter House could hardly be described as being "in the handes of one Mr. Pierce". The Paul's playhouse lay elsewhere.

Among the articles of inquiry addressed to the officers of the Cathedral Church of St. Paul, during the visitation of Bishop Bancroft in 1598, were these:

11 how is the upper Cloyster by the Chapter house imployed, and wheather is their any extraordinarie dore for any private mans use made into it, by whome and by whose consent.

12 In whose custody are the lower Cloisters, and the place called the shrowdes how are they imployd, and by whome and whose license and whether is there any doore of any private mans use made into them, and for whose use. (G.f.20ᵛ)

Two answers were received, the first from Alexander Bradshawe, verger:

Item the upper Cloister in the Chapter howse are not imployed to any use at this present neither is there any dore for any private manns use but such as were made at the buildinge of the same as I have hard
Item the lower Cloisters and the place called the shrowdes are in the Custodie of Mr gyles and by the license of the Deane and Chapter as I have heard. (G.f.47)

29. The Burbage-Keysar suit (C. W. Wallace, "Shakespeare and his London Associates", *University Studies*, Nebraska x 4 [1910]‖ 96).
30. Ibid.
31. Sisson, *Lost Plays*, pp. 60-1.
32. Ibid.

Secondly, John Sharp, Zachery Alley, and John Howe made this reply:

> Item to the xi[th] Article we saie that the upper Cloister by the Chapter howse is not imployed with any thinge nether is there any extraordinarie dore made into them for any mans private use, but onelie the dore to goe into the leades to clense and repaier them of which dore Mr Gyles hath a keye as we are informed
> Item to the 12th Article we saie that the lower cloyster and the place called the shrowdes are in the keepinge of Mr Gyles which have a longe tyme byn used of the master of the Quoristers, there is not now any dore into them for any mans private use but there is a house builte in the shrowdes by Mr Haydon sometyme petticannon of this churche which howse we take to be verie offensive in that it is close adioyinge to the upper end of the chapter howse wall. (G.f.55)

This house fulfils all the conditions imposed by contemporary descriptions for the Paul's theatre: it was, and had been for some time, under the master's control, by "license" of the Dean and Chapter; it was inside the locked area of the cathedral and there was no separate access to it; it was at once part of, and distinct from, the cathedral fabric and it was a private house—as Woodforde, the manager, described it. One end of it was built close to the Chapter House wall (the enclosing wall of the precinct) and the other end was in the "shrowdes" (probably the cloister garth). The garth was at a level lower than the main cathedral floor: the playhouse was, in a sense, built under the cathedral. Paul's house was probably located in the northwest quadrant of this garth.[33]

This playhouse was obviously small; its stage was two-storied and thus, perhaps, inside there was a spectators' gallery but since the space available for a building adjacent to the Chapter House wall was restricted, its capacity may well have been less than a hundred "select auditors". This was a private playhouse, not merely in a technical legal sense, but literally "Mr. Haydon's house".

The cloisters around it were devoted to purely secular uses for trunk-makers were in possession of them and used them as warehouses and workshops (G.f.60) and the whole area was in the

---

33. It should be noted that *c*. 1660 Flecknoe refers specifically to this house; "the Children of . . . St. Paul's Acted Playes . . . behinde the Convocation-house in Paul's" [Chambers, IV.369].

hands of the Master of the Choristers. Not merely did he control the upper and lower cloisters but also much of the property outside the Chapter House wall, for

> There are ix shedds incroched in the Alley which leadeth to the Churche and the little sowthe dore which straights the passage on both sides of the waie, the tenants . . . [of five] hold by demise from Mr Gylles. (G.f.56)

The whole precinct of the Chapter House was controlled by Thomas Gyles; it was there that the playhouse of second Paul's was located—both figuratively, and at least partially literally, our first "underground" theatre.[34]

34. My thanks are owed to Richard Hosley (University of Arizona) for a number of valuable and illuminating suggestions (most of which are incorporated in the text) relating to the staging arrangements at Paul's.

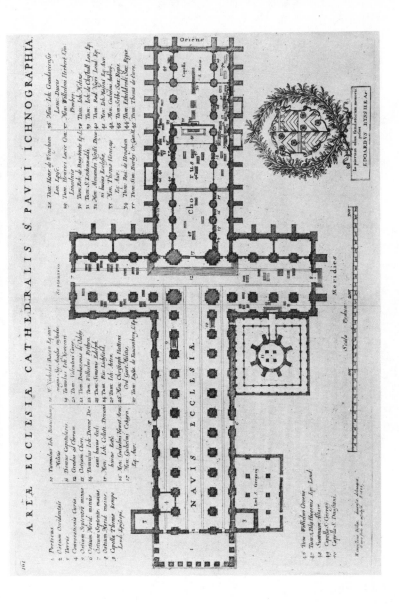

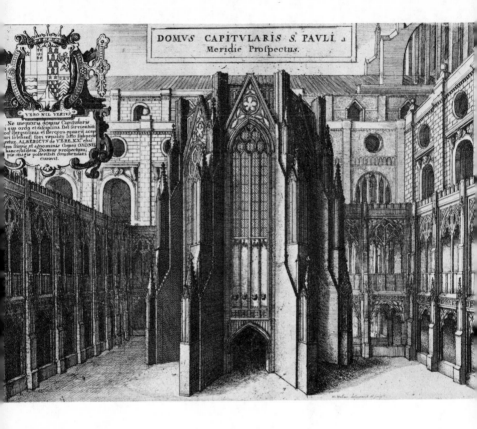

DOMVS CAPITVLARIS S. PAVLI. a
Meridie Prospectus.

APPENDIX
PAUL'S PLAYHOUSE: LOCATION

Since the main entrance to the Chapter House precinct (i.e. the whole area bounded by the enclosing wall, including the Chapter House proper, the cloisters, and the intervening spaces or garth) was from the west wall of the South Transept of the cathedral, and Flecknoe (although a late and not always accurate authority) declares that the boys of Paul's acted plays "behinde the Convocation-house in Paul's" [Chambers, IV. 369], the west wall of the precinct is indicated. By "upper" the vergers probably mean towards the main south wall of the cathedral and "end" must be "corner". The playhouse was, then, located in the northwest quadrant of the precinct.

The complaint about the house was that it was "close adioyinge" to the Chapter House wall: which wall is this? The reference cannot be to the area between the buttresses as this is an archway; the Chapter House was built upon four pillars which were inside an open octagonal undercroft. The meeting room of the Dean and Chapter was at the second-storey level, reached by a passageway which led through the upper cloister above the entrance colonnade; this room, also octagonal, had tall windows in each face.

Colonel W. Webb, Surveyor General of Bishops' Lands, surveyed the precinct on November 12, 1657: his plan is highly inaccurate, but in his accompanying description he declares that the precinct is

a Square peece of about 100 Foote each syde, bounded with the Mayne Wall of the Cathedrall on the North and East sydes thereof, and with an high old wall commonly called The Convocacon howse Wall on the West and South sydes thereof. [*P.R.O.* SP 18/179/x/K2370]

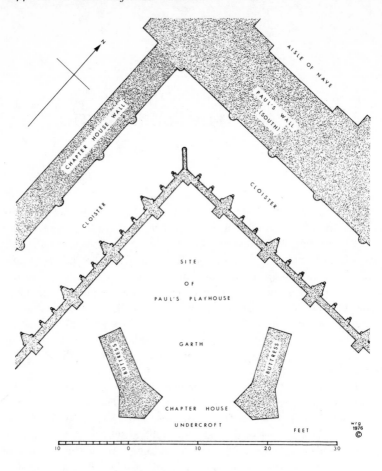

This statement, which categorically identifies the west and south walls of the precinct as the "Convocation" or "Chapter House" wall, makes it clear that the vergers were complaining because the playhouse included part of the cloisters within its structure. This would, obviously, seriously restrict access around the precinct.

The house was also in the "shrowdes". John Howe, verger, affirms in the 1598 Visitation report,

> that the Shrowdes and Cloyster under the Convocation house (were not long since the Sermons in foule weather were wont to be preached) are made a Comon laystall for boardes trunkes and chestes beinge lett out

unto trunk makers, whereby meanes of their dailie knockinge and noyse
the Churche is greatlie disturbed. (G.f.60)

This description makes it clear that the shroudes were adjacent to
and, in a sense, to be conflated with the cloister or crypt which was
formed by the undercroft of the Chapter House. The term also
appears to have been used to indicate the adjacent garth.

Confirmation of this deduction (that the garth, or area between
the cloister screen and the Chapter House undercroft, and the
shroudes, are, essentially, the same thing) is provided by the fact
that *OED* gives a figurative sense for the term [*sb.* [1] 5 *fig.*] meaning
the shadow or shade of a church. The northern part of the garth
would be permanently in the shade of the high walls of the cloister
and Chapter House.

It seems clear that the playhouse was built in the garth of the
Chapter House precinct; it included on the west (and probably also
on the north) some of the cloister bays; it extended up to the
buttresses (and perhaps projected into the undercroft) of the Chapter House.

The enlarged plan drawing of the northwest quadrant of the
Chapter House precinct is based primarily upon the report of the
excavations in this area carried out by the cathedral surveyor, F. C.
Penrose—see "Notes on St. Paul's Cathedral", *Royal Institute of
British Architects, Trans.* 29 (1878-9), 93-104 *passim*. The dimensions given in the plans which illustrate his article have been
checked against Penrose's original *Comparative Plan of the Old and
Modern Church* (Guildhall, 460/Pau (2) *pla*). A few details have
been added from Hollar's plan in Dugdale, *St. Paul's* (1658) p. 161.

The Avenger and the Satirist: John Marston's Malevole

WILLIAM BABULA

At the end of *Antonio's Revenge*, after what has been called "probably the most painful revenge—certainly ... the most horrible on-stage murder—in Elizabethan drama",[1] the Venetian senators quite incredibly offer to the avengers the "chiefest fortunes of the Venice state" (v.iii.141).[2] Antonio in particular is apparently offered the dukedom of Venice. This is indeed a rare attitude; Antonio comments on the offer: "We are amaz'd at your benignity" (v.iii.145). So too have many critics been amazed. Fredson Bowers argues that Antonio's actions "should have stamped [him] as a villain who must suffer death at the end,"[3] and Anthony Caputi writes that "Although [Antonio] claims rational control, the revenge action forces upon him acts of violence that make inescapable the inference that he suffers brutalization in the process of exercising it."[4] This is the avenger's most persistent problem: Hieronimo, Titus, and Hamlet are all virtuous men pushed into evil. But they are also dead by the end of their plays. While "the moral cost of immersion in the destructive element" was to become a crucial theme for Marston, the price did not include Antonio's death.[5]

Obviously, it is not enough to say that Antonio is a villain and should be dead; the critic must also deal with the implications of Antonio's survival. Bowers does note that while "Antonio ... refuses the dukedom and retires with no sense of moral guilt," he is reject-

1. Philip J. Finkelpearl, *John Marston of the Middle Temple: An Elizabethan Dramatist in His Social Setting* (Cambridge, Mass., 1969), p. 158.
2. My text is G. K. Hunter (ed.), *Antonio's Revenge*, Regents Renaissance Drama Series (Lincoln, Nebr., 1965).
3. In his *Elizabethan Revenge Tragedy* (Princeton, 1940), p. 124.
4. In his *John Marston, Satirist* (Ithaca, N.Y., 1961), p. 154.
5. Finkelpearl, *Marston of the Middle Temple*, p. 161.

ing "a world in which there is nothing but empty glory left him."[6]
Bowers goes on to connect this rejection of position to the "medieval
Christian theme of loathing for the vanities of the world".[7] Caputi
speaks of Antonio as a "distinctly ... Marstonian Neo-Stoic, a man
sickened by the spectacle of wrong. ... "[8] Interpreting the conclusion of the play from neither a Christian nor a Stoic position, Philip
J. Finkelpearl writes: "The vision is as darkly pessimistic as any in
Elizabethan drama. ... 'Omnipotence' treats vermin with the contempt they merit, and the natural order proceeds, indifferent to the
puny passions enacted below."[9] Antonio's final rejection reinforces
these visions of a loathsome world; his survival suggests a Senecan
tragicomedy, perhaps a contradiction in terms.

Bowers suggests that the conclusion of the play is different from
"the expiatory catastrophe of all other Elizabethan revenge
tragedies"[10] and I believe he is right. This is not society's response
to the avenger, but the avenger's response to society—an inversion
that takes one very small step towards conventional tragicomedy.
One by one the characters involved in this most grotesque revenge
reject any further participation in society. Antonio speaks of "other
vows"; Pandulpho, although attracted to suicide, speaks of life "in
holy verge of some religious order" (v.iii.152). They will remove
themselves from society, but what is important is their ability to
make this choice, for the trapped avenger, the Hamlet-figure, cannot choose his response to society. These avengers can act on their
preference to reject society completely:

> ... to meditate on misery,
> To sad our thought with contemplation
> Of past calamities. (v.iii.163-5)

It is a description of how to respond to revenge tragedy that refers to
audience and characters alike.

Thus the avengers depart because as Pandulpho says, "We know
the world" (v.iii.147). What follows is silence: the world is a calamity that one leaves alone. In *Antonio's Revenge* there is nothing to

6. *Elizabethan Revenge Tragedy*, p. 124.
7. Ibid., p. 125. G. K. Hunter, in the introduction (p. xvii) to his edition of *Antonio's
Revenge*, argues, however: "It is a gross simplification of Marston's play (and of the
revenge tradition) to suppose that either author or audience could assume a simple
assimilation of Christian ethics and revenge violence."
8. *Marston, Satirist*, p. 149.
9. *Marston of the Middle Temple*, p. 159
10. *Elizabethan Revenge Tragedy*, p. 125.

be done and nothing to be said because society cannot be rehabilitated. This is the given of revenge tragedy. In this case, the avenger lives to meditate in a "calm sequestered life" (v.iii.161) and that is all. In the final speech of the play, Marston reminds the audience of the type of play he has presented: Antonio calls for music "to close the last act of my vengeance. . . " (v.iii.172), and he mentions the "plot", a "muse", "style", a "choice audience", and an "Epilogue", and calls the story a "black tragedy". But at the same time that Marston is telling his audience that he has written a tragedy, he is also facing up to the problem of his Senecan artistic mode. A return to order is meaningless; revenge tragedy has demonstrated that there is none. Thus the silence of Antonio at the end: he has destroyed in a context of destruction. It is a Senecan education: rejection of the world is the moral for Antonio, the audience, and the artist Marston.

But the world of revenge tragedy was too limited for Marston. O. J. Campbell suggested that Antonio was only a different version of the satirist of the earlier works.[11] But the world of *Antonio's Revenge* is a radically different one from those in which the earlier figures played. It is insufficient even to argue that "like the satirist . . . [Antonio] . . . is corrective; but unlike the satirist, he . . . is incapable of the detachment required of satire."[12] One cannot be corrective as a satirist in a society that is beyond regeneration. The conventions of revenge tragedy demand death of the avenger, or at least his retreat from the world into silence; the conventions of satire, on the other hand, demand a society that can be redeemed. Finkelpearl argues that "Marston's vision [in *Antonio's Revenge*] is consonant with his satires."[13] But this is surely an oversimplification. The avenger role is not a satisfactory one, but one that must, for Marston, be modified by the satirical role. The context provided by revenge tragedy is too dismal, even for a satirist like Marston. In its very form it becomes a dead end; its morality becomes meaningless. Murder is not the material of satire. If Antonio is a satirist, he is a failure, doomed by the revenge-tragedy mode of Seneca.

Marston's best response to the problem of satirical failure is *The Malcontent*; crucial to this response is the figure of Altofront-Malevole. One approach to this figure is suggested by Samuel

11. In his *Comicall Satyre and Shakespeare's "Troilus and Cressida"* (San Marino, Calif., 1938), p. 153.
12. *Marston, Satirist*, p. 150.
13. *Marston of the Middle Temple*, p. 159.

Schoenbaum who sees little difference between Altofront and his disguise, arguing that "Marston's hero . . . is . . . a strangely tortured individual whose activities are often perversely unpleasant";[14] but such an attitude leads to a very pessimistic interpretation of the conclusion of the play. In contrast, David J. Houser comments: "An examination of the play clearly supports the position that Malevole is . . . Altofront's disguise and that the sentiments Malevole utters are not to be automatically taken to be Altofront's in either content or style."[15] Indeed, there is a sharp distinction between Malevole and Altofront. Malevole is the disillusioned and disgusted avenger who, when he is speaking for a purpose, can sound like Antonio:

> this earth is . . . the very muckhill on which the sublunary orbs cast their excrements. Man is the slime of this dung pit, and princes are the governors of these men. . . (IV.v.107-12);[16]

but when he effects the intended change he sounds like a contented and rather religious satirist: "Who doubts of Providence,/That sees this change?. . . " (IV.v.138-9). Altofront-Malevole is both satirist and avenger: destruction is but a cloak for construction. The avenger denounces, and then lapses into silence either through retreat or through death; the satirist presumably has accomplished something and will continue to attempt to improve society. Thus while Antonio rejects the dukedom of Venice, Malevole at the conclusion returns to the throne of Genoa. *Antonio's Revenge* posits a Senecan world of disaster; *The Malcontent* posits a corrupt society more in need of a scourge of villainy than an avenger of it.

Thus Marston must be very cautious about the kind of social context he creates in Genoa. A court plunged into murder is really no arena for a satirist; he would be forced into silent rejection of a damned world. There is, of course, the central act of usurpation that gives us the deposed Altofront disguised as Malevole; and there are the attempted murders and the plotted murders—but none are committed, for a corpse would create a revenge-tragedy situation and Marston would have the same problem as he had in *Antonio's Revenge*.

While the murders are never completed, another form of evil

14. "The Precarious Balance of John Marston", *Publication of the Modern Language Association of America (PMLA)*, 67 (1952) 1069.
15. "Marston's Disguised Dukes and *A Knack to Know a Knave*", *PMLA*, 89 (1974) 1002.
16. My text is Bernard Harris (ed.), *The Malcontent* (New York, 1967).

flourishes; as Caputi points out: "Practically every incident of serious matter is accompanied by or followed immediately by a brief explosion of light immoral grotesquery. . . . "[17] Here the emphasis is different from that in *Antonio's Revenge*: vice, particularly sexual vice, becomes the object of Marston's satirical thrust. Marston, of course, is returning to themes he handled earlier in *The Metamorphosis of Pygmalion's Image*, *The Scourge of Villainy*, and *Jack Drum's Entertainment*. Simply put, a sexually corrupt society is a proper target for satire, while in a world of bloody murders and cannibalism, satire is pointless. Sexual satire, as well as insisting upon education through the forms of art, is also quite in keeping with the Inns of Court tradition that Marston has been so closely tied to.[18] It is a long way from Norton and Sackville's *Gorboduc*, but *The Malcontent* can educate its audience too.[19]

While too much should not be made of Webster's Induction to *The Malcontent*, it can be seen as an attempt by a contemporary to understand the play. First in it is the audience represented by Sly and Sinklo. These are the foolish, fashion-conscious gallants who here sit on the stage, as Dekker described them doing in *The Gull's Hornbook*, and who would easily fit into Inns of Court satire, and, of course, into Marston's own verse satires. Webster is defining the audience that can best learn from this play, an audience that, because of its own predilections, finds the play "bitter". Burbage responds to this charge:

> Why should not we enjoy the ancient freedom of poesy? Shall we protest to the ladies that their painting makes them angels, or to my young gallant that his expense in the brothel shall gain him reputation? (Induction, 63-7)

Webster seems to put female folly and male sexual corruption at the centre of the play's concerns.[20] He goes on to put the revenge-tragedy elements into the background as he continues through Burbage: " . . . Such vices as stand not accountable to law should be cured as men heal tetters, by casting ink upon them" (Induction,

---

17. *Marston, Satirist*, p. 192.
18. See Finkelpearl, *Marston of the Middle Temple*, especially Chapter IV, "The Middle Temple's 'Prince D'Amour' Revels of 1597-98", pp. 45-61.
19. Finkelpearl writes of Marston's later play: "We can . . . see *The Fawne* as a latter-day, comic, more sophisticated descendant of *Gorboduc*, trying to warn the King. . . ": *Marston of the Middle Temple*, p. 236.
20. Caputi notes that "The play was constructed . . . to mend not major but minor vices": *Marston, Satirist*, pp. 181-2.

67-9). This is not a description of vice as presented in *Antonio's Revenge* or any number of revenge tragedies. An Antonio or a Hamlet cannot cure their diseased societies through satirists' words. Marston recognizes that the Genoa of Malevole cannot be the Venice of Antonio.

A second aspect of the Induction is its creation of an aesthetic distance between the audience and the play. The actor (Burbage) who is going to play Malevole walks onstage as the actor rather than the character.[21] While this is Webster's device, not Marston's, it is only reinforcing what the play implies. The distance from the action created by the Induction is only an extension of the distance created by Marston through his use of the device of the disguised duke, "the built-in guarantee in the play of a favorable outcome".[22] Both the Induction and the disguised duke tend to decrease the suspense of the revenge-tragedy plot. What follows is a tendency to concentrate on the satirical comedy rather than on the revenge tragedy. As in the later plays by Shakespeare, *Measure for Measure* and *The Tempest*, there is too much of a sense of artistic, or even perhaps divine, control to allow the audience to feel the action could degenerate into the horrors of an *Antonio's Revenge*.[23] The Induction and the disguise, that is known to the audience, reverse the kind of expectation created by the Ghost of Andrea and Revenge at the beginning of *The Spanish Tragedy*. Tragicomedy is replacing tragedy.

That Marston was in substantial agreement with Webster's interpretation of the play's main concerns is evident from Marston's additions to the third quarto: very little is added to the revenge plot; much is added to the satire. As Caputi notes, "Of the approximately 460 lines that were added practically all are satiric and relatively light in character."[24] The first major addition in Act I, scene iii, however, certainly furthers the revenge plot. Malevole urges Pietro on to revenge by means of a detailed description of Aurelia's adultery and the method works. The husband Pietro is idealized: he has selected an "inferior" lady, gone through "devoutful rites", met "her spirit in a nimble kiss", and been "true to her sheets"; he even

21. Finkelpearl interprets this device as follows: "Role-playing is shown to be a physical necessity for moral man in an immoral society": *Marston of the Middle Temple*, p. 194.
22. *Marston, Satirist*, p. 190.
23. See Bertrand Evans, *Shakespeare's Comedies* (London, 1960), especially pp. 186-219, 316-37.
24. *Marston, Satirist*, p. 200.

"diets strong his blood,/To give her height of hymeneal sweets"
(I.iii.114-5). For all this effort the adulteress

> ... gives him some court *quelquechose*,
> Made only to provoke, not satiate;
> And yet, even then the thaw of her delight
> Flows from lewd heat of apprehension,
> Only from strange imagination's rankness,
> That forms the adulterer's presence in her soul,
> And makes her think she clips the foul knave's loins.
>
> (I.iii.117-23)

Even during intercourse with Pietro, Aurelia imagines it is her lover
Mendoza instead. All of this produces the proper effect. Pietro is
urged by Malevole: "Adultery... should show exemplary punishment, that intemperate bloods may freeze but to think it"
(I.iii.141-3). This statement describes the relationship of the satirist
with his audience; he is creating examples that educate them in
morality. That is what Malevole is doing at the court of Genoa and
that is what Marston is doing in *The Malcontent*. Within this statement is a defence of the play itself. Pietro and Aurelia are not the
only audience for this tragicomedy.

For the most part, the other additions treat satirically flattery and
sexual corruption. Bilioso, in Act I, scene iv, for example, finding
Malevole in favour with the court, is ready to fawn all over him,
even offering his daughter-in-law and his wife for Malevole's pleasure, declaring: "Anything I have, stands open to thee" (71-2). The
additional scene, I.viii, comments on the same themes with references to the "sore eyes" of the cuckold Pietro, to the odd courting
practices of gallants, to the work of the old bawd Maquerelle in
inventing "woolen shoes for fear of creaking", and to Bilioso who
will "be of any side for most money".

The additions in the first three scenes of Act v follow in the same
vein although the scope of the satire widens. Bilioso's fawning is
shown to be a facet of his self-love; Maquerelle's clever method of
advertizing is satirized; the gallants' habit of duelling is mocked.
Similarly, the fool must now drink to Maquerelle's health rather
than mock her because he owes her money. Malevole comments on
the habits of young gallants who marry for money and then go travel
to avoid their wives and on hypocritical puritans and on whores. All

of these additions tend to shape the form of the play into something other than revenge tragedy.

There is, however, an important addition that requires separate examination. After Malevole has tormented Pietro in Act I, scene iii, with his "hideous imagination", the usurper exits and Marston adds a soliloquy, making it the first that Malevole speaks in the play. As such it does seem to define Malevole's ends. He certainly speaks of revenge and hints for the first time that he is the deposed duke, but his revenge is not cast in the conventional mode: as he explains, "The heart's disquiet is revenge most deep" (I.iii.151), and continues,

> Duke, I'll torment thee; now my just revenge
> From thee than crown a richer gem shall part.
> Beneath God, naught's so dear as a calm heart.
>
> (I.iii.163-5)

This is not the aim of a Vindice or a Hamlet; it is more or less the aim of a Marston, a writer of verse satire. The satirist disturbs, the satirist "breaks heart's peace", the avenger, "the life of flesh but spills". Indeed, Malevole explicitly rejects "blood" and glories rather in "a tongue/As fetterless as is an emperor's" (157-8). And it is all for a purpose, as G. K. Hunter notes: "The function of the Malcontent, Malevole, is to expose (and if possible convert) rather than punish. . . . "[25] Malevole, playing the role of an avenger in an apparent revenge tragedy, has defined that role as that of a satirist in a tragicomedy that educates.

Marston's last addition completes this development. Instead of ending with the scornful dismissal of Mendoza and the rapid handing out of judgments, he inserts a number of clearly satirical comments. The themes of flattery and sexual corruption emphasized in the additions seem as important as usurpation at the end. Malevole comments on the "strange accidents" he has witnessed at court: he has seen "the flatterer like the ivy clip the oak,/And waste it to the heart. . . " (v.iv.133-4) and also knows of

> … lust so confirmed
> That the black act of sin itself not shamed
> To be termed courtship. (v.iv.134-6)

25. In "English Folly and Italian Vice: The moral landscape of John Marston", in John Russell Brown and Bernard Harris (eds.), *Jacobean Theatre* (1960; reprinted New York, 1967), p. 100.

Sexual corruption, often the material of tragedy, is in Marston's work usually the target of satire. Thus it is fitting that the two major representatives of lust and flattery are given additional lines of ironic self-defense. Maquerelle begs not to be cast out of court into the city and Bilioso claims that he knew it was Altofront in disguise or he would not have allowed himself to be called "wittol and cuckold". The pair, however, are punished, but more by exposure than by anything else. As for Mendoza, he is simply kicked out of the court.[26] Satire and education are emphasized rather than revenge. Yet, after all, Malevole had told us early in the play, in an addition, that he was not a very conventional avenger.

Marston's additions, then, serve to emphasize Malevole as satirist rather than as avenger. Yet Malevole is an avenger; he has lost his throne and he is plotting to regain it. His role as a Machiavel gives him the effectiveness that the ranting satirist lacks. And yet his role as avenger continually slips into one of educator which is, after all, what a satirist is. Of this double role, Finkelpearl writes: "As a satirist and teacher, he shows what the world is; as a god of policy, he shows how to cope with it."[27] Thus, while he wishes to regain his throne from Pietro, he seems much more interested in educating Pietro, and Ferneze and Aurelia, than in killing them. In that sense these three can be seen as analogous to the audience. They will, depending on their sins, learn the effects of flattery and sexual corruption. Furthermore, as they learn, so too does the audience. They have become examples to be paralleled for the audience with Celso, the Captain, and Maria. The play has become "exemplary", to borrow Malevole's own word. By the end of the play both Marston and Malevole are working as proper satirists in a tragicomic mode.

Thus Marston has also discovered a proper form. Finkelpearl speaks of "theatrical innovation", but Marston is really seeking a mode that would affect the audience of wits he had apparently been trying to reach since the reopening of the private theatres in 1599.[28] Perhaps the knowledge that *The Malcontent* would be played before a much less select audience in the public theatre than in the private led Marston to emphasize the play's satirical elements. In any case,

26. Bernard Harris, in the introduction (p. xxxii) to his edition of *The Malcontent*, comments on this action: "To feel that Marston has let Mendoza off too lightly, is to ignore the peculiar satisfaction, personal and public, that this exemplary action affords."
27. *Marston of the Middle Temple*, p. 193.
28. Ibid., pp. 118, 193.

The Malcontent deals with a society that can be redeemed, although Ferneze's attempted seduction of Bianca after his reformation adds the right note of human realism. In contrast, the vision presented in *Antonio's Revenge* is in the end morally empty: the avenger deals with a society that cannot be saved. There is nothing much more to learn than the Senecan lesson. The point of *The Malcontent* is the moral education of the audience by both positive and negative examples shaped by art. That education is the aim (and can be the triumph) of the satirical, tragicomic form that denies the implications of *Antonio's Revenge*. The form Marston has developed is much more consonant with his moral vision and satirical purpose: Senecan tragicomedy has become Renaissance tragicomedy.

Involved in all of this is the crucial sense of education through art, particularly through satire in a non-Senecan tragicomic mode. Marston moves away from Senecan revenge tragedy because of the negative implications of the action it imitates. As Hardin Craig has noted, "With Seneca the very nature of things was disastrous, and calamity was irresistible and inescapable."[29] In *The Malcontent* characters can learn and change; moral education for the audience becomes crucial within the play and without. Pietro, for example, learns and changes and becomes an example who comments as he recognizes Altofront as rightful duke: "[I] world tricks abjure,/For vengeance, though't comes slow, yet it comes sure" (IV.v.122-3). And it is not too late. Similarly, as Pietro asks Altofront for forgiveness, Ferneze enters to ask Pietro to pardon him. Pietro, who has learned, offers "pardon and love"; furthermore, a final pardon will be given to the penitent and miserable Aurelia—a very unusual outcome in which a wife is allowed to survive her adultery. Marston has shifted modes because this kind of education is impossible in Senecan revenge tragedy. In contrast to the necessary abjuration of a damned world by Antonio, Altofront can say at the conclusion of his play: "And as for me, I here assume my right" (v.iv.161). Continued exertion in an imperfect but redeemable world is part of the apparent moral of *The Malcontent*. For Marston in this play calamity is neither irresistible nor inescapable.

There are also a number of references in the play that suggest the "exemplary" nature of the action. Malevole speaks of his "fantastical" dreams in which he sees "... here a Paris supports that Helen, there's a Lady Guinever bears up that Sir Lancelot" (I.iii.50-1).

29. In "The Shackling of Accidents: A Study of Elizabethan Tragedy", *Philological Quarterly*, Vol. 19 (1940); reprinted in Ralph J. Kaufmann (ed.), *Elizabethan Drama: Modern Essays in Criticism* (New York, 1961), p. 33.

Over and over the pattern is repeated in art, in history, and in the present; as Malevole says: "Common things [are] women and cuck-olds" (I.iii.19-20). The moral of the story of Aurelia and Pietro is the moral of Paris and Helen, and Guinever and Lancelot, only it is not as "bitter", to repeat a word from the Induction. There are also specific references to "those antique painted drabs that are still affected of young courtiers, Flattery, Pride, and Venery" (I.iii.24-25), which are figures out of a morality play. Marston means to educate his audience as well as Pietro, Aurelia, and the rest.

Although all of the above are negative examples, there are other kinds of "exemplary" figures, particularly the idealized duchess Maria. Malevole speaks of the dangers of a Genoa palace to such a woman:

> When in an Italian lascivious palace,
> A lady guardianless,
> Left to the push of all allurement,
> The strongest incitements to immodesty,
> To have her bound, incensed with wanton sweets,
> Her veins filled high with heating delicates,
> Soft rest, sweet music, amorous masquerers,
> Lascivious banquets, sin itself gilt o'er,
> Strong fantasy tricking up strange delights,
> Presenting it dressed pleasingly to sense,
> Sense leading it unto the soul, confirmed
> With potent example, impudent custom,
> Enticed by that great bawd, Opportunity;
> Thus being prepared, clap to her easy ear
> Youth in good clothes, well-shaped, rich,
> Fair-spoken, promising-noble, ardent, blood-full,
> Witty, flattering—Ulysses absent,
> O Ithaca, can chastest Penelope hold out? (III.ii.32-49)

Despite all the temptations Penelope can be chaste and so can the besieged Maria; there are alternatives. Marston transforms the story of Penelope into the Renaissance-court story of Maria in an Italian palace; and art and mythical history combine to create the "exemplary" actions that educate an audience. Marston has moved beyond the Senecan mode and its dismal implications. One can learn what the world is and what men must be and survive, which is something that the classical Seneca could not allow for. Not only is Malevole the avenger a satirist and educator, but so is Marston the artist.

On Marston, *The Malcontent*, and *The Revenger's Tragedy*[1]

R. A. FOAKES

In Act II of *The Revenger's Tragedy* there occurs one of a number of brilliant dramatic moments in the play, when Lussurioso, led by Vindice to think his stepmother, the Duchess, is making love with the Duke's bastard son Spurio in the Duke's bed, rushes on stage with his sword drawn to pull the curtains screening the bed, rejoicing to have an excuse to kill both. Vindice comes with him, egging him on, but Lussurioso, thoroughly provoked, and rehearsing the deed in imagination, pushes him away as he takes the final steps towards the bed:

> Away, my spleen is not so lazy;
> Thus, and thus, I'll shake their eyelids ope,
> And with my sword shut 'em again for ever. (II.iii.5-7)

Brandishing his sword, he draws the curtains screening the bed's occupants from the audience and himself, to reveal, unexpectedly, the Duchess in bed with the Duke. In a play so much concerned in language with what Vindice calls "Dutch lust, fulsome lust" (I.iii.56), and set in a court where the Duchess's youngest son

1. When I prepared this paper for the conference in July 1975, I had no idea that G. K. Hunter's edition of *The Malcontent* for the "Revels Plays" series would be published a few weeks after the conference. I have taken the opportunity to study his critical introduction, and to use the text of his edition for quotations. His introduction is full of subtle insights, deepening and extending his previous writings on the play; at the same time, although we agree on a number of matters, we approach the play from such differing perspectives, and our conclusions are so different, that the two essays may be seen as supplementing one another. In relating the play to *The Revenger's Tragedy* and the plays of Beaumont and Fletcher, I seek to define its

typically regards rape as mere "sport" (i.i.66), it is something of a
surprise for the audience to find husband and wife in bed, but for
both the Duke and Lussurioso it is an even greater, and indeed
quite devastating, shock:

> *Lussurioso* Villain! Strumpet!
> *Duke* You upper guard defend us —
> *Duchess* Treason! Treason!
> *Duke*   —O, take me not
> In sleep; I have great sins, I must have days,
> Nay, months, dear son, with penitential heaves,
> To lift 'em out, and not to die unclear.
> O! thou wilt kill me both in heaven and here.
> *Lussurioso* I am amaz'd to death. (ii.iii.8-15)

The Duke, for the moment confronting his own death, falls into a
posture of penitence, perhaps kneeling to his own son; Lussurioso,
equally taken aback and horrified to find his father there, is
paralysed, and can do or say nothing, except to indicate how completely he is disarmed. The Duke recovers first, as his guard enters
to seize Lussurioso, who speaks truer than he knows in saying "I am
amaz'd to death", for the Duke is shortly to sentence him to death.

It is, I think, worth attending to what is going on in this moment
of good drama and effective theatre. *The Revenger's Tragedy* has
achieved its present high reputation largely through the critical
efforts of writers, beginning with T. S. Eliot, who emphasized the
quality of the poetry and its imagery, and the moral intensity of the
play. There has been much less interest in its effectiveness as
drama, which was splendidly revealed in the professional production at the Pitlochry Festival in 1965, and then in the Royal Shakespeare Company's presentation of it at Stratford in 1966. The latter
production stressed another critical commonplace about the play,
its echoing of *Hamlet*, by staging both plays in the same season, and

limitations, as well as its peculiar qualities; Professor Hunter's chief concern is to
establish what can be said for the play, and he claims a greater unity and a greater
sense success for it than I do. I am not persuaded, as he is, that the serious and
absurd come together, that the satiric and comic visions are fused (as he claims on p.
lxii), or that a play "concerned with speeches, passions, and persuasions which are
rendered unreal by a context which highlights their manner rather than their matter"
(p. lxxx) can equally be seriously concerned with real issues, like "the distinction
between the power of a tyrant and the power of a true ruler" (p.lv).

using the same colours and similar costumes in both. In fact, the episode in which Lussurioso rushes in on his father in the expectation of finding Spurio may have some link with Hamlet encountering Claudius at prayer, but here, as in most of the play, the differences from *Hamlet* are more interesting and significant than the similarities to it.

Like the Duke in *The Revenger's Tragedy*, Claudius conceals his crimes behind the facade of authority, but the presentation of character is different. Claudius is portrayed in depth as a King with a conscience, and Hamlet, whose effort has been to catch Claudius off his guard and expose him, is reduced to impotence by the circumstances in which, for the only time in the play, he does have the King at his mercy, for at this moment Claudius is seriously at his devotions. The action is, so to speak, contained within the play, and is realistic in the sense that we have the illusion that it springs from the characters themselves, who are wholly engaged in what they are doing. Shakespeare here avoids the theatricality of a surprise confrontation between Hamlet and Claudius and brings out instead the deeper resonances of Hamlet's moral uncertainties and Claudius's guilt; Claudius never knows that Hamlet stumbled upon him at prayer. When Lussurioso rushes into the bedchamber of his father in *The Revenger's Tragedy*, he is directed there by Vindice, whose aim is to prevent him seducing his sister Castiza, but neither Vindice, nor Lussurioso, nor, for that matter, anyone in the audience, expects that the Duke will be in his own bed. Lussurioso is reduced to impotence by sheer amazement, and the Duke's hypocrisy is exposed as, in the threat of immediate death, he is driven to acknowledge his sins. Here the action is, so to speak, imposed by the dramatist, and is non-realistic in the sense that it exploits the theatricality of a wholly unexpected confrontation between characters who are manipulated to this end by the author.

In this way the simultaneous exposure of Lussurioso and the Duke has connections with farce; in the Royal Shakespeare Company's production this episode was very funny, as were other incidents in the play, such as the scenes portraying the mistaken zeal with which Ambitioso and Supervacuo rush to bring about the execution of their own brother, while supposing they are ridding themselves of the heir to the dukedom, their stepbrother Lussurioso (III.i; III.vi). Here the humour has a macabre edge to it, and it becomes even more bizarre and gruesome in the scenes in which Vindice as dramatist designs the most effective staging of the death of the Duke, using the skull of his mistress "dressed up in tires", delighting in his own skill as artist:

> O sweet, delectable, rare, happy, ravishing! (III.v.1)

At the same time, *The Revenger's Tragedy* impresses itself in the theatre as a disturbing and serious play. On the one hand it shows the dramatist manipulating his characters into situations and confrontations that can border on the farcical, and exploiting a self-conscious theatricality that even has Vindice's request for the sound of thunder answered (IV.ii.199), the character cueing his own stage effect; on the other hand, it involves the audience by its sustained challenge to their moral complacencies:

> Does every proud and self-affecting dame
> Camphor her face for this? and grieve her maker
> In sinful baths of milk, when many an infant starves
> For her superfluous outside—all for this? (III.v.84-7)

So Vindice preaches, displaying the skull of his dead mistress, and we all feel the chill.

In recent years we have come to understand much about the "self-conscious dramaturgy including discontinuous action emphasizing scenes rather than plot, and exaggerated characters manipulated for debates and passionate declamations"[2] that was developed notably by Jonson and Marston, was used in a rather different way by Beaumont and Fletcher, and had an influence on Shakespeare's last plays. It would be hazardous to point to any particular origin for this. It involves the use of elements of burlesque, farce, and parody, all of which can be found in earlier drama, as in the work of Lyly, or in Peele's *Old Wives' Tale*. However, in so far as it is linked to the rise of formal satire based on Latin models, which achieved currency in the 1590s in the writings of poets like Donne, Hall, and Marston, it can be said to emerge at the end of this decade with peculiar strength. As a dramatic technique it is especially associated with the revival of the children's theatres in 1599-1600 and with the new mode of "comical satire"

---

2. Arthur C. Kirsch, "*Cymbeline* and Coterie Dramaturgy", *ELH, A Journal of English Literary History*, Vol. XXXIV (1967) 293; Professor Kirsch has developed his argument in his important book, *Jacobean Dramatic Perspectives* (Charlottesville, Va., 1972).

introduced at this time by Jonson and Marston. In such plays there may be "no continuous plot, but rather a serial arrangement of episodes designed to further various intrigues and expose various characters";[3] the plays were acted by children, who could be used by the dramatist with a conscious reference to adult actors, to imitate, mock, or parody, with the effect of translating the spectators' awareness into a "dual consciousness of the actors as actors and characters".[4]

It is important not to overemphasize the element of parody or burlesque, and categorize these or other plays of the period too simply, so giving force to the reasonable complaint that a bad play may too readily be transformed into a good one by the discovery of unsuspected ironies or burlesque in it.[5] It is equally important not to ignore these aspects and treat plays like Marston's *Antonio* plays and *The Malcontent* too solemnly. Arguably, the best dramatic achievements of Marston lie in these plays, especially *The Malcontent*. By comparison, *The Dutch Courtesan* and *The Fawn* seem slight, possessing local and topical interest in relation to London life and the probably satiric allusion to James I in the weak figure of Duke Gonzago, and *Sophonisba* contains ceremonious artificialities that reflect, in Marston's conscious straining for epic grandeur, the limitations of children as actors of serious tragedy. The critical difficulty of Marston's central plays is that, while everyone seems to agree that they are interesting and important, opinion is divided about what sort of plays they are, and the degree of their success. Most see an earnest, even passionate, moralist in Marston; a few see a dramatist primarily occupied with comic or absurd effects; some see both aspects, and, in the case of *The Malcontent* especially, rescue the moralist and dismiss the clown in order to claim for it a serious world-view, for recent criticism of Jacobean drama has taken this more than anything else to be the measure of a successful play.

It is possible to extract from *The Malcontent* a notional moral vision, and, by dwelling on particular speeches, to find a weighty thematic content—to claim, for example, that "Malevole's sombre vision of man's desperate state moves Pietro beyond the limits of his

---

3. "*Cymbeline* and Coterie Dramaturgy", p. 290.
4. Michael Shapiro, "Children's Troupes: Dramatic Illusion and Acting Style", *Comparative Drama*, Vol. III (1969) 48.
5. See Richard Levin, "The New *New Inn* and the Proliferation of Good Bad Drama", *Essays in Criticism XXII* (1972) 41-7.

personal grief into a declaration of his political guilt,"[6] or that the
play is unified by its imagery into a satire with simony as its
principal target.[7] Perhaps Marston intended to express these
things, and to evoke in his readers "a profound sense of moral
distress",[8] but I suspect it is only the *reader*, placing his emphasis
where he likes, and attending to what he wants, who can find in this
or the *Antonio* plays anything like a coherent ethical vision. In his
dedication to Ben Jonson, and address "To the Reader", Marston
calls the play a comedy, and refers to it as "this trifle", while at the
same time claiming that his satire is directed only at "those whose
unquiet studies labour innovation, contempt of holy policy, rev-
erend, comely superiority, and established unity". Readers can
attend to the concern with policy and disorder, but most have not
had the opportunity (not, at least, until 1973, when it was performed at the Nottingham Playhouse in a version somewhat adapted
by John Wells, and directed by Jonathan Miller) of seeing the play
professionally staged and of discovering whether, as acted, it turns
out to be a mere "trifle" after all. This production stressed the comic
and grotesque aspects of the play, which took on something of the
nature of a series of satirical sketches, in what John Wells described
in his programme note as an atmosphere of "tragic slapstick". The
characters tended to turn into caricatures, and although it may have
been Jonathan Miller's design to emphasize the comedy, and make
the play as funny as possible, what he did has warrant in the text.
So, for example, when Mendoza has a soliloquy at the end of I.v
praising "sweet women, most sweet ladies... preservers of mankind,
life-blood of society", echoing Hamlet's praise of man, "In body how
delicate, in soul how witty, in discourse how pregnant, in life how
wary", it is immediately followed by a scene in which we see the

6. See Bernard Harris's introduction to his New Mermaid Series edition of *The
Malcontent* (New York, 1967), p. xxix. Philip J. Finkelpearl also finds in the play a
"nightmare" vision of "what it must cost the morally innocent to participate in a
degraded society": *John Marston of the Middle Temple: An Elizabethan Dramatist in
His Social Setting* (Cambridge, Mass., 1969), p. 194.
7. Einer Jensen, "Theme and Imagery in *The Malcontent*", *Studies in English
Literature*, Vol. x (1970) 367-84; for him the central theme of the play is "the conflict
between the forces of order and disorder", p. 380.
8. The phrase is from Anthony Caputi, *John Marston, Satirist* (Ithaca, N.Y., 1961), p.
198. Caputi, in fact, acknowledges elements of burlesque in the play, and notices that
a latent evil never becomes active, but yet claims there is a successful fusion of "the
solemn and the grotesque". For an emphasis on the comedy and conscious histrionics
as distancing and curbing the effect of what might have been sombre and disturbing,
see Brian Gibbons, *Jacobean City Comedy* (London, 1968), pp. 98-103.

court-ladies for the first time, led by Aurelia, the Duchess who freely cuckolds her husband with Mendoza and then tries to do so with Ferneze, and Maquerelle, whose very name implies what she is, a hideous old bawd. Mendoza's speech could be read in serious terms, but whether interpreted as satirical or as straightforward praise of women, it is, so to speak, disarmed by the nature of the action in which it is set, and rendered comic. It is difficult to see how Maquerelle and her troop of "ladies" could be presented on stage without at any rate verging on caricature; it is what her very name implies.

This production confirmed for me a sense that the "main interest is in intrigue; the insistence on the externality of the action, the intricate arrangements of effects, as in the use of multiple disguises, the conscious staging, and the exaggerations of the language, all establish a tonality that undermines Malevole's attacks on court corruption and his enthusiasm for 'fearless virtue'."[9] At the same time, this has to be set against the experience of critics who, studying the play as readers, treat it with varying degrees of seriousness, even solemnity; perhaps the most persuasive of these is G. K. Hunter, who argues that "*Antonio and Mellida* asks us to see the matter of court intrigue as at once passionately serious and absurdly pointless,"[10] a phrase that might be applied equally well to *The Malcontent*. The question to ask is how may a connection be made between seriousness and absurdity? The first is likely to appear more prominent in a reading, while the second dominates in the theatre.

Marston's "seriousness" is to be found chiefly in the emphasis on corruption in the state, the sententiae, and quasi-philosophical reflection in certain speeches of Malevole and Mendoza. At the beginning of the play, for example, Malevole informs Duke Pietro that he is being cuckolded by Mendoza, and urges him to take revenge in an exchange of dialogue that is so extravagant that it borders on the comic:

> *Malevole* A cuckold. To be made a thing that's hoodwinked with kindness, whilst every rascal fillips his brows; to have a coxcomb with egregious horns pinned to a lord's back, every page sporting himself with

9. R. A. Foakes, *Shakespeare, the Dark Comedies to the Last Plays* (London, 1971), p. 71.
10. "Introduction", G. K. Hunter (ed.), *Antonio and Mellida*, Regents Renaissance Drama Series (Lincoln, Nebr., 1965), p. xvii.

delightful laughter, whilst he must be the last to know it. Pistols and poniards! pistols and poniards!
Pietro Death and damnation!
Malevole Lightning and thunder!
Pietro Vengeance and torture!
Malevole Catso!
Pietro O, revenge!...
Malevole I would damn him and all his generation: my own hands should do it; ha! I would not trust heaven with my vengeance anything.
Pietro Anything, anything, Malevole! Thou shalt see instantly what temper my spirit holds.... (I.iii.97-106, 149-53)

Pietro rushes off, as it seems to execute something, but, as always in this play, to no effect. Maquerelle, bribed by Ferneze, has led the Duchess to transfer her favours from Mendoza to him, so that when, in Act I, scene vii, Pietro storms in (not "instantly", as he said he would in Act I, scene iii, but three scenes later), sword in hand, to attack Mendoza, Marston has cut the ground from under him. Mendoza is as mad at being jilted by Aurelia, as Pietro is mad at being cuckolded by her, and the scene is emptied of all danger as Mendoza jests his way out of death:

Pietro Say thy prayers.
Mendoza I ha' forgot 'um.
Pietro Thou shalt die!
Mendoza So shalt thou. I am heart-mad.
Pietro I am horn-mad.
Mendoza Extreme mad.
Pietro Monstrously mad. (I.vii.2-8)

Mendoza simply does not take Pietro's threats seriously and Marston continues a moment of good theatre by having him in effect mock the revenge stance, and then proceed to turn Pietro's anger against Ferneze.

In citing the passage from Act I, scene iii in which Malevole provokes Pietro to rush off to do something "instantly", I quoted what Marston first wrote. In the text as we read it, this scene incorporates two substantial additions, included for the first time in the third quarto: one begins just after Pietro's line "O, revenge", and consists of about thirty-five lines in which Malevole dilates on the theme of adultery and incest; the second is a soliloquy given by

Malevole after Pietro's exit, in which he takes pleasure in the idea of afflicting Pietro with "heart's disquiet", and contemplates his own revenge upon the man who has usurped his dukedom:

> Duke, I'll torment thee; now my just revenge
> From thee than crown a richer gem shall part. (I.iii.170-1)

These additions seem to be conceived more in the spirit of a serious revenge play, but the writer knew that no deaths occur in the play; even Pietro's losing his peace of mind, the "richer gem" than his crown, is a theme that evaporates as Mendoza turns Pietro's anger against Ferneze, and Malevole's intrigues begin to focus on Mendoza. Marston's concern seems to have been to make a comedy (as his address to the reader calls it), or tragicomedy (as the Stationer's Register entry calls it), embodying, as the Prologue says

> the freedom of a pen,
> Which still must write of fools, whiles't writes of men.

The additions confuse here the tone of a play which in any case seems uncertain in its direction; they simultaneously toughen the dialogue of Malevole and enlarge the comic dialogue by adding the role of the fool Passarello, and expanding that of Bilioso, an old courtier.

However "serious" the speeches of Malevole and Mendoza may be, the tendency of the action is to dissipate their effect; railing against vice seems in the end a bit pointless when the vicious are so ineffectual and villainy never achieves its end. Marston prefers in this play to exploit opportunities for theatricality, as in the confrontation between Pietro and Mendoza, when Pietro rushes in with "his sword drawn", as the stage direction puts it, and Mendoza, showing no sense of danger, turns aside the threat by his witty response. By contrast, the scene in *The Revenger's Tragedy* in which Lussurioso rushes into his father's bedchamber with drawn sword produces its moment of comedy, as both are taken aback and the Duke, petrified with fear and thinking he is at the point of death, bursts, we may imagine for the first time ever, into prayer, but the overall effect is contained within the serious action of the play; the danger is real, and the Duke recovers quickly to have Lussurioso arrested and sentenced to death. Even the wit of the dialogue becomes secondary to the action, as Lussurioso is reduced to silence, except for his comment, "I am amaz'd to death", which has a deeper meaning than he suspects, as he is shortly taken off to be sentenced. Marston's play reaches a climax when Mendoza hires Malevole and the disguised Pietro to poison one another, a (deliberately ?) implausible device designed to lead to the scene (IV.iv) in which these two echo one another in revealing all:

> *Pietro* I am commanded to poison thee.
> *Malevole* I am commanded to poison thee—at supper.
> *Pietro* At supper!
> *Malevole* In the citadel.
> *Pietro* In the citadel!
> *Malevole* Cross-capers, Tricks! (IV.iv.8-13)

The emphasis is upon the "cross-capers", and the effect one of comic bathos, in a ludicrous descent from the sententiae with which Mendoza closes the preceding scene:

> Then conclude,
> They live not to cry out ingratitude,
> *One stick burns t'other, steel cuts steel alone;*
> *'Tis good trust few; but, O, 'tis best trust none!*   (IV.iii.141-4)

Not content with making the following action undo any effect these lines might have, Marston gives to Malevole a topical joke that invites the audience not to take such speeches seriously; Pietro enters speaking in the same vein as Mendoza, that is to say as if he is in a serious revenge-play:

> *Pietro* O let the last day fall, drop, drop on our cursed heads!
> Let heaven unclasp itself, vomit forth flames!
> *Malevole* O do not rand, do not turn player; there's more of them
> than can well live one by another already. (IV.iv.2-5)

Here Marston deflates the "serious" speeches of Mendoza and Pietro in both action and dialogue. Again, the contrast between this and *The Revenger's Tragedy* is revealing. In this play Vindice, disguised as Piato, carries through his scheme of poisoning the Duke, and casts off the disguise he has been using; he is then hired by Lussurioso to kill Piato, that is, himself, so he is put to his "inventions" (IV.ii.202) and comes up with a "device" (IV.ii.208) of dressing up the body of the Duke in Piato's clothes, so that Lussurioso will discover the body, and believe he was murdered by Piato, who has disappeared from court. All this is wholly motivated by and contained within the sustained action of the play, so that when Vindice bursts out into what Malevole calls "rant" in this scene, his speech has powerful and serious resonances:

> O, thou almighty patience! 'Tis my wonder
> That such a fellow, impudent and wicked,
> Should not be cloven as he stood, or with
> A secret wind burst open.
> Is there no thunder left, or is't kept up
> In stock for heavier vengeance? There it goes! (IV.ii.194-9)

There is a comic edge to the successful deception he practises on Lussurioso, but this speech, like the whole episode, works with a savage irony, making us aware of deeper deceptions in the action, as Vindice fails to recognize in himself someone as "impudent and wicked" as Lussurioso. Even the theatricality of the thunder that sounds at Vindice's request is subdued so that the action predominates; he does not ask for whom it sounds, but we know it is directed at him as much as anyone.

The Malcontent seems by comparison almost frivolous, exploiting "cross-capers", sudden turns, coincidences, and surprises for their own sakes. In performance these things predominate, and although the characters sometimes take themselves seriously, they inhabit a sort of cartoon version of a corrupt court, in which revenge motifs are deployed for comic and melodramatic effects. This is not to suggest that the play is merely trivial; the contrast drawn with *The Revenger's Tragedy* illustrates the extent to which its serious concerns are brought home to us in the total effect of the drama through the comic; it has the kind of seriousness that caricature can have, freeing the grosser energies of humanity into inflated and grotesque proportions in character and language, but containing them at the level of gesture, by denying them fulfilment,[11] so that as spectators

---

11. G. K. Hunter remarks, in specific relation to Bilioso and Maquerelle, that "the play achieves tragicomedy because it is able to frustrate their intentions while liberating their energies": *The Malcontent*, p. lxxxiii. My point is that it equally releases the energies of Malevole (as Altofronto he is one-dimensional), Mendoza, and Pietro, and this release creates something very different from tragicomedy in the mode, say, of Beaumont and Fletcher.

we can be amused, and enjoy the exhibition, which exposes potential violence, horror, and obscenity, but allows us to contemplate the spectacle with relief and pleasure because it is all playful and exaggerated, and never issues in action.

So the play has power, marked in the vigour of its language and its dramaturgy, and it also has, with the *Antonio* plays, a special importance as an innovative work. It provided a new slant on the malcontent figure, and the ways in which such a dramatic character could be used; it constituted a kind of critical comment on *The Spanish Tragedy* and *Hamlet*, showing how the exaggerations of revenge tragedy could be made comic—and if there are hints of this in earlier plays like Marlowe's *The Jew of Malta*, no one before Marston did it with such wit and sophistication; and it revealed new ways in which entertaining stage effects could be obtained by exploiting various kinds of theatrical artifice for the conscious enjoyment of the spectator.

So in the Induction to *Antonio and Mellida* Alberto reproves the boy-actor who is to take the role of Antonio, and who is worried at having to "play a lady" when Antonio is disguised as an "Amazon", saying it is "common fashion" to "play two parts in one", and goes on, "Nay, if you cannot bear two subtle fronts under one hood, idiot go by, go by, off this world's stage." The echo of Hieronimo suggests Marston's point of departure, but his innovation is indicated too, in extending the idea of playing two parts in one, as in *The Malcontent*, where Act IV, scene iv, brings together Malevole, the disguised Duke Altofronto, and Pietro, the usurping Duke disguised as a hermit, to reveal that they have been hired by Mendoza, who has been playing "two parts in one" in another sense, to kill each other. The parts they play generate most of our interest and most of the dramatic excitements of *The Malcontent*, and go near to obliterating any sense of character, of identity; all seem chiefly involved in playing games, and the action has something of the nature of a charade.[12]

Malevole is also playing two parts in one in yet another way: on

12. In relation to this, T. F. Wharton, in an important essay, *"The Malcontent* and 'Dreams, Visions, Fantasies'", *Essays in Criticism*, Vol. XXIV (1974) 271, argues that "The play founders because Marston refuses to exploit the ambiguities of Altofronto's position. Although the way in which his disguise absorbs him into the fantasies and fictions of the Genoese court is clearly demonstrated, the play stops short of recognizing that his performance at the end of the play (as pious and magnanimous ruler), is a further piece of role-playing, a self-glorification quite as involuntary as the 'dreams' of Mendoza."

the one hand as he indulges himself in the sheer pleasure of "cross-capers" and tricks, and on the other hand when he moralizes in lofty terms, as in his speech in this scene, "World! 'tis the only region of death, the greatest shop of the devil, the cruellest prison of men . . . there's nothing perfect in it but extreme, extreme calamity" (iv.iv.27-31). At this point the repentant Aurelia enters, being led away apparently to banishment, but the prevailing tone, and the sentimental excesses of her rhetoric, anticipating Fletcher,[13] undermine her stance, and her happy reunion with her husband a few scenes later is hardly surprising. There is, in other words, no sustained connection between Malevole's fooling and his moralizing, between action and speech. Hence arises that sense G. K. Hunter has of Marston's court intrigues as being "at once passionately serious and absurdly pointless";[14] the weakness of *The Malcontent* is that it lacks a shaping vision that might control and unite these contraries. Marston is content in the end to let his play see-saw between them, and since there is nothing to sustain in action what is serious in dialogue, the total effect is weighted towards the absurd.

Some might argue that Malevole himself is a kind of spokesman for Marston, and so becomes a controlling voice in the play; and in some senses it is true that the play we witness is "created" by Malevole, who pulls the strings and arranges much of the action. However, if he is to be identified with Marston, this merely confirms the view of the play I have been presenting, since Malevole does not so much exercise an overall control as indulge himself in a kind of variety show, a display cabinet of humours and fantasies—for this is what he "dreams" and brings to life, as he says when we first see him in Act I, scene iii:

Pietro ... I hear thou never sleep'st?
Malevole O no, but dream the most fantastical... O heaven! O fubbery, fubbery!

13. The anticipation of Fletcher is convincingly argued by Kirsch, in "*Cymbeline* and Coterie Dramaturgy" and *Jacobean Dramatic Perspectives*.
14. In this estimate I differ from G. K. Hunter, as indicated in note 1. His claims for the play are more guarded than those of a number of other critics, such as Brian Gibbons, who finds in it a "rich organic coherence": *Jacobean City Comedy*, p. 98. These arguments do reflect a general tendency to claim for *The Malcontent* qualities it does not in my view possess. An exception to the general pattern is T. F. Wharton, who argues in "*The Malcontent* and 'Dreams, Visions, Fantasies'", p. 272, that it is not possible to "Make sense of the play's contradictory, cynical and didactic elements."

Pietro Dream? What dreamest?

Malevole Why, methinks I see that signior pawn his foot-cloth, that metreza her plate; this madam takes physic, that t'other monsieur may minister to her; here is a pander jewelled; there is a fellow in a shift of satin this day, that could not shift a shirt t'other night. Here a Paris supports that Helen; there's a Lady Guinever bears up that Sir Lancelot—dreams, dreams, visions, fantasies, chimeras, imaginations, tricks, conceits! (I.iii.45-56)

The world of the play seems to be something like a realization of Malevole's chimeras and conceits, and however pungently satirical his comments are from time to time, what the action shows is his relish in bringing to life and playing out fantasies, tricks, and conceits.

In spite of this the play is important because it is so "theatrically ambitious",[15] and it suggests new dramatic possibilities. Marston may possibly have been less innovative than he now seems, and other dramatists, like Ben Jonson, had been developing ways of using child-actors to good effect, by exploiting their aping of adults and the possibilities they offered for satire and burlesque; but the daring and range of Marston's dramaturgy mark him out as an original. *The Malcontent*, however, has too much in it. It invites its audience to delight in "cross-capers", in the consciousness of its clever theatrical devices, in its use of conventions, and in the wit of its presentation of action and of characters like Malevole and Maquerelle. In one direction the play points towards *The Revenger's Tragedy* and the tragedies of Webster, the only non-Shakespearian tragedies of the period that can be claimed as masterpieces. These achieve a difficult and precarious balance by subduing a similar witty, striking, and conscious theatricality to an overall shaping vision, a total artistic control. In *The Revenger's Tragedy* in particular, our sense of the author's control and of a marvellously well-shaped artifice is more important than our sense of the characters, since the play builds its multiplying ironies out of the ever-widening gap between the author as dramatic moralist, and Vindice as the artist who comes, like Marston, so to delight in his own cleverness that he ends by confounding serious issues in the pleasures of successful intrigues and "cross-capers". In this play the control is

15. The phrase is from Bernard Harris's introduction to his edition of *The Malcontent*, p. xvi.

shown also in the brilliance and tautness of the dialogue, in which every line contributes to the play's ironies, and to the maintenance of a consistent tonality.

Webster achieves a sense of artistic control through the creation of a dense poetic atmosphere; the characters of his major tragedies are subdued by this sense of atmosphere, of the mood of the world they inhabit; again, the vehicle of the author's vision is more important than the individual characters. Perhaps only in *The Revenger's Tragedy* and in Webster's plays is a fully successful fusion achieved of those elements that tend to separate in *The Malcontent*, in a precarious balance which yields a special kind of tragic effect. Even in Webster this effect is perhaps more poetic than dramatic, and his plays are difficult to stage convincingly. It is arguable that no other non-Shakespearian tragedy of this period really deserves to be regarded as better than a near-miss. The tragic balance was immensely difficult to achieve because the natural mode of drama in which to exploit these discordant and incongruous elements was tragicomedy.

Tragicomedy is the other direction in which *The Malcontent* points, it being the mode of drama which came to dominate the Jacobean stage. From the first entry of Malevole to "out-of-tune" music, Marston jars his audience with a series of discontinuities and surprises, displaying for their appreciation a series of theatrical cross-capers, perhaps partly in an effort to shock. Some of the most notable of these, such as the threatened deaths which turn out to be empty of danger, climaxed in the "poisoning" by Mendoza of Malevole, who seems to die, but jumps up to speak, full of life again, a few lines later (v.iv.45-84), and the "repentance" of Aurelia, lamenting her sin, and wishing for death, when the audience knows she is on the way to the cell of a hermit who is, in fact, her husband (iv.v), become the stock-in-trade of Beaumont and Fletcher. These playwrights focus in a narrower and more limited way on theatrical gestures which issue in melodramatic effects, as in the final scene of *Philaster*, in which the hero twice offers to stab himself, but is prevented on both occasions from doing so. Tragicomedy of this kind, stemming from *The Malcontent*, relies a good deal upon the exploitation of the audience's conscious awareness of the play as artifice. To achieve a serious and compelling depth in this mode it was necessary, as in tragedies like *The Revenger's Tragedy*, to strike a difficult balance, making the conscious theatricality of the play secondary to its overall shaping vision and purpose. Only Shakespeare found the way to do this in tragicomedy, by matching the obvious contrivances of the action in his late plays to a sense of life itself as theatrical and full of tricks and surprises, so that the artifices of *Cymbeline* and *The Winter's Tale* paradoxically embody a curiously free and vital sense of life's continuing strangeness.

In seeking to identify more sharply the importance and limitations of *The Malcontent*, and the nature of the special dramatic achievement of *The Revenger's Tragedy*, I have been trying to consider them both as texts experienced by readers, and as plays experienced by audiences. The theatre experience is especially difficult to assess, because a modern production may not have a lot in common with what went on in the Jacobean theatre, and no absolutely secure conclusions can be drawn from the available evidence about the special features of the children's theatres, and the acting and style of production in them.[16] At the same time, it seems to me that far too much commentary treats Jacobean drama as a species of literary texts to be read as one might read a novel, with the consequence that many plays are over-valued, or treated too simply in terms of what can be extracted by way of thematic interpretation from a selection of the more prominent speeches in them. Recently a vigorous attack has been launched[17] on those (like myself) who have sought to account for some puzzling plays of the period, ones generally regarded as unaccountable or unsatisfactory in serious terms, by noting in them the possibilities for irony and burlesque. Perhaps there has been a bit too much of this, and an over-eagerness to challenge traditional readings; but in so far as such reassessments are based on an attempt to get inside the play and understand how it would work on stage, they take the exploration and understanding of Jacobean drama a step further. The alternative offered is to treat plays as "straight", "as meaning what they seem to mean", or "what generations of spectators and readers have taken them to mean".[18] The trouble with this is that few spectators, if any, have had an opportunity of seeing most of the plays concerned since the seventeenth century, and the notion of

16. See J. A. Lavin, "The Elizabethan Theatre and the Inductive Method", David Galloway (ed.), *The Elizabethan Theatre II* (Toronto, 1970), pp. 78-80.
17. Richard Levin, "The Proof of the Parody", *Essays in Criticism,* Vol. XXIV (1974) 312-27; this was a retort to my comment on his earlier essay (see above, p. 63), "Mr. Levin and 'Good Bad Drama' ", *Essays in Criticism*, Vol. XXII (1972) 327-9.
18. Richard Levin, "The Proof of the Parody", pp. 315-16.

"meaning" is too circumscribed if it depends on particular emphases or themes in the language of the play, or on "key" speeches. The meaning of a play is only to be grasped through a sense of its nature as a piece for the theatre, and while it is easy to have this sense in relation to Shakespeare's plays, which are regularly staged, it is much harder to enter into the life of other Elizabethan and Jacobean drama. The effort needs to be made, for, as Marston himself reminds us,[19] "the life of these things consists in action", and a "straight" reading of a play like *The Malcontent* is likely to undervalue or ignore its complex manipulation of theatrical effects, and so misjudge the overall nature and quality of the play.

19. In his address, "To my equal reader" prefacing *The Fawn* (published in 1606).

John Webster:
The Apprentice Years

NEIL CARSON

Honest disagreement among readers is a familiar and necessary feature of literary criticism. Ordinarily, of course, such disagreement occurs in a context of assumptions about which the disputants have no quarrel. What is striking about discussions of the work of John Webster is the absence of that larger area of agreement within which meaningful arguments about detail can take place. There is no universally acceptable definition of Webster's peculiar genius, nor even a general consensus about wherein, precisely, the admitted greatness of the mature tragedies can be said to lie. One critic, for example, decries Webster's weak characterization, noting the absence of what he calls "significant inner revelation",[1] while another claims that "deepened insight into character... [is] Webster's greatest strength."[2] The extent of the playwright's conscious control over his material is also a subject of debate. One reader thinks that Webster has "little realization of the effect of his plays",[3] while another concludes that his "structures are too deliberate, too intellectual."[4]

These glaringly contradictory opinions about the nature of Webster's mature art are paralleled by an ambiguous attitude towards his early collaborated plays. It is generally agreed that the

1. Travis Bogard, *The Tragic Satire of John Webster,* quoted in G. K. Hunter and S. K. Hunter (eds.), *John Webster* (Harmondsworth, 1969), p. 175.
2. M. C. Bradbrook, "Fate and Chance in *The Duchess of Malfi*", *Modern Language Review*, Vol. 42 (1947), quoted in Hunter and Hunter, *John Webster*, p. 133.
3. Clifford Leech, *John Webster* (New York, 1970; first published 1951), p. 32.
4. G. K. Hunter, "Introduction to Part Three", Hunter and Hunter (eds.), *John Webster*, p. 107.

great tragedies of 1612-14 are "old-fashioned", but many critics are reluctant to admit that Webster learned much of value during that period of his writing life, when such plays were in vogue. Rupert Brooke gives, perhaps, the clearest expression of this conviction. He asserts:

> Writing for Henslowe was not the best school for genius. No high artistic standard was exacted. It rather implies poverty, and certainly means scrappy and unserious work. It may have given Webster... a sense of the theatre. But he emerged with so little facility in writing, and so little aptitude for a good plot (in the ordinary sense), that one must conclude that his genius was not best fitted for theatrical expression, into which it was driven.... None of his collaborators left much mark on his style.[5]

Such a view of Webster's development, implying as it does that the poet learned nothing from his early association with the popular theatre and yet a decade later wrote two masterpieces reminiscent of work produced by that theatre, seems neither consistent nor reasonable. I would like to suggest that Webster did, in fact, gain something from his early associates, and that certain characteristics of his later style are most easily understood as a logical development of his apprentice years.

Very little is known about Webster's early career, but he almost certainly had not been writing long when he began contributing to the repertoire of the Lord Admiral's Men in 1602. The theatrical accounts of Philip Henslowe show that between May 22 and May 29 of that year he collaborated with Drayton, Middleton, Munday, and Dekker on a play called variously *Sesers Fall* and *Too Shapes*. There is no evidence that the work in question was ever produced, and Webster appears to have left the company that spring. The following autumn he began a short association with Worcester's Men who were then probably performing at the Rose. Between October 15 and October 21, 1602, Webster received a share of £8 along with Chettle, Dekker, Heywood, and Smith for his contribution to *Lady Jane Part I*. This work went into rehearsal early in November, and probably opened about the middle of the month. Meanwhile, Webster was hard at work on a second play, for between November 2 and November 26 he received payment, along with Chettle,

---

5. Rupert Brooke, *John Webster and the Elizabethan Drama* (New York, 1967; first published 1916), pp. 79-81.

Dekker, and Heywood, for *Christmas Comes but Once a Year*. The title suggests the play's seasonal nature, and it was almost certainly first performed shortly after December 18 when the last expenditure for properties was recorded. Worcester's Men continued playing until the theatres were closed by the Queen's final illness in March 1603, but Webster (and Dekker) stopped writing for the company towards the end of November, and can be assumed to have departed.

Nothing is known of the playwright's movements during the next year or so. In 1604, however, he wrote an Induction for Marston's *The Malcontent* (presumably at the request of the King's Men who wished the work lengthened for performance in the popular theatre), and collaborated with Thomas Dekker on *Westward Ho* for Paul's boys. The latter comedy seems to have been an instant success, inspiring the compliment of imitation on the part of the Children of the Chapel, who produced *Eastward Ho*, and justifying a sequel, *Northward Ho*, which Dekker and Webster probably completed for Paul's the following year. *Westward Ho* and *Northward Ho* seem to have established Webster's reputation. They both appeared in print in 1607, probably immediately following the dissolution of Paul's boys; and about the same time an enterprising publisher issued the old *Lady Jane* which, under the title of *The Famous History of Sir Thomas Wyat*, he described as yet another collaboration of Dekker and Webster.

Perhaps the most remarkable feature of this sketchy biography is the continuing relationship between Webster and Dekker. For there would seem, on the face of it, to be little similarity between the two men. The elder, a facile contriver of exuberant bourgeois comedies and vigorous pamphlets about London life, seems an unlikely friend and mentor for the young poet who was to make his own reputation later as an explorer of the exotic world of Mediterranean lust and intrigue. Even more surprising than the relationship itself is the success of their collaboration, for in spite of the prevalence of joint dramatic authorship in the Elizabethan theatre, there is evidence that it was regarded, even then, as artistically makeshift. Apart from some notable exceptions, such as the plays of Beaumont and Fletcher or Rowley and Middleton, the works most highly regarded, then as now, were by individual authors. It is doubly surprising, therefore, that the Dekker-Webster plays of 1604-05 are of such high quality.

In some ways, the very success of this collaboration makes analysis difficult. To begin with, it is virtually impossible to distinguish satisfactorily between the contributions of the two partners. Since no uncollaborated plays of Webster's earlier than *The White Devil* survive, our only reliable evidence for the dramatic style of one of the contributors post-dates the citizen comedies by five or six years. This fact seems to me to undermine seriously the efforts of critics such as Pierce[6] and Brooke[7] to differentiate the collaborators' hands. Discussion of authorship is further complicated by our very imperfect knowledge of the methods of collaboration employed in the Elizabethan theatre. We know almost nothing, for example, of how aesthetic judgments were arrived at. Did the authors agree on a general plot outline and then write different sections of the play independently, or did they collaborate on individual scenes and speeches? Did they revise each other's work, and if so who had the final authority? If the writers worked separately, how were problems of continuity and consistency of characterization solved? Until we can answer at least some of these questions with reasonable certainty any conclusions we draw about a particular playwright's share of a play will be unreliable. One possible solution to the problems posed by the collaborated play is to ignore the question of authorship altogether. By so doing, one can regard the stylistic inconsistencies of a work such as *Westward Ho* not as evidence of two imperfectly aligned creative imaginations, but as the reflection of certain aesthetic tensions characteristic of the time.

Such tensions seem to me to be particularly prevalent in the drama of the period 1600-07. The cause of such strains (and of the confusion of artistic purpose which they reflect) was, I believe, the re-emergence of the boys' companies at the turn of the century. During the 1590s, the popular-theatre dramatists had been moving fairly consistently in the direction of what I would call naive illusionism. The aim of the playwrights and the actors for whom they wrote was to make the spectators believe totally in the imaginative world of the play. I could cite expressions of this purpose from many plays and by many dramatists of the popular theatre, but I would like to quote just two, both of them by playwrights with whom Webster was intimately associated during his apprentice years. The

6. Frederick E. Pierce, *The Collaboration of Webster and Dekker* (New Haven, Conn., 1909).
7. Brooke, *John Webster and the Elizabethan Drama*, pp. 79-81.

first is Thomas Heywood, resident dramatist for Worcester's Men and collaborator with Webster on *Lady Jane* and *Christmas Comes but Once a Year*. In his *Apology for Actors*, written sometime between 1607 and 1612, Heywood states his belief that what he calls "liuely and well spirited action" can literally "bewitch" an audience and convince its members that the "Personater [is] the man Personated."[8] Webster's closest collaborator, Thomas Dekker, also believed that a true dramatic poet was one who could hypnotize an audience, making a spectator "applaud what [his] charmed soule scarce understands."[9] Both playwrights stress the drama's power to still the rational or critical faculty, and to exert an influence directly on the imagination. What they advocate might be described as a theatre of enchantment.

The re-establishment of the boys' companies provided a stimulus to, and a focus for, a very different dramatic aesthetic. It seems fairly certain (Ben Jonson's tribute to Salomon Pavey notwithstanding) that the boy-actors cannot have conveyed a wide range of mature male passion with anything like the convincing realism of their adult rivals. Most critics now assume that the emphasis on satire and burlesque in the private theatres was an attempt to compensate for the boys' physical and vocal limitations. With little hope that the spectators at the private theatres could be persuaded of the credibility of what they saw, the dramatists sought to engage them intellectually rather than emotionally. Instead of striving for illusionism, the writers sought to prevent close identification with the characters. The attitude they encouraged was one of detachment in which the world of the play was clearly recognized to be one of artifice. The response solicited was much more sophisticated than that aimed at in the popular theatres. It was essentially rational, combining a critical awareness of formal charac-teristics of the drama as artifact with a judicious appreciation of the moral or intellectual problems raised by the dialogue. I know of no wholly satisfactory term for this aesthetic, but it might be described as a theatre of estrangement.

One effect of the emergence of the boys' companies then was to make playwriting an even more self-conscious art than it had previ-ously been. As Thomas Heywood expressed it some years later, "New Playes [were] like new fashions,"[10] and dramatists vied with

8. Thomas Heywood, *An Apology for Actors* (1612), B4.
9. Thomas Dekker, "Prologue", *If This Be Not a Good Play*.
10. Thomas Heywood, Epilogue, "A Maidenhead Well Lost", R. H. Shepherd (ed.), *The Dramatic Works of Thomas Heywood* (London, 1874), Vol. IV, p. 165.

one another to establish a novel style. While the highly experimental nature of late Elizabethan and early Jacobean drama is widely recognized, however, it is not always understood that the experimentation touched all aspects of dramatic construction. The rival "traditions" that developed were not simply different schools of thought about such topics as court sycophancy, business enterprise, or the pliability of city wives. They involved as well conflicting theories about how to present character, establish environment, manipulate plot, and manage catharsis. It is scarcely surprising that a play such as *Westward Ho*, written during a period of aesthetic uncertainty, should reveal certain confusions of style.

The extent to which an audience will be enchanted by a performance depends very largely on the skill of the actor and on his ability to disappear entirely in the character he portrays. In *Westward Ho* Dekker and Webster seem to exploit the ambiguous nature of live performance. At certain times the authors want to convince the audience of the reality of the dramatic characters. At its simplest, this is achieved by a believable presentation of motive and emotion. While it is impossible to be dogmatic in these matters, it seems to me that there is a deliberate contrast evident in the play between certain speeches intended to bewitch the audience and others intended to evoke their laughter or censure. For example, the Earl's courtship of Mistress Justiniano in Act II, scene ii seems to be in a very different mode from the parallel scene in Act IV, scene ii. In the former, the lover's protestations, though conventional, seem designed to win assent from the audience as well as from the lady:

> *Earl* Y'are welcome: Sweet y'are welcome. Blesse my hand
> With the soft touch of yours: Can you be Cruell
> To one so Prostrate to you? Euen my Hart,
> My Happines, and State lie at your feet:
> My Hopes me flattered that the field was woon,
> That you had yeilded, (tho you Conquer me)
> And that all Marble scales that bard your eies
> From throwing light on mine, were quite tane off,
> By the Cunning Womans hand, that Workes for me,
> Why therefore do you wound me now with frownes?
> Why do you flie me? Do not exercise
> The Art of woman on me? I'me already
> Your Captiue: Sweet! Are these your hate, or feares. (II.ii.70-82)[11]

11. Thomas Dekker, *Dramatic Works*, Fredson Bowers (ed.) (Cambridge, 1955),

In the latter scene, the emotion seems presented in a deliberately inflated, almost grotesque manner to prevent any close identification between spectators and character.

> *Earl* A woman! Oh, the Spirit
> And extract of Creation! This, this night,
> The Sun shal enuy. What cold checks our blood?
> Her bodie is the Chariot of my soule,
> Her eies my bodies light, which if I want,
> Life wants, or if possesse, I vndo her;
> Turne her into a diuel, whom I adore,
> By scorching her with the hot steeme of lust.
> Tis but a minutes pleasure: and the sinne
> Scarce acted is repented. Shun it than:
> O he that can Abstaine, is more than man!
> Tush. Resolu'st thou to do ill: be not precize,
> Who writes of *Vertue* best, are slaues to vize,
> The musicke sounds allarum to my blood,
> Whats bad I follow, yet I see whats good. (IV.ii.38-52)

Here the effect is more of a commentary on, than the presentation of, passion. The performer seems to step aside from the role he is playing to reflect on the implications of actions and feelings. The effect reminds me of Brecht's description of the ideal performance as that of a witness describing an accident.

Audience engagement is determined in part, therefore, by the extent of the actor's submersion in the character he is playing, but it is also controlled and varied by the relationship of the character with the audience. At one extreme, the dramatist breaks down the conventional barrier between the worlds of the stage and the auditorium, and invites the audience to participate actively in the game of the play; at the other, he creates a closed dramatic world into which the spectator is permitted to enter, if at all, only as a passive observer. Playwrights wishing to distance the spectators can do so in two ways.

The first is anti-mimetic in that the dramatist deliberately breaks the actor's spell to remind the audience that what it is watching is art and not life. For example, at one point in *Westward Ho* Jus-

---

Vol. II, p. 339. Subsequent quotations from *Westward Ho* will follow the text of this edition.

tiniano draws attention to theatrical convention: "Haue amongst you Citty dames? You that are indeede the fittest, and most proper persons for a Comedy" (I.i.225-6).

The second method of excluding the spectators is more dramatic. It eliminates the possibility of direct contact between performer and audience by presenting soliloquies and asides in such a way that they are completely self-contained. This estranging technique can be understood by comparing two soliloquies in *Westward Ho*. Justiniano's first speech alone in Act I, scene i seems to demand that the actor take the audience into his confidence:

> why should a man bee such an asse to play the antick for his wiues appetite? Immagine that I, or any other great man haue on a veluet Night-cap, and put case that this night-cap be to little for my eares or forehead, can any man tell mee where my Night-cap wringes me, except I be such an asse to proclaime it? (I.i.211-15)

Elsewhere, however, soliloquies are treated in such a way that the actor must ignore (or appear to ignore) the spectators. Mistress Justiniano, for example, although alone on stage, frames her words as an invocation rather than as an address to the audience:

> Pouerty, thou bane of Chastity,
> Poison of beauty, Broker of Mayden-heades,
> I see when Force, nor Wit can scale the hold,
> Wealth must. Sheele nere be won, that defies golde.
> But liues there such a creature: Oh tis rare,
> To finde a woman chast, thats poore and faire. (II.ii.142-7)

Here the effect is to distance the spectators slightly by making them eavesdroppers rather than participants in a one-sided conversation.

The presentation of character in *Westward Ho* is therefore somewhat inconsistent. At certain moments the *dramatis personae* are given a life of their own which they manifest in their relations both with other characters and with members of the audience, while at other times they are represented as frankly conventional creations, embodying not life but art, and bound within the confines of their artificial world.

Similar differences can be observed in the treatment of setting. Certain scenes in *Westward Ho* show the dramatists attempting to establish a fully credible environment surrounding the characters. One way in which this is done is by devoting detailed attention to the use of properties and furniture, or to scenes of pantomime which will help convey an impression of time and place. For example, in Act IV, scene i the dramatists use a card game to give a sense of location, and to lend an air of probability to the long silences between certain characters necessitated by the divided stage. In the same scene, the discovery space and the upper stage are established in the dialogue as architectural features of the imagined scene. When Honeysuckle is anxious to hide, Birdlime shows him into what he calls a "closet". The upper area is referred to as a "dining Chamber". The effect is to establish a wholly logical relationship between the main stage, the two entrance-doors, the discovery space, and the upper stage in such a way that the action of the scene can be imagined flowing through an environment which extends back into the tiring-house. This tendency to give attention to details of offstage, or background environment as well as to the immediate foreground is also evident in Act V, scene i. There the playwrights make clever use of offstage voices to establish separate bedrooms adjoining the main stage.

A very different treatment of stage environment can be seen in Act IV, scene ii where the dramatists either carelessly or deliberately make no attempt to create an illusion of "real" space. To begin with, the scene is set conventionally using a dumb show:

> Whilst the song is heard, the Earle drawes a Curten, and sets forth a Banquet: he then Exit, and Enters presently with *Iustiniano* attird like his wife maskt: leads him to the table, places him in a chaire, and in dumbe signes, Courts him, til the song be done. (IV.ii.52)

The ensuing action is difficult to follow because the playwrights make no effort to explain either in the dialogue or in the stage directions exactly how they intend certain effects to be achieved. For example, the disguised Justiniano takes off his mask, but continues in the first part of the scene to pretend that he is a woman. When he is threatened by the Earl, however, he reveals himself as the wronged husband. Presumably some hood or cloak is thrown off when Justiniano says, "there drops your Ladie" (IV.ii.101), but the precise management of the revelation is left to the actor or the book-keeper. In the same way, the discovery of Mistress Justiniano's body is regarded by the playwrights as a problem for stage management. Modern editions of the play usually include some appropriate stage direction such as "Draws a curtain and discovers Mistress Justiniano as though dead", but we do not know how the authors themselves visualized the scene. It is quite possible that here they did not think in terms of environment at all. They may have imagined the characters more as poetic or symbolic abstractions, like those in a Lord Mayor's pageant, requiring no "real" space in which to live.

The contrasting technical means of creating an illusion of character or space are paralleled by different ways of handling narrative. Here again, the inconsistency is between an artistry which works in "depth", creating a world with background as well as foreground, and one which strives for discrete effects. Certain scenes are conceived of as integral parts in a continuing story taking place in a fictional but credible space and time. Others seem to exist almost in isolation without cause or consequence. It is sometimes difficult to know if this disconnected effect is aimed at or is simply a result of ineptitude or careless collaboration. For instance, the revelation of Justiniano's motivation in the early scenes is made so casually that it suggests an open defiance of realistic conventions. After telling his wife that he had sold his house to cover his debts, Justiniano confesses to the audience:

> I haue told my wife I am going for *Stoad*; thats not my course, for I resolue to take some shape vpon me, and to liue disguised heere in the Citty. (I.i.218-21)

This casual handling of exposition is comparable to the indifference manifested in other parts of the play to the elementary requirements of foreshadowing and causality. In Act IV, scene i the three husbands, Honeysuckle, Tenterhook, and Wafer (whom we had not previously had cause to suspect of lechery), are shown visiting Luce. Towards the end of the scene Justiniano appears, says that he has received a letter from his wife, and asks the men to accompany him to Putney—although why he should have interrupted his journey thither to visit the three citizens is not made clear.

The different handlings of character, setting, and narrative in the various parts of *Westward Ho* reflect contradictory or confused ideas about the nature of comic catharsis. Certain scenes seem to show the dramatists using all their art to engage the audience in the dramatic fiction. Characters are sympathetic and speak directly to the audience, inviting it to participate in the action and intrigue of the play; the environment is credible and represented in depth; the actions of the *dramatis personae* seem consistent and logically connected. In other scenes the playwrights seem intent on distancing the spectators. Characters view their own actions objectively, and either remind the audience of the conventional nature of theatrical performance or else exclude them from the world of the play; events seem to occur in two dimensions, and to lack both spatial and temporal connections.

Whether the contrasting dramatic styles in *Westward Ho* reflect the idiosyncrasies of the individual collaborators, or are the result of the two playwrights writing now in one mode and now in another can not, perhaps, be determined. But Northrop Frye is probably right to remind us that "the word 'collaborator' does not have to be used in its wartime sense of traitor, and that collaboration often . . . creates a distinct and unified personality."[12] The unity and coherence that Frye posits in a collaborated work might be the product of a determined effort on the part of the dramatists to conform to a common style. Or it might result from a kind of artistic symbiosis by which each partner learns from and even imitates the other. The "personality" of *Westward Ho* as I have described it is not unified in the simplest sense of that word. As I have shown, it reflects an uneasy alliance between very different dramatic techniques. The play is not incoherent, however, and even goes some way to show that a workable synthesis of the techniques of enchantment and estrangement is possible. What I find interesting is that when we come to look at Webster's unaided mature work we find the same uneasy tension between naive and self-conscious dramaturgy. Much of what has been described as "baroque"[13] in Webster's work results from the alternation between moments which involve us totally in the emotions and fortunes of the characters, and passages that invite us to remain detached, critical, and reflective. What the painters of the baroque period achieve by a violent contrast of light and darkness, Webster accomplishes by shifts between conventions of realism and stylization, between scenes of carefully motivated and logically described action, and scenes in which deeds seem deliberately grotesque, exaggerated, or emblematic. Webster's power comes, to a large extent, from his capacity to fuse these seemingly

12. Northrop Frye, *A Natural Perspective* (New York, 1965), p. 38.
13. Ralph Berry, *The Art of John Webster* (Oxford, 1972).

contrasting methods of dramaturgy into a satisfactory whole, a sort of metaphysical drama created by the yoking together of heterogeneous styles. In the end, the dramatic technique seems so individual that one feels that Webster simply speaks in his natural voice. I think it unlikely, however, that he would have written in quite the same way if he had not served his apprenticeship in both the public and private theatres.

Shakespeare and the Multiple Theatres of Jacobean London

M. C. BRADBROOK

In venturing on a topic to which these conferences have contributed so much, I would wish to emphasize a shift in general approach, seeking to relate both the archaeological and the purely thematic or literary approaches by considering primarily the audience structure of the Jacobean theatre. In spite of the large enterprises of G. E. Bentley and Glynne Wickham, reinterpretation proceeds sporadically from a wide range of studies in other fields—the political, the iconographical, and the philosophical, still sometimes divorced from theatrical considerations.

My views must necessarily be speculative, but I hope they will not be termed sociological, since the end of study is the understanding of the plays themselves which is, as we now recognize, a matter of performance.

Recent presentations in England, though experimental and often bizarre, derive not only from study of the original theatre buildings but of the social background of the time. The programmes issued by the Royal Shakespeare Company, with their many extracts from sixteenth-century authors, as well as from the latest critics, sometimes read like the syllabus of a university course. We will hear of one such performance from Dr. Stanley Wells; I want to take a look at Shakespeare in his Jacobean development, since the Jacobean period is our main concern, but perhaps in conclusion to say something about modern recreations of the Jacobean plays.

Since the theatre evolved in relation to public demand, built for people and for actor-audience relationships, its very shape first expressed, but thereafter was to condition those relationships, as well as the relations between one part of the audience and another.

We have learnt much recently from these conferences about alternative forms of playing places, from the innyard to the private theatre of Whitehall, and Reavley Gair's fascinating description of the second theatre at Paul's. His account achieved a connection, all too rare, between the structure of the theatre and the plays performed there, a connection which for instance is absent from the new *Revels History of Drama in English*, which, so disparate are the contributions of the distinguished authors, might rather be termed "Four Histories in One".

At least four forms of theatre survived from late medieval times. The perambulating wagons of the craft plays involved something like the "blocking" that governed royal entries and processions.[1] The chief actors moved past watching crowds, but also halted here and there to become audience for a show or a speech, or to receive a gift. Processional drama lay in two-way traffic between royal or civic dignitary and the crowd, as well as in the matter presented; there were many plays-within-the-play.

Shakespeare catches up this dramatic activity in the description of Henry IV's entry to London for his coronation, followed by Richard the disgraced actor; yet more dramatically it is actually staged in the final scene of *King Henry IV Part II*, where the new King makes his coronation entry. Falstaff, who should have been content with the role of loyal spectator, aspires to a part, breaks decorum. The clown often did this, especially if the show was domestic, as for example it had been in *The Princely Pleasures of Kenilworth*. In the solemn, indeed religious rite—part of the coronation ritual itself consists still in the showing of the monarch to the people—Hal did not offer Falstaff the indulgence that, at Kenilworth, Elizabeth had extended to Laneham.

Until about a dozen years ago, thinking about the Elizabethan theatre was largely dominated by consideration of the "game places"; even a social orientation, such as that of Alfred Harbage in his pioneering *Shakespeare's Audience* (1941), oversimplified the problems between the open stages and the private theatre of the hall, the theatre of privilege. The open stages had their noble equivalent in the tilts, tourneys, and other "closed" courtyard

---

1. Alan H. Nelson, *The Medieval English Stage* (Chicago, 1974), argues that in one case at least craft performances did not take place on the wagons, but only in the guild-hall.

entertainments which played such an important part in the dramatic ritual surrounding Elizabeth, especially, as Frances Yates has shown, in the Accession Day Tilts.

The fourth type of theatre, the innyard, was used not only by touring troupes in the provinces, but by London troupes until the Privy Council decision of 1597 excluded them from the City inns. The most popular of all Jacobean theatres, however, the Red Bull in Clerkenwell, emerged, and much light has been thrown on these innyard theatres by the work of Herbert Berry and the late Charles Sisson on the Red Bull's predecessor, the Boar's Head in Whitechapel.[2]

The special social aspects of the innyard theatres may be hard to isolate, but even if they no longer functioned as inns, opportunities for coming and going into the private rooms opening on the galleries, the full provisions for eating and drinking, and the accommodation available for the players and managers in the actual building itself must have given the audience a life of its own, distinct from that of the play. In 1557, at a small theatre in Islington, then a village north of London, plays had served as a cover for prohibited religious meetings.

Audience participation at the Red Bull meant that an Elizabethan audience here survived into Jacobean times; as a boy, Thomas Killigrew learnt to be an actor on the stage of the Red Bull at the invitation of the players: "Who will go and be a devil on the stage and he shall see the play for nothing?"[3] This innyard theatre survived until the Restoration.

Up and down the countryside local theatres still stand, from the little "game place" at the Suffolk village of Walton-le-Willows[4] to the most beautiful and least utilized by historians, the Tudor Guildhall at Leicester, where travelling troupes regularly performed. But theatre had not been separated from other "games" and ritual pastimes.

On any of these stages, the icon of the Queen herself could be presented; though she herself travelled widely and met her people,

2. Herbert Berry, "The Playhouse in the Boar's Head Inn, Whitechapel", David Galloway (ed.), *The Elizabethan Theatre I* (Toronto, 1969) and *The Elizabethan Theatre III* (Toronto, 1973); C. Leech and J. M. R. Margeson (eds.), *Shakespeare 1971* (Toronto, 1972); C. J. Sisson, *The Boar's Head Theatre* (London, 1972).

3. See G. E. Bentley, *The Jacobean and Caroline Stage*, Vol. VI (Oxford, 1968), p. 243.

4. See Kenneth Dodd, "Another Elizabethan Theatre in the Round", *Shakespeare Quarterly*, Vol. XXI (Spring, 1970).

her image was dispersed pictorially in forms increasingly conventional, which gradually transformed a recognizable woman to a mask of formal majesty. Although a procession or progress in which the image miraculously came to life was the culmination of this rite, the Inns of Court might venture on advice or allegory; the Chapel Boys might reproduce in miniature the courtly wooing game; even on popular stages, the divine Cynthia might appear in epiphany. The evidence of the cult has recently been gathered in Frances Yates' collection *Astraea* (1975); but it has become so familiar through exhibitions, television programmes, and the like as to permit popular articles for the middle page of *The Times* (March 8, 1975).

In his history plays, Shakespeare had offered a parallel but distinct form, which allowed the audience to see themselves reflected in images from those troublesome times before "all tragedies are fled from state to stage".[5] The tableau of the father who killed his son and the son who killed his father, an emblem for civil war, gave the king only a passive role. The entry of a noble with the cry "Montague, Montague for Lancaster" might so stir the Earl of Southampton, Montague's descendant, as, in 1601, to prompt that notorious staging of *Richard II* as the curtain raiser to the Essex rebellion.

The great unifying force of chronicle histories spent itself before the physical death of the old queen; as Irving Ribner showed, it vanished around 1600, except for the innyard theatres.

The trouble which followed the playing of the scurrilous *Isle of Dogs* in 1597 not only sharply reduced the number of London theatres, but actually caused the demolition of the little theatre at Newington Butts, which pleasant and reputable site had seen in 1594 some Shakespearean productions. It does not appear that any compensation was offered, and I can hardly credit Glynne Wickham's suggestion that such consideration prevented the demolition of the Curtain, and other houses; the idea of compensation is surely a modern one, and Cromwell, for instance, did not find it needful, half a century later.

In a few years, the accession of King James brought not only a further concentration of drama in the leading London companies, a decline of provincial progresses and plays, but the replacement of the Tudor myth by the far less potent one of Troynovant or of

5. Thomas Hughes, Prologue to *The Misfortunes of Arthur* (1587).

M. C. Bradbrook

Reunited Britannia. Rivals like Dekker and Jonson united in coronation pageants to celebrate the peaceful change of crowns, since by joining three kingdoms, James had reversed that old unhappy fall from grace, the division of the island between the three sons of Brut. On his coins James inscribed "Henricus rosas, regna Jacobus" (Henry united the roses, James the kingdoms). Much use was also made of that old commonplace, the marriage of the monarch to his kingdom, but James found his new subjects and his old far from ready to accept a complete union, and perforce remained subjected to an uneasy state of political polygamy.

An increased interest in dramatic entertainment under the Stuarts, especially the court masque, which has been pursued both by Glynne Wickham and, in Jonsonian studies, by Stephen Orgel and Roy Strong, has brought about some reinterpretation of Shakespeare's Jacobean plays, which tend to be seen as reflecting themes of the masque and of court entertainment. The new Stuart myth has been postulated by Glynne Wickham as sharply altering the emphasis in *King Lear*. The play is seen as reflecting events of the years 1605-06. Among the last plays, *The Winter's Tale* is explained as celebrating the installation of the Prince of Wales as Knight of the Garter, and simultaneously the reinterment of Mary Queen of Scots in Westminster Abbey. In these interpretations Wickham has recently been supported by Frances Yates.[6] Shakespeare, so runs the argument, as one of the King's Men, directed his plays in grateful and dependent adaptation towards the royal auditory.

I find myself dissenting from several assumptions; in particular that the new Stuart myth embodied in the City triumphs retained its currency for very long, or the court masque proved a stable source of emblems to be reflected in the public theatre. The *staging* may have shown some influence of court; the *dramatists* tended to develop a counter-movement. Revenge tragedy satirized court masques, and "tragedies of state" did not spare the court or even the monarchy.

Despite the contention of Leeds Barroll in *The Revels History of*

6. Glynne Wickham, "From Tragedy to Tragicomedy: King Lear as Prologue", *Shakespeare Survey 26* (1973); "*The Winter's Tale*, A Comedy with Deaths", in Glynne Wickham, *Shakespeare's Dramatic Heritage* (London, 1969); "Shakespeare's Investiture Play", *Times Literary Supplement*; "Romance and Emblem: A Study in the Dramatic Structure of *The Winter's Tale*", Galloway (ed.), *The Elizabethan Theatre III*. Cf. Frances Yates, *Shakespeare's Last Plays* (London, 1975).

Drama in English that in the sixteenth century patronage had played a part in keeping troupes on the London scene, the Jacobean stages were relatively established and independent; and the fees for productions at court could hardly have supported the large establishments that now flourished. Interplay between the different types of Jacobean theatre depended on recognizing that each was catering for a different type of audience. So different *genres*, already established, could be identified with certain theatres, and parodied at others. The second theatre at Paul's, as we have heard, specialized in certain kinds of appeal, and with such a small auditorium was best-suited for the camarist plays of Marston, who exploited critical interchange between different groups. Yet the "little apes", varying the tart flavour of their railing with the sweetness of their songs, were but one part of the scene; if opposition between children's playhouses and the common stages was not quite of the rigid simplicity postulated by Alfred Harbage in *Shakespeare and the Rival Traditions* (1952), this must be attributed to the other theatrical traditions of the court and the Inns of Court.

The close-knit interaction was intensified by the decline of provincial tours and of independent provincial playing.[7] Settled in "their usual houses of playing", the companies evolved specific styles of performance, based on their leading dramatists (whose influence could also be felt as working members of the team, in the cases of Shakespeare at the Globe and Heywood at the Red Bull) and their leading actors.

Although the common players moved into the closed Theatre of the Hall at Blackfriars, this is no warrant that they reflected the forms of the City pageants or the Court Masque. The City myth of Troynovant had its brief hour at the time of James's coronation, but the courtly masque, dependent on variety, evolved no single and stable set of images, which James could succeed in presenting to his people. If his eldest son showed signs of remedying this, an early death deprived the poets of such binding and cohesive force; most of the tributes to Henry Prince of Wales take the form of elegies. The style of the "Astraea" icon could not be translated to serve the Stuarts, and literary habits themselves had become iconoclastic.

The older icons of the last reign were both regretted and mocked.

---

7. See L. G. Salingar, "Les comédiens et leur public en Angleterre de 1520 à 1640", Jean Jacquot (ed.), *Dramaturgie et société* (Paris, 1968), Vol. 2.

In *The Widow's Tears* (1605), a famous song in praise of Elizabeth as Cynthia is applied in joyous irony as the frailty of another Cynthia is disclosed:

> She, she, she and only she,
> She only queen of love and beauty.

But in *Bussy D'Ambois*, Chapman whilst reflecting satirically on the English court for making "Of their old queen/An ever young and most immortal goddess" praises the state and worth of her court, suggesting that the French court is, by comparison, a "mirror of confusion", which he fears the English will soon take to imitating.

A sharpened awareness of the different responses of different audiences is attested by the inductions and commentaries of early Jacobean theatre, above all by the treatment of the Grocer and his wife in that slice of theatrical history, Beaumont's *The Knight of the Burning Pestle* (1607). They betray ignorance and inexperience in every action, from the moment the lady steps on the stage. No lady, I think, would have been so immodest as to seat herself on the stage, or come in by the players' door unless indeed as Chief Spectator she was placed in a Chair of State; even as late as Jonson's *The Staple of News* (1626), the invasion of the stage by women is considered surprising. Jonson's inductions, indeed, seem indebted to Beaumont's play, which in turn may owe something to the habit of using members of the audience as clowns (which can be found in the private Christmas revels of the Inns of Court).

At the apex of all London performances, the court masque established a ritual not merely theatrical; the theory of the masque as a reflection of Platonic harmony in a divinely instituted kingdom, a rite which enacted and induced a state of due devotion in the subject for his king, was expounded many years ago by D. J. Gordon, especially in relation to Jonson's *Hymenaei*, the supreme example of this form.[8] Recently, Stephen Orgel has very fully developed the implications.

But there was another side to Jonson, who in *Sejanus* (1603) had already depicted a court full of every vice, presided over by a homosexual, and peopled by ladies skilful in painting and disguise of

---

8. D. J. Gordon, "The Imagery of Ben Jonson's *The Masque of Blacknesse* and *The Masque of Beautie*" and "*Hymenaei:* Jonson's Masque of Union", *Journal of the Warburg and Courtauld Institutes*, Vol. VI (1943) and Vol. VIII (1949).

a less innocent kind than Queen Anne's "game" of appearing in blackface. As I have indicated elsewhere, Jonson spoke with two voices,[9] and the theory of harmony became dispersed in favour of an increasing cult of grotesque and varied antimasques, which finally took over in *The Gypsies Metamorphosed.*

The political implications of the Jacobean masque were worked out as long ago as 1913 by Mary Sullivan. Presented in the presence of ambassadors, whose struggle for precedence replaced harmony by conflict, the brief show was but the prelude to that mingling of actors and audience, whose separation had carefully been built up in the public theatre.[10]

As one of the King's Men, Shakespeare must have had a free entry, indeed have been called for duty to the masquers' scene; but he was never given a commission to write a masque. Whatever the explanation, he could have felt some chagrin, some humiliation, as he waited on his friend Jonson's efforts. Nor could he have failed to observe the dark side of the revels, the drunkenness, the rifling of food and even of jewels from the masquers' costumes, the bawdry, the quarrels, the undertow.

Spenser, long ago, in *Colin Clout's Come Home Again*, had juxtaposed the seamy side of court life with its glories, but the Jacobean court offered far more glaring contrasts. Christopher Hatton may have danced himself into the Queen's favour at a masque but he earned his promotion by solider qualities; the captivation of James by George Villiers had much more corrupting effect.

Roy Strong observed that whenever the Medici or the Valois were in difficulty, in times of financial crisis or religious conflict, they used masques and shows to simulate a state of harmony which could be seen to prevail. Many courtiers bear witness to the squalid qualities of Jacobean masquing; the contrast between what was professed and what occurred could not fail to present itself as a dramatic motif.

On the Elizabethan stage, treacherous revels had provided the climax to *The Spanish Tragedy*, the Bartholomew massacre of *The Massacre at Paris*; in *Woodstock*, the good Duke Humphrey is kidnapped by treacherous revellers, headed by the king. The force

9. M. C. Bradbrook, "The Nature of Theatrical Experience in Ben Jonson", *Studies in the Literary Imagination*, Georgia State University, Vol. VI (April 1973).
10. See Anne Righter (Barton), *Shakespeare and the Idea of the Play* (London, 1962).

of such revels, however, is much more strongly developed in the
"second wave" of revenge tragedy, above all in that play of the
King's Men, *The Revenger's Tragedy*, with its reiterated horrors all
based on "the pleasures of the palace", that we are to consider:

> Nine coaches waiting, hurry, hurry, hurry —
> Ay, to the devil

and its private masquerade of the poisoned skull:

> Does the silk-worm expend her yellow labours
> For thee? for thee does she undo herself?
> Are lordships sold to maintain ladyships
> For the poor benefit of a bewitching minute?

The silk-worm which is also a grave-worm, the implicit sexual
violence, the entwined images of copulation and death as subjects of
meditation belong to the powerful new revenge convention; but the
drive behind this passage is an inverted form of that which fills the
great speech of Volpone to Celia, or at a lower level, the raptures of
an Epicure Mammon. It is common to tragedy and comedy but is
directed against court luxury and vice. [11]

All these plays belong to the period around 1604-10, the early
years of James's reign. His honeymoon of a wedding to the realm
was brief. The general public had no image to sustain it, and the
court masque became to them a subject for irony. The strongest
testimony is found in Act I of *The Maid's Tragedy*, where, as
Inga-Stina Ewbank has shown, [12] the masque provides as exact and
savage a refutation of the subsequent action as could be found,
equaled only in real life by the conduct of Lady Frances Howard,
the bride of Jonson's *Hymenaei*, and the infamous cause of the
Overbury murder.

What evidence of the influence of the masque is to be found in
Shakespeare's Jacobean plays, comparable to the manifest influence
of the choristers' theatre on *Hamlet*?

Macbeth certainly has its political aspect, in the spectacular

11. See note 9, p. 95, and Joel Hurstfield, "The Politics of Corruption in
Shakespeare's England", *Shakespeare Survey* 28 (1975).
12. See Inga-Stina Ewbank, "'These Pretty Devices': A Study of Masques in Plays",
T. J. B. Spencer and Stanley Wells (eds.), *A Book of Masques: In Honour of Allardyce
Nicoll* (Cambridge, 1967).

scenes which Shakespeare did not find in his sources: the haunted coronation festivities, and the ghastly inversion of a coronation masque proffered by the witches. Both invert the true royal rites; the witches themselves were later to supply an antimasque for Jonson's *Masque of Queens* (1609). (These "stage" figures may have included Shakespeare and Burbage, since in masques speaking parts were taken by professional players.) *Macbeth* is the sublimation of spectacle into poetry, but it does not directly reflect masquing, rather contrasts with it.

King Lear inverts the unification of the three kingdoms, and into Lear's household Shakespeare brings the most archaic form of entertainer, the household fool. The speeches of praise proper to a masque are given to Regan and Goneril. In readmitting the fool and the beggar, with their strange cries that so deeply pierce to the centre of Lear's tragedy, Shakespeare was reintroducing to his stage the wildness and freedom of the old clowns, an anarchy which had seemed to be buried in the grave with Yorick.

The spectator is challenged to his limits by mummery and mocking of greatness. I would concur therefore with Glynne Wickham in sensing some connection between *King Lear* and the revival of old stories about the division of the kingdom, some sense of what "court holy water" was dispensed in the masque; but that Shakespeare "prudently chose to refrain" from "a public declaration that the second Brutus had finally arrived in the person of King James" whilst "admitting the possibility through making Albany the agent of Lear's reunion with Cordelia"[13] seems to me unacceptable in face of what the play says and shows to any audience. The icon of Lear entering with the dead Cordelia in his arms, the stark monosyllables of "Howl", "Dead as earth", and the fivefold "Never" do not suggest prudent reservations to me. Shakespeare gave a new mythology to the world, which has outlived that of Troynovant. "Mythology is not about something; it is itself that something" as Samuel Beckett has remarked. If he could not compete with the royal splendours of the court, its jewels and machinery, Shakespeare could turn to his own resources, and carry them to the very limits of language, where words fail. If, later, he was able to use and adapt the material of the masque for his theatre, it was as one who had recognized the gulf between these two forms, who was

13. The quotations are from Glynne Wickham, "From Tragedy to Tragicomedy", p. 43.

seeking a new way to reconcile popular and courtly audiences.

The King's Men's plays had to fit either the Globe or the Blackfriars. In 1615, seven years after the King's Men opened their second theatre, the little Cockpit in Drury Lane was being adapted by one of Burbage's former prentices to serve the popular company from the Red Bull. It must have had a minute audience-capacity;

> Can this cockpit hold
> The vasty fields of France?

was said in deliberate depreciation of a theatre with a capacity of between 2,000 and 3,000. A cockpit might have suited a "young company" of boys; prices were presumably much higher, and if it were roofed in, performances could have been repeated in the afternoon and evening, thus compensating for the size of the house (it is worth recalling that in Jonson's *Bartholomew Fair* Lantern Leatherhead the puppet man reckoned to hold nine performances in one afternoon!), and it could be be used all the year round as well.

However, within a few weeks, the city prentices, presumably deprived of the cheap entry they had enjoyed at the Red Bull, wrecked the new theatre. Rebuilt and named the Phoenix, it eventually housed Beeston's Boys.

The noblest halls available in Jacobean times were those of the Inns of Court. It was the young gentlemen of the Inns who provided the critical part of any audience; like modern undergraduates, the "termers" were happiest when they could parody existing institutions. Parody did not exclude admiration.

We know of their burlesques from *Gesta Grayorum* (1594) and as I would hold, from the anonymous *The Comedy of Timon*, which I take to be a burlesque of Shakespeare's play,[14] in a revelling play of the Inner Temple. To the same genre I would assign the newly discovered manuscript play of *Tom a Lincoln*, recently discovered in the library of the Marquis of Lothian at Melbourne Hall in Derbyshire, and sold by auction. In the sale catalogue, Sotheby's ascribed it to Thomas Heywood; I would prefer to read it as a burlesque both of Heywood and of Shakespeare, and, if an author is to be sought, the scribe who signed the colophon may well have been the author.

---

14. M. C. Bradbrook, *"The Comedy of Timon"*, *Renaissance Drama* (1966).

Finis Deo soli gloria
Quam perfecta manent, strenuo perfecta labore
Metra quid exornat, lima, litura, labor
Morganus; Evans;

The couplet contains one obvious false quantity (strĕnuo, which should be strēnuo) but derives from Horace, *Ars Poetica*, II.290-94. If *quam* is read as *quae* it may be translated "What adorns the measures that have been completed and made perfect by strenuous toil? Polishing, erasure, (the "blot"), more toil." I would hazard therefore that he had reworked the play into a burlesque for his Inn, using a playhouse text obtained from the manager of the Red Bull, a neighbouring theatre to Gray's Inn.[15] This play came from that Inn with the papers of the great Sir John Coke; Morgan Evans was admitted there on June 12, 1605.

The story of Tom a Lincoln, the Red Rose Knight, is found in the romance of Richard Johnson (1599). It is the sort of tale that Shakespeare began to act in—*Sir Clyamon and Sir Clamydes,* such a one, is recalled in *Cymbeline*—the sort of play that Francis Flute asked for when he hoped Thisbe was a "wandering knight". But this drama echoes several popular successes of 1611, especially Heywood's *Golden Age* and Shakespeare's *The Winter's Tale*, and it can be dated round the Christmas season of that year or the next, and offers a parody of romance.

The story relates how King Arthur, caught in a love-situation closely resembling that of his descendant Edward III in a play attributed to Shakespeare, behaves with much less restraint; approaching the lovely Angelica, daughter of the Earl of London, as she sits in a summer bower, he lays passionate siege to her and after twelve days' wooing, conquers. Conveniently removing herself from her father's eye (in the romance), Angelica is professed a nun at Lincoln, and gives birth to a son who is found and fostered by a poor shepherd, after being exposed on the King's orders. Overjoyed by a rich purse of gold tied round the child's neck, Antonio adopts the infant and names him Tom a Lincoln. The birth is displayed by Time as Chorus, in a dumb show but with words not unfamiliar to students of *The Winter's Tale*; or *The Four Ages*.

---

15. This was Thomas Greene, the celebrated clown, who might have obliged his young patrons.

> I that have been ere since the world began
> I that was since this orbed ball's creation,
> I that have seen huge kingdoms' devastations,
> Do here present myself to your still view —
> Old, ancient, changing, ever-running Time,
> First clad in gold; then silver; next that, brass,
> And now in iron, inferior to the rest,
> Yet more hard than all.

Having shown the fate of the babe, Time concludes his speech

> thus in short time
> Time briefly hath declared what chance befell
> This hopeful infant at his happy birth —
> By your imagination, kind spectators,
> More quick than thought, run with me, think the babe
> Hath fully passed sixteen years of age.

The adventures of Tom combine aspects of Shakespeare's lost princelings with the instincts of a Cloten, the predations of an Autolycus, and the unsinkable resources of a Stephano. His career makes *Pyramus and Thisbe* seem like an exercise in classic restraint. He also recalls Heywood's Four Prentices, and some of Heywood's more peculiar coinages appear in the text. When the enamoured Fairy Queen is about to raid Tom's bedchamber she compares herself to "lust-spotted Tarquin" thus combining Shakespeare and Heywood in one thundering incongruity.

Christmas plays often dealt with times and seasons, being part of the festive calendar, and frequently they united grandeur and burlesque. (W. R. Elton would put *Troilus and Cressida* among such plays.) There were often heraldic puns, and the griffon or dragon who provides the climax of Tom a Lincoln's adventures constitutes not only the arms of the Principality of Wales, but of Gray's Inn also. Compare the use of Pegasus, the heraldic device of the Inner Temple, in *The Comedy of Timon*. The clown's jests about his native Lincoln may be aimed at Lincoln's Inn, the nearest neighbour to Gray's Inn, rather than embodying memories of Heywood's native county. What would any audience care where the playwright came from? Topical and local "hits" were what counted; and Rusticano's recollections of the dung carts of Lincoln could recall a local quarrel about the disposal of refuse from Gray's Inn in

Lincoln's Inn Fields. The familiar jokes of Christmas time take this local line anywhere.

There was not one Jacobean theatre, but many; and they took to parody and jest of one another, without necessarily feeling rancour. Indeed a little of this kind of popular success would be good for the box-office, and professional players might well help amateurs in their "send up", for it was after all a form of advertisement and no one would pause to parody a failure.

What finally is to be deduced about Shakespeare's romances from such parodies? How then are we to read Shakespeare's last plays? As direct celebrations of the royal family, as suggested by Glynne Wickham and more recently by Frances Yates?[16]

To me, as to Philip Edwards when he reviewed the critical history of these plays for *Shakespeare Survey*, they have too distinct an individual life to be treated as variants on the masque, emblems of Prince Henry, vehicles of Rosicrucian doctrine. The difficulty with such theories is that they can neither be proved nor disproved. The eye of faith will detect such latent meanings everywhere, as when Miss Yates would see in Cranmer of *King Henry VIII* an attempt to reconcile Catholic and Protestant views, or, in defiance of commonly accepted chronology, take *The Alchemist* as Ben Jonson's attack on the Rosicrucian doctrines that Shakespeare proffers.

I take it, what we meet in *The Winter's Tale* is an open form which invites the audience to fill it out. This is not an indeterminate form; but it is free from that "application" which playwrights grew to fear and strenuously to deny. All sorts of lovers could and did use the wooing speeches; the conscious archaism of *Pericles* was bettered in *The Winter's Tale*, where Shakespeare took for refashioning an old romance of his first enemy, Robert Greene, subtitled *The Triumph of Time*. He also took the antimasque of satyrs from Jonson's court masque *Oberon, the Fairy Prince* (an even more famous antimasque was later embodied in *The Two Noble Kinsmen*). This is not the same as imitating a form; as T. S. Eliot once said "Bad poets imitate; good poets steal." Although he had not been invited to produce one, Shakespeare was now capable of adapting the masque form—but this does not imply that he was subordinated to its conventions; quite the contrary.

The Tempest is so Protean and mysterious a play that it has recently been seen as a satire on colonialism, as a dream play, or, as

16. See note 6, p. 92.

represented by Sir John Gielgud, as subsuming within itself the masques it presents. In *The Sea and The Mirror* Auden drew out some of the varied implications it might hold for a modern mind. Any single application must be reductive of the riches of the play.

This "poetry of the gaps" invited everyone to supply what they themselves could bring. As Middleton put it in a prologue of the year 1613:

> How is't possible to suffice
> So many ears, so many eyes?
> Some in wit and some in shows
> Take delight and some in clothes.
> Some for mirth they chiefly come,
> Some for passion—for both, some;
> Some for lascivious meetings, that's their arrent;
> Some to detract and ignorance their warrent.
> How is't possible to please
> Opinions toss'd on such wild seas?
> Yet I doubt not, if attention
> Seize you above, and apprehension
> You below, to take things quickly,
> We shall both make ye sad and tickle ye.
> (Prologue to *No Wit, no Help like a Woman's*)

It is a commonplace that the modern stage approximates more closely to the Elizabethan and Jacobean public stages than anything in the intervening ages. Thrust platforms, theatre in the round, multiple entry, through the auditorium if need be, have dismissed Inigo Jones and his innovations of the proscenium arch, the shutters, the curtain. Only lighting retains all advantages of the electronic era, reinforces the imagination, and embodies the dream world behind the play, the subtext. We know that we cannot reproduce with fidelity any one old stage, for our evidence is always incomplete, but we can produce workable stages that enable all sorts of obscure Elizabethan works to be acted, although in general Shakespeare's lesser known plays, rather than the masterpieces of his contemporaries, have continued to hold the stage.[17]

His plays are now being adapted to supply the mythology for a

17. See the concluding chapter in the new edition of M. C. Bradbrook, *The Growth and Structure of Elizabethan Comedy* (London, 1973).

world stage, from the Zulu *Umabatha* to the American burlesque, *Macbird*. His mythology has replaced that of the Bible for the medieval stage and of the classical deities for later ages. The vast multiplicity of acting forms enables the student of Renaissance drama to feel something of the original variety of the multiple stages of Jacobean times. That drama also was "mungrel" (Sidney's word). Experience alone will supply authentic "recreation".[18] Some modern "recreations" cannot be accepted easily. I could not myself accept the much applauded "pop" version of the sheep-shearing in *The Winter's Tale* put on by the Royal Shakespeare Company in 1969, nor the pop version of *The Two Gentlemen of Verona* running in 1975 at Stratford, Ontario. It seems to me to justify Q's remark "by now, there are *no* gentlemen in Verona", for the absurdities of decorum cannot be exposed where they are not even acknowledged to exist. On the other hand, in a great reconstruction, like that of Peter Brook's *A Midsummer Night's Dream*, there emerged a deep unity. The clowns recreated that feeling of holiday which the Elizabethans associated with Midsummer Night in the greenwood—the feeling that called out the execrations of a Philip Stubbes against such paganism, the feeling Shakespeare revives for *The Two Noble Kinsmen*—recaptured for a modern audience energy and agility which could not be regained by archaeologizing. It embodied material which "sank to the depth of feeling, was saturated and transformed there—and brought up to daylight again", for "what one makes in this way may succeed in standing the examination of a normal frame of mind; it gives me the impression of a long incubation, though we do not know till the shell cracks what kind of egg we have been sitting on."[19]

The great film director Kozintsev declared of Shakespearean films, "One has to seek out and decipher the poetic sign, the code. It's in the lines, and as always happens with poetry, it's between the lines as well."[20]

However, as I have said, an open form is not an indeterminate form; coherence lies in the delicate balance between surrender to the tale and mockery of it. This balance seems also to have been

18. That is, the removal of conventions and associations unconsciously imposed by tradition, exposing the play freshly to the modern world; the process may be compared with the cleaning of an old painting.
19. T. S. Eliot, *The Use of Poetry and the Use of Criticism* (Cambridge, Mass., 1933), pp. 144, 146 (he is speaking of Coleridge's "Kubla Khan").
20. Grigori Kozintsev, "*Hamlet* and *King Lear*: Stage and Film", Leech and Margeson (eds.), *Shakespeare 1971*, p. 193.

present in the more complex Jacobean audience, versed in the multiple stages, the many and divergent dramatic conventions of the drama's full maturity. The skilled director may now painlessly supply what the modern reader must painfully acquire from much reading and many footnotes. Of course a multiplicity of performances is a *sine qua non* of this process. There is no longer a single central classic tradition for the presentation of plays; but when the Jacobean theatre was at its greatest, there was no single tradition either.

Players had used to be scornfully termed chameleons rather than comedians; but the Protean art sustained its integrity by tension between manifold styles: between Shakespeare and Jonson, and Jonson and Middleton, between the Red Bull and the Inns of Court, between all of these playwrights and theatres and the Court rituals, or the civic triumphs.

The Revenger's Tragedy
Revived

STANLEY WELLS

The Revenger's Tragedy has, I suppose, a thinner stage history than any contemporary play of comparable reputation. Most of the better-known tragedies of Webster, Middleton, Massinger, and Beaumont and Fletcher have been professionally performed, often in adaptation, at some time or other between the time they were written and our own age. But when R. A. Foakes prepared his Revels Plays edition of *The Revenger's Tragedy* the only professional production to which he could refer was that at the Pitlochry Festival, still in the future.

There had, of course, been performances by amateur groups, especially in universities, of the kind that leave little trace behind. One at Toynbee Hall in 1954 drew from the critic of *The Times* (February 18) an expression of surprise that the play was "so much neglected". Although it had a ludicrous plot and was deficient in humanity, few of Tourneur's less neglected contemporaries could equal him in the narrative of crime, and "the character of the revenger has a sustained force and consistency and a fidelity to its own rough conception of justice that finally overcomes incredulity. As for dramatic language, pungent, pointed, and intensely theatrical, one leaves this revival in the conviction that Tourneur is a master of it". The only performances that could be taken wholly seriously were those of Lussurioso and Vindice. Perhaps the reviewer had more wholly serious expectations of the tragedy than later critics would have felt appropriate. He found that "the inexperience of the other actors does not enable them to suppress in us the notion that crime and punishment on such a scale are somehow comic." Ten years later, Professor Foakes praised an

Oxford college performance for bringing out "the ironic humour of the play", stating that its director felt that "the play, as 'black comedy', had been theatrically effective".[1] Here an explicit link was being made between Tourneur's dramatic style and the modes of modern drama. A reviewer of the first recorded professional production, by Brian Shelton at the Pitlochry Festival in July 1965, similarly referred to its "black humour", and wished "that the first night audience had appreciated it more".[2]

A Cambridge production given jointly by the Marlowe Society and the ADC in November 1965 provoked similar comparisons. *The Times* reviewer (November 25) found that it presented "the skeletal outline of the tragedy", not helped by "a distracting attempt to restore the Jacobean pronunciation" and "a set resembling upturned garden furniture". Still, it provided a reminder "that there is a rooted tradition of horrific violence in English drama which outdoes anything on the contemporary stage. What modern dramatist would dare show a man making love to a poisoned skeleton and being subsequently trampled to death?" (a rhetorical question answered in the next day's issue in a letter from Pamela Hansford-Johnson saying, "Oh, come now, pretty well any of them.") The reviewer was left with the desire to see the "skeletal outline ... filled in by a professional company". The critic of the *Financial Times* (November 25) also said that the play "ought soon to be given a full-scale professional production."

So there was a distinct upsurge of interest in *The Revenger's Tragedy* in the mid-1960s, and it was not surprising that the Royal Shakespeare Company, which was showing an interest in plays by Shakespeare's contemporaries, should consider it for their repertory. Other factors too may have drawn them to the play. The company was deeply involved in the "Theatre of Cruelty" movement. David Addenbrooke points out that "nearly every play staged by the RSC during 1964 was, in some way, influenced by 'cruelty'." A "result was a year of productions which virtually compelled audiences to leave the theatre with their senses and intelligence jolted and disturbed as never before."[3]

Perhaps the most important of these productions in relation to *The Revenger's Tragedy* was Clifford Williams's presentation of

1. *The Revenger's Tragedy*, Revels Plays series (London, 1966), p. xlv.
2. *Theatre World* (August 1965), p. 33.
3. *The Royal Shakespeare Company* (London, 1974), pp. 137-8.

Marlowe's *The Jew of Malta*, given at the Aldwych in 1964 and at Stratford the following year. This brilliant production has been largely responsible for a critical revaluation of the play since, as *The Times* (April 17, 1965) said, it was "a classic demonstration of how far a play's theatrical impact can differ from the impression it makes on the page." It, too, provoked comparisons with contemporary playwriting. James L. Smith writes "Time and again, Williams' production emphasised the prime tenet of 'black comedy': that laughter mounts in direct proportion to the threatened violence of the action it anaesthetises." And: "the audience accepted the play as a 'black comedy' and untroubled by embarrassing uncertainties of genre were free to concentrate wholly on Marlowe's dramatic purpose."[4] The great achievement of this production was to hit upon a mode of performance which released the play's latent energies in a manner that seems never to have happened before. Marlowe's mode, whether one refers to it as "black comedy" or, perhaps more accurately, as ironic tragedy, is close to that of *The Revenger's Tragedy*, and I have no doubt that the company's liberation of a play with an ostensibly tragic framework from the irrelevant and stifling associations of romantic tragedy was a major factor in preparing the ground for its production of Tourneur's play.

Theatrical fashions relate, of course, to life; and Trevor Nunn has stated that his interest in *The Revenger's Tragedy* stemmed from its contemporary relevance:

It was a play that I'd read at university . . . and I was just overwhelmed by it. . . . It seemed to me a play that was extraordinarily about aspects of our own world . . . where the relationship between sex, violence and money was becoming increasingly popular, and expressed through all sorts of things—spy novels—James Bond. The "good life"—the life of extraordinary opulence and comfort—was also connected with something fundamentally immoral. . . . I was also fascinated by a society which reviled this development, but could [not] stop talking about it. . . . What fascinated me about the Revenger—about the character Vendice—was that he was totally schizophrenic; a completely modern study. He was somebody utterly dedicated to the destruction of this world, and he was—at the same time—totally fascinated by it.[5]

4. "*The Jew of Malta* in the Theatre", in Brian Morris (ed.), *Christopher Marlowe*, Mermaid Critical Commentaries (London, 1968), pp. 15,18.
5. Addenbrooke, *The Royal Shakespeare Company*, pp. 144-5.

The theatrical and intellectual climate seems then to have been particularly favourable for a major revival of *The Revenger's Tragedy* in 1966 when Trevor Nunn asked to be allowed to direct it as his first independent Stratford production. It was announced in September as the play's "first professional staging for nearly 300 years", a claim which had to be hastily amended to allow for the Pitlochry Festival performances of the previous year. The Stratford repertory also included a revival of Peter Hall's distinguished production of *Hamlet*, with David Warner as the Prince. When *The Jew of Malta* had been performed at Stratford the previous year, Eric Porter had played Barabas, and also Shylock in *The Merchant of Venice*. Publicity statements had made much of links between the two plays in what seemed like a defensive justification for playing Marlowe at Stratford, partly no doubt for fear of adverse effects on the box-office. In the announcements for *The Revenger's Tragedy*, links with *Hamlet* were similarly stressed. A commercial success was obviously not expected. Only eight performances (along with two previews) were planned, and the budget was low. For the sake of economy, the *Hamlet* set was used.

This background to the production is reflected in the programme, a typically eclectic document which includes a note on the play mentioning the revenge genre, morality plays, and "the Malcontent (whom we now call the Angry Young Man)"; a note on Tourneur; a note on revenge from Gāmini Salgādo's introduction to the play; a photograph of the last scene of Peter Hall's *Hamlet*, showing four corpses; a sexy still from a James Bond film and another from Fellini's *La Dolce Vita*; rehearsal photographs of *The Revenger's Tragedy*; a drawing of the Dance of Death; and miscellaneous quotations of varying degrees of relevance from, among others, Bacon, Burton, Bryden, Nashe, *The Guardian* (on murder for honour in modern Italy), Swinburne, Allardyce Nicoll, Robert Ornstein, Irving Ribner, and R. A. Foakes.

After its eight performances in 1966, Trevor Nunn's production was revived in Stratford for nine more performances in 1967. The intention was to take it to London later that year, but this was abandoned. It eventually reached the Aldwych in November 1969, and had thirty-one performances, including a gala one in the presence of Princess Margaret. Material relating to it is deposited in the theatre's archives in the Shakespeare Centre in Stratford. There are three promptbooks. The one for 1966 is made from a cut-up

copy of the Gāmini Salgādo edition of 1965.[6] Pages of this edition
are mounted on foolscap sheets, with typescript additions and
manuscript annotations. The 1967 promptbook is similar in format,
but shows changes in the text. There are two versions, one with
detailed notes, the other in simplified form with "cues only",
marked "used in performance". The 1969 promptbook is a
photocopy of a typescript of the 1967 text, with only minor changes.
The bound volumes of theatre records include many newspaper
clippings and similar documents, and there are photographs of both
rehearsals and performance.

Salgādo's text was much adapted. Many lines were omitted. The
order of several episodes was rearranged, with some consequent
revision of linking passages. There were minor changes and
substitutions in the dialogue. Most important, seven substantial
passages written by John Barton were added. There is also evidence
that other editions were consulted. Salgādo's error of "bound" for
"bold" at v.i.138 is corrected, and an alternative reading not
recorded by Salgādo ("To be miserably great" instead of "Great, too
miserably great!") is followed at iv.iv.74.

The complex textual revisions made in 1966, along with other
changes made in 1967 and a few minor ones in 1969, make this a
difficult text to describe, and the situation is complicated by the fact
that the production records are not entirely reliable. Those who
have worked with theatrical materials will not be "amazed to death"
by this. Promptbooks are not infallible evidence of what happens
at each performance. There is a glaring instance in that the
promptbook for 1966 has no trace of Act iii, scene iv, in which the
Junior Brother is shown shortly before execution, although this
scene was certainly acted on the first night. It was dropped during
the run, and no doubt the promptbook was amended to take account
of this. The scene was not included in the revivals. I saw several
performances in both 1966 and 1967, but none in London. My
account is based on the performances that I saw and my reading of
the archives. There were few reviews of the 1967 production, at the
request of the management, because of the proposed revival in
London. My own impressions have become a bit blurred, and the
different promptbooks are variously helpful at different points of the

6. *Three Jacobean Tragedies* (Harmondsworth, 1965); all references are to this
edition of *The Revenger's Tragedy*.

action, so my account of the production must be regarded as a composite one. My aim is to give an objective account of some features of the production, and of its reception, rather than to explore in detail its critical implications.

I should like to look first at the textual changes, and will begin with those affecting the overall structure. One was anticipated before any words were spoken by the addition of a mimed episode portraying a masque dance, and culminating in a stylized representation of a rape. In Act I, scene i, Vindice's determination to take on the office of pander to Lussurioso was followed by an abbreviated version of Act I, scene iv, showing Antonio's grief over his dead wife's body. This made the rape episode more clearly a part of the play's exposition, and may also have made the plot easier to follow since it caused Antonio's grief to precede the scene (I.ii) in which the Junior Brother is tried for the crime. In the 1966 production the action then moved straight into the trial scene, omitting the passage at the end of Act I, scene i which introduces Gratiana and Castiza. (This passage was restored in the later revivals.)

The original structure was then followed, bypassing Act I, scene iv, up to the end of Act II, scene ii, where a brief insertion caused Spurio to enter reporting his failure to find Lussurioso. This perhaps increased suspense before Spurio's entry into the following bedroom scene. The next rearrangement of scenes occurred at the end of Act III, scene iii, in which Ambitioso and Supervacuo give to the Officers the Duke's signet which will accidentally result in the execution of their own younger brother. The omission after the first few performances of the Junior Brother's main scene probably reduced the serious implications of Ambitioso's and Supervacuo's action, and emphasized the macabre comedy of Act III, scene vi, in which they discover their error, and which followed immediately. The action then moved back to Act III, scene v, showing Vindice's vengeance on the Duke. The single interval came at the end of this scene: a strongly climactic point, especially since the conclusion of the Junior Brother episodes came into the first half of the play as acted. The first part lasted about ninety minutes, the second about an hour.

The second half began with Act IV, scene i and went on till the end of Act IV, scene iii, showing Ambitioso's and Supervacuo's resentment at the liaison between Spurio and the Duchess. Act IV, scene iv, which shows Gratiana's admission of her sin and her

reconciliation with her sons and daughter, was bypassed to bring
together the scenes of Vindice's final vengeance on the Duke. The
omitted scene was played just before Act v, scene ii, in which the
culminating murders are plotted, and the action then followed the
original design till the play's last line.

The shape and effect of the play were of course changed not only
by the reordering of scenes but also by the added passages. John
Barton had already had much practice in writing blank verse in the
fourteen-hundred-odd pseudo-Shakespearian lines that he had
added to the three parts of *Henry VI* and *Richard III* in order to
turn them into *The Wars of the Roses*.[7] His additions to *The
Revenger's Tragedy* were not on so large a scale. They are printed
below, by kind permission of Mr. Barton, who tells me that some of
the alterations were arrived at after rehearsals had started, as the
result of actors' requests for clarification of particular passages. I
should like to comment on a few points in the additions.

The first was partly necessitated by advancing Antonio's scene of
grief to a time before the trial of his wife's rapist. The new dialogue
anticipates, instead of reports, Antonio's complaint that judgment
"cools and is deferred" (i.iv.51) because the Duchess wishes to save
her son. More importantly, it removes from Hippolito his oath to
ensure that Antonio is avenged, and transfers the determination for
vengeance to Vindice:

> Nay, 'twill ne'er please me
> Till we that love you may her vengers be.

So a link between Vindice and Antonio in their grievances against
the ducal family is established early in the play instead of in the last
scene, as in Tourneur. No less important, Antonio is explicitly
shown to be content to leave vengeance to heaven:

> 'If you love me, or law,' he says, 'you'll hold your hand.'

The contrast between the virtuous Antonio's insistence that revenge
be left to heaven, and Vindice's desire to effect it himself, seems
intended to evoke modern beliefs about the Elizabethan revenge
ethic, and to point to Vindice's final fate at Antonio's hands.

7. *The Wars of the Roses* (London, 1970), p. xvi.

The second, brief insert came at the end of Act II, scene ii, causing Spurio to enter reporting his failure to find Lussurioso. It is based on the lines given by Tourneur for Spurio's entry into the bedroom scene (II.iii.39-45) along with a line omitted at v.i.169: "The Duchess is suspected foully bent." The cut in the bedroom scene removes the awkwardness of a conversation between Spurio and his servants in the midst of the dramatic episode of Lussurioso's humiliation—an awkwardness which was probably not felt in the non-representational original staging.

In Act III, scene v Hippolito is given an additional speech on vengeance, stressing its pleasures. His phrase "Sure, 'tis a violent joy" picks up Vindice's "the violence of my joy forgot it" (III.v.27). This fourteen-line speech replaces an eight-line one (III.v.35-42), also spoken by Hippolito; perhaps Vindice needed more time than this would have allowed him to go out and return with the bony lady.

The fourth insert expands the dialogue between Spurio and the Duchess, watched without their knowing it by the dying Duke. It increases the sexual innuendo of the original, expands on Spurio's expression of hatred for his father, and adds a statement of contempt by the Duchess for her husband's coldness. The reference to dancing is derived from Act II, scene v of *The Atheist's Tragedy*, "... dance the beginning of the world after the English manner—Why not after the French or Italian?—Fie! They dance it preposterously, backward" (II.v.66-9); the later line, "Man's is humble till a woman moves it", is based on one from the same play: "The flesh is humble till the spirit move it" (IV.i.92).

The fifth insert comes before Act IV, scene iii and picks up the imagery of the previous one, but applies it to Spurio's political ambitions instead of his sexual exploits. The Duchess makes it clear that he should not "hope too high". The Duke's absence from court, already reported (IV.i.83), is emphasized again, with sexual imagery, in a clear attempt to increase suspense. Act IV, scene iii follows, with Ambitioso and Supervacuo watching with annoyance the departure of Spurio and the Duchess. At the end of the scene, according to the promptbook, two courtiers cross the stage calling "My Lord!", evidently seeking the Duke.

In Act V, scene i, at line 167, John Barton adds a representation of the Duchess's banishment, merely reported by Tourneur. Again her guilty sexuality is emphasized. She is spurned successively by Spurio, her sons, Antonio, and Lussurioso who, the promptbook says, "spits on her and throws her to [the] ground." She leaves "Amidst laughter". At line 172, Vindice speaks a couplet based on one from the end of Act IV, Scene ii:

> And by the way too, now I think on't, brother,
> Let's conjure that base knave out of our mother.

This is obviously the result of the transposition of the scene showing Vindice and Hippolito visiting their mother and sister. A brief insert shows Spurio inciting Ambitioso and Supervacuo to kill Lussurioso.

Besides these extensive additions there were other, minor additions and substitutions. Names were added to help the audience to identify characters, as in Hippolito's first line: "Still sighing o'er death's vizard [, Vindice?]". At the end of Act I, scene iii Vindice has the couplet,

> So touch 'em,—tho' I durst almost for good
> Venture my lands in heaven upon their blood.

This is rather obscure: Foakes annotates "The meaning seems to be, 'I dare almost for good and all stake my hopes of salvation on their disposition (or strength of character)'."Barton alters the lines to

> I durst almost for good
> Venture my soul upon my sister's blood,

which both removes the obscurity and provides a pointer to the following, transferred scene.

A few passages are rewritten in an obvious effort to achieve greater clarity of exposition. An example at Act V, scene ii (ll.11) perhaps provides the most useful illustration of the procedure. The original reads:

> revels are toward,
> And those few nobles that have long suppressed you
> Are busied to the furnishing of a mask
> And do affect to make a pleasant tail on't.
> The masking suits are fashioning.

This was altered in 1966 to

> revels are toward,
> The Bastard Spurio and the Duchess's sons
> Are furnishing a masque and mean to make a pleasant tail on't.

But apparently this was still not felt to be clear enough, because in 1969 the last line was altered to "And mean to make a mortal end to it." It is not surprising that an attempt should be made to increase the audience's preparation for the play's climax.

There was also some reassignment of speeches; for instance, Antonio's role was built up by giving him some of the anonymous Lord's speeches in Act V, scene i.

Naturally enough, the additions to the dialogue were at least counterbalanced by omissions. Among the more substantial passages omitted were ones having contemporary social relevance, such as Act I, scene iii(ll.46-55), most of Vindice's speech on women in Act II, scene i (ll.217-2ᵋ and 227-35), and much of the legal satire in Act IV, scene ii. The static panegyric of Antonio's wife was cut (I.iv.3-26 and 48-66), and so was Dondolo's introduction of Vindice in Act II, scene i (ll.10-27), Dondolo's only appearance. Among short passages omitted are some lines of inessential amplification, some rather obscure ones, and a high proportion of moralizing and sententious remarks, such as "Ladies know Lucifer fell, yet still are proud" (I.iii.75). Changes in theatrical conventions probably account for the omission of a number of asides. Conspicuous among these are Vindice's expressions of affection and concern for Castiza in Act II, scene i, including the two invocations,

> Troops of celestial soldiers guard her heart,
> Yon dam has devils enough to take *her* part. (137-8)

and

> O angels, clap your wings upon the skies
> And give this virgin crystal plaudities! (245-6)

Similarly Vindice sacrificed (IV.ii.162):

> Has not heaven an ear? Is all the lightning wasted?

To deprive Vindice of these powerful acknowledgments of a divine scheme of things is to reduce his own perspective upon himself, and may make it more difficult for the audience to accept Tourneur's final assertion of orthodox morality—and to understand why Vindice himself accepts it.

The principal aim of the alterations seems to have been to clarify the action and to speed it up, increasing the amount of dramatic preparation, reducing static and discursive elements and passages with mainly topical relevance. Sexual suggestiveness was increased, especially in relation to Spurio and the Duchess, whose roles were enlarged; so was violence, in the episode of the Duchess's banishment. The textual alterations worked towards particularization rather than generalization. The play's Christian frame of reference was reduced, and some of Tourneur's moral and social reflectiveness was sacrificed. Though there was a gain in pace, it evaded the challenge of Tourneur's emblematic, tableau-like stylization of action, which Professor Foakes referred to (see p. 63) as "a serial arrangement of episodes" rather than "a development of plot", and which might conceivably have been exploited rather than denied.

The set for *Hamlet* against which the production was presented is described by David Addenbrooke as "an open, black, shining 'box', with two huge doors opening at the rear. . . . The basic material used was black formica."[8] B. A. Young in the *Financial Times* (October 6, 1966) complained that Christopher Morley's designs "lean rather heavily on Royal Shakespeare Company clichés... dark panelled walls at the back are hinged to create various shapes of acting area, and a tall canopy throne of familiar aspect floats down the centre of the stage for the Duke." The version of the design for *The Revenger's Tragedy* "was given a formal structure which centred on a huge silver circle on the black floor of the stage. This circle imposed a hierarchical order and formalized grouping on the court: the centre of the circle was the 'centre of the Court' (the Duke), and the Duke was costumed in bright glittering silver. As one moved further from this centre, the costumes and stage became less silver and more black."[9] Christopher Morley's costumes were particularly striking. He explained that he "started with three silhouette designs—dresses and stomachers for the women, breeches for the men, basic colour of silver over black. Everyone was to have the same basic costume with various additions depending on status or

8. *The Royal Shakespeare Company*, p. 130.
9. Ibid., p. 145.

rank.... Trevor told me we were dealing with a decadent, narcissistic court with incest at the centre and a family in mourning on the periphery. Out of this came the monochromatic idea."[10] Hippolito, asked by Vindice "How go things at Court?", replies "In silk and silver, brother: never braver" (I.i.51-2), which may have given a hint to the designer.

The masque with which the production opened stimulated several critics to description. D. A. N. Jones wrote in 1969: "The glittering, silvery courtiers of the Duke's household surge forward from a deep black box, brandishing masks and torches: as they swish in patterns about the stage, like brilliants juggled on black velvet, we get a clue about who's being raped, who's in charge, who's paying court to whom." After a dance episode, the rape of Antonio's wife was mimed. It is vividly, if technically, described in the 1969 promptbook: "All exit except men. Men surround [the actress playing Antonio's wife] in circle. [Wife] runs from one side to other in circle. She is pushed down in centre of circle, head facing down-stage. [Junior] leaps on top of her. Men raise cloaks to hide them. Men rhythmically raise and flap their cloaks as vultures' wings. [Actress] screams. Men exit."[11]

The opening of the play proper formed a deliberately ironic contrast. As Vindice described the ducal family, they "silently introduce themselves to us, as if they were in church, bowing as they cross themselves; we, the audience, are treated as the altar, the eyes of God".[12] At "Thou sallow picture of my poisoned love" Vindice "whips out from behind his black cloak the skull of his beloved."[13] It was an impressive moment, with Ian Richardson in full control of the audience's reactions.

I have said that the adaptation of the text worked towards particularization; the same was true of the settings. The critic of *The Times* in 1966 (October 6) commented that the producer succeeded "in striking the right balance between a stylized and a realistic treatment. On the one hand, he has the courtiers uniformly clad in black and silver as if to remind us that Vendice is fighting a corporate evil rather than isolated individuals; on the other hand, he places every scene in a precise and meaningful context." Thus the first encounter between the disguised Vindice and Lussurioso was

10. "The Designer Talks", *Plays and Players* (January 1970), p. 54.
11. *The Listener* (December 4, 1969).
12. Ibid.
13. *Glasgow Herald* (October 8, 1966).

set in a fencing school. There were two lines of fencers, all masked when the scene opened. The fencing between Vindice and Lussurioso was treated as a display of their opposing wills: the promptbook (1966) calls for a sign of dismay when Vindice scores a point, and when Vindice and Lussurioso are left alone they "fight. Finally Vindice is disarmed. Masks off." When Vindice swore to be true, he kissed Lussurioso's sword.

The next scene, between Vindice and Castiza, was played with a number of dressmakers' dummies on stage, as if to suggest a profession for Castiza. When Vindice had to show Gratiana gold, he took material from a dummy, spread it on the ground, and put jewels on it. Gratiana went on her knees to them.

Act II, scene ii, which is mostly a conversation between Vindice and Lussurioso, showed Lussurioso, practically naked, lying on a slab and being oiled and stroked by a plump masseur who looked like a dumb eunuch.

One of the most successful scenes was one for which Tourneur himself provides a localized setting of the bedroom in which Lussurioso hopes to surprise Spurio with the Duchess. Lussurioso leapt on to the bed and tore down the curtains, to reveal the disconcerted Duchess, wigless and bald, and the half-naked Duke, gibbering with penitential fear until Lussurioso dropped his dagger and fell to his knees on "I am amazed to death!", when the Duke snatched his own dagger from under his pillow. When the Court entered, the Duchess's ladies helped her to dress, and Guards dragged Lussurioso to the side. After the Duke had assured the Duchess that Lussurioso would die, she exultantly slapped Lussurioso's face before departing. This interpolated piece of business served as preparation for the later, added scene of her banishment, in which Lussurioso was to spit at her.

Most of the broad comedy in the production came from Ambitioso and Supervacuo, played respectively as a tall, mincing figure with earrings and high heels, and as a squat, dumpy, cowardly boaster. Ronald Bryden wrote: "the duchess's idiot sons appear as chalk-faced clowns from a silent film, bickering and cuffing like Laurel and Hardy in ruffs";[14] Gareth Lloyd Evans found them "entirely evil while being completely comic";[15] Benedict Nightingale, discussing whether burlesque elements in the

14. *Observer* (October 9, 1966).
15. *Stratford-upon-Avon Herald* (October 13, 1966).

production were justified, wrote of them: "As Tourneur sees it,
they're spoiled, callous, greedy and stupid–cunning but
incompetent, as becomes clear when they arrange the execution of
their envied stepbrother and find their own brother's head in a
basket.... In Nunn's production they... mince about the stage,
whispering, and bob and chirrup in crises.... It's hard to take them
seriously... but that doesn't invalidate their conception... [Nunn]
shows us a state that's been taken over by its Osrics."[16] Their scene
with the basket containing the head of their executed brother
provided an episode of brilliantly macabre comedy, not least when
Supervacuo swung the basket in the Officer's direction, threatening
him: "I'll brain thee with it" (III.vi.79).[17]

This scene was followed climactically by the one described in the
promptbook as the First Lodge Scene (III.v), for which the main
feature of the setting was a tomb. On this Vindice seated the "bony
lady", a scarecrow figure dressed in a robe and topped by the skull
of his dead mistress. The promptbook calls for the lecherous Duke
to "climb on top of figure on tomb, kiss it, Hippolito at head of
tomb, Vindice to upstage of it." When the Duke realises he has
been poisoned, the direction reads "Hippolito onto tomb, fist 3
times into Duke's face." D. A. N. Jones wrote:

> They force the duke's face down on this thing... then they pin him–one
> dagger at his heart, the other at his tongue–compelling him to silently
> watch his wife making love to his bastard son. If he closes his eyes, they'll
> remove his eyelids–'and make his eyes, like comets, shine through
> blood'. Then comes the author's brilliant, rhyming joke: 'When the bad
> bleed, then is the tragedy good'. This takes place under cover of loud
> music from a banquet. The duke shows the audience his butchered face,
> the lips eaten away, and dies.[18]

16. *New Statesman* (December 5, 1969).
17. Dr. Lois Potter tells me that in the Pitlochry production, although this scene was
given its full value as comedy, nevertheless the actor succeeded in chilling the
audience on the line "I see now there's nothing sure in mortality but mortality"
(III.vi.89). She continues: "Then, when the brothers had gone off in a huff, the gaoler
was left holding the head and obviously wondering what to do with it. The stage set
was a modified Elizabethan one, with projecting forestage and skeletal wooden pillars
with nasty-looking spikes projecting from them. At last the gaoler shrugged his
shoulders and stuck the head on one of these spikes as the lights came up for the
interval."
18. *New Statesman* (October 14, 1966).

The interpolated love scene between Spurio and the Duchess was played as a kind of walking torch dance, with much erotic suggestiveness in their movements and their manipulation of the torches as they raised them above their heads and mingled their flames. It was not authentic, but it was certainly memorable.

The first scene after the interval, in which Lussurioso seeks to replace Vindice disguised as Piato by Vindice himself, was played in a torture chamber, with suffering figures stretched on racks. The director may have taken his hint from Lussurioso's

> Push, I shall prove too bitter with a word,
> Make thee a perpetual prisoner
> And lay this ironage upon thee. (IV.i.38-40)

Cruelty was clearly to the fore here. D. A. N. Jones regarded the setting as a mistake, since the verse was "punctuated by shrieks every time Lussurioso presses a lever: this kind of staged horror can spoil the author's climaxes."[19] In 1969 at least, court ladies were present to share the entertainment offered by the victims' sufferings.

In the following scene there was a deliberate and, I thought, timid evasion of the implied stage direction:

> Is there no thunder left, or is't kept up
> In stock for heavier vengeance? [*Thunder.*] There it goes! (IV.ii.205-6)

But we heard no real thunder; instead Vindice drummed angrily with his fists on the table. In itself it was effective enough, but it denied Tourneur's suggestion of divine concern, and became one element of the more general process of secularization.

The first words of John Barton's fifth addition, which preceded Act IV, scene iii, were always good for a laugh. The promptbook directs a court entrance to the centre of the stage: "All stare outwards then general exit leaving Duchess and Spurio." The Duchess (arms akimbo, if I remember rightly, and glowering) spat at the audience "I do not like the morning." Several critics noticed the line; not all approved of it. Jeremy Kingston, writing in *Punch* (October 12, 1966), said, "when the Duchess... enters stiffly after a night of bedwork and pauses after the phrase, 'I do not like the

19. Ibid.

morning', the laugh seems to me improper." (He appears to refer simply to the way the line was delivered, not to its inauthenticity.)

After this episode followed the "Second Lodge" scene, in which the Duke's corpse is discovered, and which includes another line that always succeeded in raising a laugh. It was vulgarly described in *The Sun* (October 6, 1966), whose critic (David Nathan) wrote "These old classics can be something of a lark, I can tell you . . . the laughs . . . lie in the direct, often inadequate language in which the bloodcurdling events are chronicled. The old duke, for instance, lies dead . . . and his evil, bastard son confides to the audience 'Old dad, dead!'"

In the following scene, the representation of the banishment and spurning of the Duchess was not to everyone's taste. D. A. N. Jones, who had disliked the torture chamber, wrote in 1966 "Nunn overdoes it again when Lussurioso, driving his stepmother from court, spits in her face",[20] and in 1969 he expanded this: "Nunn has built up the Duchess's expulsion from court into something needlessly sadistic, from a mere hint in the text."[21] Benedict Nightingale, however, listed among the production's "striking aperçus" the episode in which "courtly lovers dally and snicker while a prisoner screams from the rack", and that in which "the whole hilarious aristocracy amuses itself by aping Patience Collier's Duchess as she pleads and wails after being condemned to exile."[22]

Act IV, scene iv, in which Gratiana repents, was played as a bedroom scene. D. A. N. Jones wrote "The scenes concerning enforced chastity are in dead earnest and the women . . . play them so, more movingly than the author deserves."[23]

One of the great set-pieces of the production was, justifiably, the dumbshow representing the investiture of Lussurioso. The walls at the back of the stage opened to admit guards with torches. A procession in five ranks, led by Lussurioso, advanced from the back of the stage in slow and ritualistic fashion. The empty throne followed them. The members of each rank of the procession turned their backs to the audience, the stiff fabric of their robes swishing sinisterly with each obscene thrusting forth of their bodies till Lussurioso mounted his throne in corrupt splendour and turned to face his courtiers, who knelt and kissed his hand in hypocritical

20. Ibid.
21. *The Listener* (December 4, 1969).
22. *New Statesman* (December 5, 1969).
23. *New Statesman* (October 14, 1966).

adoration. He raised his arm in a totalitarian salute, which the courtiers returned. The blazing star was not represented but imagined as if in the audience; on seeing it (v.iii.15) Lussurioso collapsed and had to be supported by the lords.

For the climactic dance of revengers the director devised a mime of skull-masked figures dancing metronomically to the insistent rhythm of an off-stage drum. They bore swords which they raised above their heads and clashed together in the dance, like morris dancers, associating this dance of death with the erotic dance in which Spurio and the Duchess had used torches in a similar manner. Finally they leapt on to the table, killing their carousing victims, who themselves wore skull-masks, with downward stabs.

The director was fortunate in his cast. Ambitioso and Supervacuo could not have succeeded as well as they did without the stongly individual contributions of John Kane (later to play Puck in Peter Brook's production of *A Midsummer Night's Dream*) and Terrence Hardiman. As Hippolito, Patrick Stewart was entirely reliable, a good foil to the brilliance of Ian Richardson's Vindice. The Duke was played initially by David Waller, a stocky, bull-necked actor who brought to the role a weighty, glowering coarseness. In 1967 Nicholas Selby took over, and Gareth Lloyd Evans wrote "Last season's Duke was a gross, slobbering, unctuous thing; this year he is a thinner, dry-voiced, pathetic lecher."[24] In all the performances that I saw his Duchess was played most forcefully by Brenda Bruce, aggressive, brassy, and tough (Patience Collier took over the role in 1969). Norman Rodway complemented her well as Spurio. He played a lot of bastards, actual and metaphorical, around this time. He had an incisive earthiness that made easy contact with an audience.

The two outstanding performances were in the roles of Lussurioso and Vindice. Alan Howard, as Lussurioso, received mixed notices. He is a tall, lean actor, highly mannered in both voice and movements, and he played the role very much as a languorous, decadent sensualist. Philip Hope-Wallace referred to his "wonderful arrogant sneering pride";[25] B. A. Young saw him as "a kind of decadent Lohengrin, tall and blond and looking smashing in his ducal robes."[26] Ronald Bryden, in *The Observer* (October 9),

24. *Stratford-upon-Avon Herald* (May 12, 1967).
25. *Guardian* (October 6, 1966).
26. *Financial Times* (October 6, 1966).

spoke of him in 1966 as "a nervous, sometimes over-busy actor", but found that he established "the character with imaginative, balletically sharp physical strokes—an empty, small-toothed smile, a twitching cheek, a convulsive, prowling walk." *The Times*, in 1966 (October 6), however, found his performance "a crucial interpretative flaw": "he makes Lussurioso a bisexual exquisite, more absurd than evil. Consequently one feels the court is being rid less of a contaminating presence than of a rather temperamental dandy; and the case for Vendice is thereby weakened." Harold Hobson, too, saw him as "an effeminate and gilded fop".[27] Lussurioso was certainly portrayed as an introverted, neurotic character, but he did not seem to me to create a less evil impression as a result.

As Vindice, Ian Richardson had a triumphant success. He has a highly developed technique, a strong sense of comic irony, and a real power of conveying intelligence. He is a bold, attacking actor, able to make the most of those moments of direct address in which Tourneur, through Vindice, chills the spectators into awareness of their participation in the guilt of the characters of the play. *The Times* (October 6, 1966) found that "he meticulously conveys the ambiguous nature of the character's desire for revenge, motivated partly by genuine justice and partly by a zest for bloodletting." In the *Financial Times* (October 6, 1966), B. A. Young found that he addressed "some of his lines to the audience with the confiding glance that characterizes the best playing in French farce", and extracted "double meanings from the most unpromising lines". Nevertheless, "the serious passages are sometimes spoilt by a suspicion that at any moment Mr. Richardson will reveal that he has been working up to a laugh all along." This suspicion of a hint of burlesque in his performance, as in the production, was voiced by several critics. Gareth Lloyd Evans countered it with "Ian Richardson is not inconsistent in his characterization when, one minute, he is both laughing and making us laugh and, the next minute, pulling himself and us into a frightened, serious silence. . . . One could have wished . . . that [he] had occasionally shown more 'inner' consciousness of the character's complexities, but . . . [his] performance is on the right lines and has a superb verbal resonance."[28] In 1969, Philip Hope-Wallace said he "handles the

27. *Sunday Times* (October 9, 1966).
28. *Stratford-upon-Avon Herald* (October 13, 1966).

part with the ease of a man drawing on gloves, cool, witty, terrible in his guile and intent",[29] and D. A. N. Jones spoke of his "three Jacobean voices: posing as a malcontent thug for hire, he has the dark, melancholy tone of a Jacques; disguised as a courtier, he sounds as bright and silly as his own Bertram; when in earnest he uses his fine personal blend of the Gielgud quiver and the Olivier yelp."[30]

A popular success for the production was not expected, and critics of some newspapers did not feel able to recommend it. The *Birmingham Mail* (October 6, 1966) neatly headed its notice "The Black and White Murder Show", and was pleased to remark that there were "some flashes of language well above the merely serviceable level." The *Evening News* (October 6, 1966), noting some "atrocious rhyming couplets", doubted if, "a few laughs apart", the play was worth doing; the *Daily Express* (October 6, 1966) found it "a common-or-garden Jacobean thriller-diller" which "should delight everyone except the merest toddlers"; the *Leamington Spa Courier* (October 7, 1966) spoke of "a graceless play", "a verse play without poetry", "a scrofulous corpse" in "a sickening exhumation". Even the *Sunday Telegraph* (October 9, 1966) found it "one of the most vicious, perverse and evil tragedies in English drama", with "clumsy characterization and poor poetry". As usual, some of the remarks cancelled one another out. In 1969 the *Daily Telegraph* (November 28) found the plot "unusually well-constructed and easy to follow", whereas the *Sheffield Telegraph* (November 29) found the "tortuous, salacious plot . . . too complex to bear repetition." The *East London Advertiser* (December 12, 1969) went one step further and accused the play of having no plot at all: "Of course there is a theme of sorts . . . but it is almost lost in the mystic layers of treason and assassination."

These comments are insensitive, of course, but perhaps it is right for us to be aware of the Philistine point of view. And it is not far removed from an attack on the play by one of our most influential critics. Harold Hobson, citing the programme's claim that the play "has something to do with exposing a corrupt society", found it rather "an encyclopaedia of moral obscenities, an incursion into the filthy recesses of the Jacobean mind. Some exercises of this sort are

29. *Guardian* (November 28, 1969).
30. *The Listener* (December 4, 1969).

at least interesting. . . . But Tourneur. . . deals only in elementary
misdemeanours, and the splendour of language on which he
occasionally hits is tarnished in this production by a spirit of
burlesque."[31]

Hobson's condemnation was not shared by most of his more
responsible colleagues. J. C. Trewin referred to "language of an
often startling splendour" and regarded the performance as "an
important night in our classical theatre".[32] The *Listener* (May 25) in
1967 referred to "this virtuoso production of a great and neglected
play"; Ronald Bryden felt that "the tilt of macabre comedy" Trevor
Nunn gave it "revealed it not as the uneven second-rank tragedy
most scholars considered it, but a masterpiece in a genre of its own:
satiric melodrama";[33] and Martin Esslin found the production
"magnificent, a real classic of insight and style, unforgettable as a
spectacle, a vindication of a great and much neglected
playwright."[34]

Hobson's moral objections to the play are linked, we notice, with
the accusation that the production was informed "by a spirit of
burlesque". He was not alone in discerning this. Philip
Hope-Wallace's "only cavil" was that it "occasionally and no doubt
excusably slips into self-parody".[35] B. A. Young suggested that the
play's impact had been "distorted by mocking its weaknesses."[36]
Punch's critic (October 12, 1966) had "the impression of a director
seeking to make fun of the characters for taking themselves so
earnestly." Yet this is exactly what Tourneur himself does, when,
for example, he causes Vindice, after his brutal treatment of the
Duke, to retreat into ironic comment with "When the bad bleeds,
then is the tragedy good" (III.v.200).

It is interesting that the line the *Punch* critic singles out as raising
an "improper" laugh is the Duchess's "I do not like the morning",
written by John Barton. In quoting these criticisms of the 1966
production it is only fair to record that in 1969 Philip Hope-Wallace
had modified his judgment, referring to a "marvellously sharpened
and intensified production" which transformed the play "from a
curiosity to a play gripping in its own peculiar right", even if there

31. *Sunday Times* (October 9, 1966).
32. *Birmingham Post* (October 6, 1966).
33. *Observer* (November 30, 1969).
34. *Plays and Players* (January 1970), p. 46.
35. *Guardian* (October 6, 1966).
36. *Financial Times* (October 6, 1966).

were still "occasional lapses into pantomime buffoonery".[37] (This probably refers mainly to the manner of playing Ambitioso and Supervacuo.) Similarly, Milton Shulman in the *Evening Standard* (November 28) felt that "it has toned down its more blatant extravagances and flourishes so that it has considerably reduced its ever-present dangers of toppling over into parody."

But even in 1966 such accusations had been countered. The *Stratford-upon-Avon Herald* (October 7, 1966) reported the presence in the first-night audience of "Professor Reginald Foakes, who edited the last edition.... Yesterday he told the *Herald* the great difficulty with the play is achieving balance between its tragic and comic elements. 'I think it is a tragic satire on the follies and vices of society, strikingly applicable now as it was in its own time. The company did marvellously well to achieve the balance so that they could shift from one mood to another very rapidly.'" In the same newspaper, Gareth Lloyd Evans (October 13, 1966) wrote "It is both pointless and wrong, firstly, to call it a merely dirty or violent play and, secondly, to say that the RST has 'sent it up'." D. A. N. Jones felt that the production "takes... almost exactly the right tone."[38] In 1969, in the *New Statesman* (December 5), Benedict Nightingale offered an extended discussion of whether the "burlesque" was justified and came to the conclusion that "the satire introduced by Nunn... enriched the play and brought it closer to the audience's experience of reality, without distorting Tourneur." And Martin Esslin, referring to critics who had rebuked the director for playing "too much for laughs", wrote "this precisely is what it is all about: we are shown two attitudes which are both equally perverse and which ultimately are identical; pursuit of lust for its own sake and the perverse preoccupation with the fight against the flesh which is only experienced by those who have to suppress just such lustful preoccupations. Both perverse stances are equally reprehensible and sick and we can gain the true distance to them merely by healthy laughter."[39]

There was then a conflict in the reviewers' reactions to the production, and I think it stems from a basic discrepancy in critical response to the play, and perhaps even more fundamentally from preconditioning aroused by associations of the word "tragedy".

37. *Guardian* (November 28, 1969).
38. *New Statesman* (October 14, 1966).
39. *Plays and Players* (January 1970), p. 47.

Should a tragedy make people laugh? Is it not irreverent to laugh at a tragedy? Where has all the catharsis gone? In the Prologue to *The Jew of Malta* are the lines

> I come not, I,
> To read a lecture here in Britain,
> But to present the tragedy of a Jew. . . .

I remember the actor who played the Governor in the Royal Shakespeare Company's production saying that if the word "tragedy" here was not spoken with an ironic inflection, it took half an hour to coax the audience into the right mood for the play. This production too was accused by some critics, including Philip Hope-Wallace[40], of not taking the play seriously enough, of "sending it up". Yet both plays succeeded in hitting the mood of the mid-sixties. The 1966 reviews of *The Revenger's Tragedy* include a number of references to "black comedy" and "Theatre of Cruelty". By 1969 the phrase "permissive society" had entered our jargon, and is several times invoked. The director was successful in relating his production to the era without blatant contemporaneity. Most critics probably did not realize the extent of John Barton's additions. The programme simply said "Text edited and adapted by John Barton". His additions do add to the cruelty and sexuality of the original text. They do not, it seems to me, add to its comedy or increase the element of self-parody that Tourneur himself allows to his characters. If accusations of unwarranted comic effects had any justification, it was mainly in relation to the portrayal of Ambitioso and Supervacuo. Here there was unquestionably a layer of comedy deriving from the way the roles were played rather than from the way they were written. But playwrights must always expect actors to make their personal contribution, and I did not myself feel that these performances ever got out of hand.

The other major source of comedy in the production was in the performance of Vindice. It is, I think, inevitable that we should be more aware of the role's inherent comedy when we see the play than we are likely to be when we read it. The disguises are an open invitation to the actor to exercise virtuosity in character creation. And the ironic situations in which Vindice finds himself have comic as well as tragic aspects. It is true that, as Gareth Lloyd Evans

40. *Guardian* (April 15, 1965).

suggested, Ian Richardson is a rather "external" actor, sometimes even giving the impression of an ironic objectivity about his own plight within the character he is playing, rather than of living and suffering through it. But such an attitude in Vindice is helpful to the audience as it struggles to maintain its awareness of the complex situations, and Ian Richardson's individual handling of the role seemed to me to go no further beyond the legitimate limits of interpretation than we consider quite customary in Shakespeare. His performance had a pervasively incisive wit that seemed entirely appropriate. The almost hysterical laughter, half-smothered, with which, carried beyond himself by exultation in his own ingenuity as he boasted to Antonio of how Hippolito and he had carried out their plan, took the audience along with it so that they shared his shock at Antonio's stern reaction. This was, moreover, the culminating reversal of the relationship between Vindice and the audience that had been carried on throughout the play: a relationship in which the audience alternately shared Vindice's amoral fascination with corruption and recoiled from it in a revulsion expressed by Vindice himself. When he confided in Antonio, as he had been confiding in us, his expectations of sympathy were rudely shattered. But we accepted his recovery as one side of his personality gallantly condemned the other:

> 'Tis time to die when we are ourselves our foes.
>   ... We have enough
> I'faith, we're well, our mother turned, our sister true,
> We die after a nest of dukes. —Adieu.

It seems to me that reviewers who accused the director of burlesquing or parodying the play revealed a lack of understanding, perhaps as a result of preconditioning about what properly constitutes tragic effect. They were troubled by "embarrassing uncertainties of genre" such as had sometimes inhibited a proper response to *The Jew of Malta* (see p. 107). But, as I have said, an examination of the textual alterations suggests that some interpretative slanting was effected, particularly by the reduction of the play's ethical and religious framework. This, along with the emphasis on sexuality and cruelty in some of the additions and in the staging, increased the "cynicism, the loathing and disgust of humanity" which Eliot found excessive in Tourneur. Yet the firm insistence on Antonio's virtue, and the relative lack of tampering with the scenes showing Castiza and

Gratiana, allowed some power to human virtue, if not to divine protection.

This version of *The Revenger's Tragedy*, like practically every production of a play out of its time, went some way towards adapting the play to the intellectual and theatrical fashions of the time of the production. But, in its realization of the ironically comic energies of the text, it was, I thought, faithful to the spirit of the dramatist. Perhaps one day another director will do as much for the farcical savagery of *The Atheist's Tragedy*, or the anarchic satire of *The Malcontent*.

John Barton's additions to 'The Revenger's Tragedy'

INSERT 1: *after* i.iv.50

Antonio	His trial's appointed.
Vindice	Who shall judge him, think you?
Antonio	Grave men. Albeit the Duke must give the sentence.
Hippolito	He'll never doom him: what?–the Duchess' youngest son.
Antonio	Yet he'll be judged.
Vindice	But when?
Antonio	When heaven shall please.
Vindice	Deferr'd till doomsday? Nay, 'twill ne'er please me Till we that love you may her vengers be.
Antonio	If you love me, or law, you'll hold your hand.
Vindice	Nay, Sir —
Antonio	Nay, nay, Sir. That must not be scanned: There are two laws, the Duke's and God's above. Learn this a little ere you talk of love.
Hippolito	And yet 'twere pity [*on to line 67*]

INSERT 2: *after* ii.ii.176 (*end*)

Spurio	He was not there ! You are all villains, fablers !
Servant	O good my Lord.
Spurio	Lussurioso was not there !
Servant	'Twas his intent to meet there.
Spurio	Not there, not there ! I wonder where he went ?
Servant	Wher'er I doubt not he was foully bent.
Spurio	Go find him, villains, and report him right: 'Tis certain he's at foulness now 'tis night.

INSERT 3: *after* III.v.34

Hippolito A witness: to what ? Why, to my brother's vengeance.
What's that to me ? I like't, and like it not.
This vengeance is a law prompted by nature,
Promulgate by our blood, which when we broach it
Makes that blood thrill, as now my brother's doth.
Sure, 'tis a violent joy, and I suspect it;
Nay, I must doubt myself, for mine own veins
Joy, too, i'th' very moment of suspect.
Why do they so ? Alas, we dare not know:
Most perilous actions, dire and dangerous,
Are lesser danger than to search ourselves, —
Masks off, that's fearful. Yet the masks being on,
I fear the first fires of our outward flames
Are fouler than our vices' outward names.
[*On to line 43*]

INSERT 4: *after* III.v.201.

Spurio Like you the music ?
Duchess   Ay, and long to dance.
Spurio Shall's do't by torchlight ?
Duchess   Yes.
Spurio   Or in the dark ?
Duchess Fie, an your torch be out our dance is done:
I mean to dance till morning by the maypole.
Spurio In the English manner then ?
Duchess   Or in the French.
Spurio Fie, they dance backward.
Duchess   So: let's try out [other] countries
And learn new ways to climb.
Spurio   Ay, to the mountain,
Duchess There's many ways.
Spurio   Yet all meet i' the shrine
Where torches kiss, thus, i' the fiery circle.
Duchess Hot brands should be thus brandished and enmixt.
Spurio And cold sheets warm'd thus by the twain betwixt.
This place is cold and craveth such a fire.
Duchess Cold as the icicle i' the old Duke's bed,
Whose touch is loathsome to me. Come your fire.
Here is a vault for vaulting.
Spurio   'Tis e'en so;

> Court-panders whisper oft of such a quaintness,
> And swear that here where great men end, most grave,
> Others begin, or were begun, in dancing.
> There are some luxurs, so the sheet-spies murmur,
> That lust so curiously that in their doting
> They spend them here.

Duchess   Then even as thou art lustful,
Be spendthrift too.

Spurio   I muse where my dad got me:
My thoughts being deadly, sure I think it was
In some such place of death. Could I once find it,
In vengeance on my sire I'd slake you there
On that vile slab where I was seminar'd.

Duchess Think not on him.

Spurio Why it adds sweets to sweetness:
Sharp'st spices make the feast more cruel-great.
And lust's not lust till it be sauc'd with hate.
To think on him is fiery.

Duchess   'Faith I find
My own affections flame to think on's coldness,
And now I could embrace the air to cool them.

Spurio 'Tis thy natural Eve's-flesh.

Duchess Ay. Man's is humble till a woman moves it.
I'll make you proud.

Spurio   I am.

Duchess   The dance must prove it.

Spurio Be more demure.

Duchess   Why so ?

Spurio   You'll burn too quick.

Duchess Tush, I'll burn long.

Spurio   Ay, when thou find'st the wick.
The music quickens. Come, I long to feed;
My father's dish shall be the bastard's meed.
[*On to line 215:* 'Why, now thou'rt sociable.']

INSERT 5: *at the beginning of* IV.iii.

Duchess I do not like the morning. Give me nights
For my court pleasures.

Spurio   So I do, yet think me
The court i'the day may serve for sweeter pleasures.

Duchess Nay, now I see thou art political.

Spurio   Thyself did say there's many ways to climb.
Duchess I spoke of bed-tricks. Thou'rt a bastard; think on't.
Spurio   So do I ever.
Duchess   Thou'rt a proper man;
          But for advancement, —
Spurio   Ay ?
Duchess   Hope not too high.
                    (*Enter* Antonio)
Antonio Good-morrow, madam. Saw you the duke this morning ?
Duchess Why ask you, sir ?
Antonio   He's miss'd i'the council.
Duchess   Well ?
Spurio   'Tis thought that he's rid forth; (but on what mare
          Is not surmised).
Antonio   Rode forth in private, then ?
Spurio   It is reported so.
Duchess   So tell the council.
Antonio Madam, I will; farewell.   [*To* Spurio] Your servant sir.
                    (*Exit* Antonio)
Spurio   And yours. Perchance he's dead.
Duchess   I would he were.
Spurio   There's portents: whiles we flam'd the heavens were stirr'd;
          It lighten'd. And our court-intelligencers,
          Astrologers of state, divine in's absence
          Some ill, some smell of blood, some doom of state:
          'Tis strange he's not returned.
Duchess   Delay'd at night-work ?
          That is not strange; 'was ever slow to kindle.
          Would he were charnell'd.
Spurio   Doubt not he'll die soon.
Duchess Good.
Spurio   Ay; for thy nights. Not for thy days i' the court —
          Lussurioso being duke, and thou
          A widow-duchess, then, thy power being out,
          Thy pleasures bate.
Duchess   Yet thy power being in — .
Spurio   E'en so.
Duchess   E'en so, sweet. (*Embracing him*)
Spurio   Nay, that's not my meaning.
Duchess 'Tis mine. Would it were night now ! [*On to* IV.iii.1:
          'Unlock yourself'].

                    131

INSERT 6: *after* v.i.167 ('Griefs lift up joys, feasts put down funerals')

Lussurioso	But for you, lady, thus: I muse you weep.
Duchess	Have I not cause ?
Lussurioso	I know not, but thou shalt.
	What say you, shall the new duke make decrees ?
Duchess	Doubtless, in time.
Lussurioso	Nay, at this time: you're banish'd.
Duchess	Banish'd ? For what ? Alas, what have I done ?
Lussurioso	That thou know'st best; much done and much been done.
Antonio	This is not known.
Lussurioso	Ah, she's much known, my lord.
	Mark how she blushes.
Antonio	That is not modesty.
Lussurioso	Nay, 'tis hot thoughts. 'Tis known she hath an itch,
	And itches token tetters, fevers, foulness.
	Sir, she's no sooner tingled but she coins;
	To banish her's a balsam for her loins.
Duchess	You slander me; if this is so, then prove it.
Lussurioso	Put you to proof ? Not I, although you love it.
Duchess	Try me.
Lussurioso	You're tried enough.
Duchess	This is false rumour.
Lussurioso	To make it holy-writ is our court humour.
	Thy humour is too hot. Is it not so,
	Spurio ?
Spurio	Aye, 'tis so; she's better from the court,
	And shall do well i' the country.
Lussurioso	That's my thought.
Duchess	My sons, speak for me.
Ambitioso	Nay, it may not be:
	To speak you true were little charity.
Supervacuo	Thou art an old bed-reveller, that's pure truth.
Spurio	Out of the mouth of babes and sucklings, sooth !
Duchess	I challenge law.
Antonio	Thou'st challeng'd it enough,
	And law requites thee.
Lussurioso	Law gives thee the snuff.
	Suffice thou art suspected foully bent:

Now I'll 'gin dukedom with thy banishment.
So to our revels, lords. Our music, strike:
Feasts, banquets, masques make dukes more monarch-
like.

INSERT 7: after Insert 6, Tourneur's v.i.171-2 *followed by*
iv.ii.233-4; *these four lines are given below before the Insert begins.*
(*Exeunt* Lussurioso, Nobles *and* Duchess)
Hippolito (*aside*) Revels !
Vindice (*aside*) Ay, that's the word, we are firm yet;
　　　　　Strike one strain more, and then we crown our wit.
　　　　　And by the way too, now I think on't, brother,
　　　　　Let's conjure that base knave out of our mother.
Spurio Brothers, —
Ambitioso 　　　　Ay, my brother bastard ?
Supervacuo 　　　　　　　　　What's your will ?
Spurio The new duke loves you not.
Supervacuo 　　　　　　　　We hate him, too.
Spurio Then think on this: he has unmask'd your mother.
Ambitioso He smok'd her, sure.
Spurio 　　　　　　　　And he may be your smother.
Ambitioso Let's kill him then.
Supervacuo 　　　　We often thought to do it.
Spurio Be your thoughts acts; let's think on't and then do it.
　　　　A mask is treason's licence, that build on:
　　　　'Tis murder's best face when a vizard's on.
　　　　Farewell. I'll pierce his heart, or near about,
　　　　Then have at any—a bastard scorns to be out.
　　　　　　　　　　　　　　　　(*Exit*)
Note: *The second and third lines of Spurio's last speech are*
Tourneur's v.i.184-5, *transferred from Supervacuo. The scene con-*
tinued from Tourneur's v.i.177, *omitting lines* 184-5.

Love, Marriage and Money in Shakespeare's Theatre and Shakespeare's England

G. R. HIBBARD

Sir Francis Bacon, a man not much given to romantic illusions, except, perhaps, about the benefits of scientific discovery, begins his essay "Of Love", in the final version of it published in 1625, with the following words:

> The Stage is more beholding to *Loue*, then the Life of Man. For as to the Stage, Loue is euer matter of Comedies, and now and then of Tragedies: But in Life, it doth much mischiefe: Sometimes like a *Syren*; Sometimes like a *Fury*.[1]

Bacon clearly saw a marked discrepancy between love as it was portrayed in the theatre, where it generally led to the happy ending of comedy in a marriage which, it is assumed, will be completely satisfactory, and love as it existed in real life, where, as it seemed to him, it was productive only of trouble and disaster, either luring its victims to destruction or driving them to it. In his main contention that love on the stage was in general something quite other than love in the big world outside the theatre he was undoubtedly right. Love as the essential preliminary to marriage and the only sound basis of it, which is indeed the assumption underlying the great romantic comedies of Shakespeare and his contemporaries, was not, in fact, the basis of marriage in the England of his time, except,

1. Francis Bacon, *A Harmony of the Essays*, ed. Edward Arber (London, 1871), p. 445.

possibly, among some of the very poorest members of society who had nothing but love to marry for. The audience that first saw *As You Like It*, for example, somewhere about the year 1599-1600, was witnessing an action which, measured by the standard of contemporary habits and practices, was both highly improbable and extremely reprehensible; for in this play Rosalind, the daughter of a duke, albeit a banished one, and Orlando, a young gentleman and third son whose worldly prospects look distinctly poor for the greater part of the time, fall in love with each other at first sight, enjoy the pleasures of a protracted wooing with no interference whatever from parents or relations, and finally marry without so much as consulting a lawyer. Moreover, the Duke, Rosalind's father, who does not learn of the marriage until the last minute, is perfectly happy about it, and actually gives the couple, and the other couples, his approval and his blessing.

Things were managed very differently from this at the court of Queen Elizabeth, or, if they were not, there was serious trouble. Sir Walter Ralegh's clandestine marriage to one of her maids of honour, Elizabeth Throckmorton, who was five-months pregnant by Ralegh when it took place in November 1591 —not the most fitting state for a maid of honour to be in —so enraged the Queen when she eventually learned of it some eight months later that she had the pair of them sent to the Tower. Ralegh, who was too useful to be kept there for long, was let out again after five weeks, but his unfortunate Bess had to remain in the Tower for five months, from August 1592 until the end of the year. It is true that the offence was exacerbated in this case by the fact that Ralegh was one of the Queen's favourites, with the result that she looked on his marriage as a personal affront, and also by Lady Ralegh's return to her office of maid of honour after the child was born; but it is also true that Elizabeth expected none of her maids of honour to marry without her personal consent and approval.[2]

Ralegh's courtship of Elizabeth Throckmorton was, incidentally, if that old gossip John Aubrey is to be believed, of a rather different kind from Orlando's delicate playful pastoral wooing of Rosalind, though it too took place in a sylvan setting. Here is what Aubrey says in his *Brief Lives*:

He [Ralegh] loved a wench well; and one time getting up one of the

2. See Joel Hurstfield, *The Queen's Wards* (London, 1958), pp. 52, 140.

Mayds of Honour up against a tree in a wood ('twas his first Lady) who seemed at first boarding to be something fearful of her Honour, and modest, she cryed, sweet Sir Walter, what do you me ask? Will you undoe me? Nay, sweet Sir Walter! Sweet Sir Walter! Sir Walter! At last, as the danger and the pleasure at the same time grew higher, she cryed in the extasey, Swisser Swatter Swisser Swatter.[3]

Whether that story is apocryphal or not—and it receives some measure of support from Cecil's smug reference to Ralegh's "brutish offence"—there can be no doubt that Ralegh's love for his wife and hers for him were the real thing. He took her without a dowry—her portion of £500 had been lent years earlier and was never recovered[4]—a most unusual event in those days; and, despite its inauspicious beginnings, the match proved a thoroughly happy one. Ralegh came to know his wife so well that he could jest with her in the grimmest of all possible situations. According to John Chamberlain, the great letter-writer of the early seventeenth century, this is what happened on the night before Ralegh's execution in November 1618:

his Lady had leave to visit him that night, and told him that she had obtained the disposing of his body, to which he aunswered smiling yt is well Besse that thou mayest dispose of yt dead, that hadst not always the disposing of yt when yt was alive: and so dismissed her anon after midnight when he setled himself to sleepe for three or fowre howres. . . .[5]

Ralegh's way to marriage was, as befitted the man, unconventional. Bacon's was far more typical of the age. His first move in the direction of matrimony came, so far as I know, in 1597, when he was thirty-six. He was in financial difficulties at the time, as, indeed, he was for most of his life. At this juncture Sir William Hatton died, leaving behind him a young widow who was, like Emma Woodhouse, "handsome, clever, and rich". Bacon decided to try his luck, and set about the matter much as Claudio begins the wooing of Hero in Shakespeare's *Much Ado About Nothing*. He wrote to the Earl of Essex, asking him to use his influence with the lady's

3. John Aubrey, *Brief Lives*, ed. O. Lawson Dick (Harmondsworth, 1962), p. 318.
4. A. L. Rowse, *Ralegh and the Throckmortons* (London, 1962), p. 57.
5. John Chamberlain, *The Letters of John Chamberlain*, ed. N. E. McClure (Philadelphia, 1939), Vol. II, pp. 179-80.

parents, and with the lady herself, on his behalf. Essex duly obliged; but there were other suitors in the field; and in November 1598 Lady Elizabeth Hatton was married to Bacon's great rival in law and politics as well as love, Sir Edward Coke. Bacon, prudent as usual, waited five years before taking the next step, and this time he did not fly so high. On July 3, 1603, he wrote to Sir Robert Cecil to ask for his help over some money troubles he was in, and to express his rather reluctant willingness to be made one of James I's new knights. He ends his letter thus:

> Lastly, for this divulged and almost prostituted title of knighthood, I could without charge, by your Honor's mean, be content to have it... because I have found out an alderman's daughter, an handsome maiden, to my liking.[6]

Bacon knew that the prospect of becoming a titled lady was a good bait to dangle before the alderman's daughter and her family. The maiden in question was almost certainly Alice Barnham, the second of the four daughters and co-heiresses of Benedict Barnham, a wealthy London merchant who had died in 1598. Alice was only eleven years old at the time when Bacon wrote to Cecil, so the wedding did not take place until three years later,[7] in 1606, when it was recorded in a letter from Dudley Carleton to John Chamberlain in these terms:

> Sir Francis Bacon was married yesterday to his young wench in Maribone Chapel. He was clad from top to toe in purple, and hath made himself and his wife such store of fine raiments of cloth of silver and gold that it draws deep in her portion.[8]

At this date, Alice, like Shakespeare's Juliet, was fourteen, and her husband forty-five. How did this match so carefully entered upon between this young girl and the middle-aged lawyer, statesman, and philosopher turn out? We do not know for certain, but it is possible to read something into a remark Bacon made to his friend Lord Chancellor Ellesmere in a letter written a month after the wedding, where he says that a married man is "seven years elder in

6. J. Spedding, *An Account of the Life and Times of Francis Bacon* (London, 1878), Vol. I, p. 417.
7. Catherine D. Bowen, *Francis Bacon* (London, 1963), p. 90.
8. Spedding, *Life and Times of Francis Bacon*, Vol. I, p. 484.

his thoughts the first day". Alice, it would appear, had something to teach him. After that all is silence for the next twenty years. What we do know is that there were no children, which must have been a great disappointment to Bacon, and that something went badly wrong between husband and wife towards the end, because after making a will in which he left Alice well provided for, with lands that would enable her to keep up her rank of viscountess in fitting style, he added a codicil in which he stated:

> Whatsoever I have given, granted, confirmed or appointed to my wife, in the former part of this my will, I do now, for just and great causes, utterly revoke and make void, and leave her to her right only.[9]

Bacon does not specify what these "just and great causes" were, but Alice's conduct immediately after his death supplies a likely clue. Bacon died on April 9, 1626. On April 20 of the same year, less than two weeks later, Alice, moving at double the speed of Gertrude in *Hamlet*, married her gentleman-usher, John Underhill. It seems probable that the two of them had been having an affair for some time, and that it was Bacon's discovery of it which led him to alter his will. After all, Alice was still only thirty-four when her husband died, whereas he was sixty-five. Incidentally, the marriage of a newly-made widow to a member of her household staff was by no means uncommon, for the very good reason that officials such as stewards—one recalls *The Duchess of Malfi*—were often the only men, apart from the husband, that the woman had seen much of since the time of her marriage.

I have described these two marriages, contracted by two of the greatest men of their time, because they have a certain representative quality. Ralegh's tempestuous love for Elizabeth Throckmorton, for the sake of which he jeopardized his career, coincides substantially with the kind of love Shakespeare depicts in his romantic comedies, in *Romeo and Juliet*, in *Othello*, and in *Antony and Cleopatra*. But if, on that score, we think of it as being in any way typical of the age, we are hopelessly wrong. It is Bacon's careful selection of a girl with a good fortune that conforms to the basic norm of Elizabethan marriage, at least among those classes of society about which we have much reliable information. The main considerations were lands, rank, and money, not love. The evidence

9. Quoted from Bowen, *Francis Bacon*, p. 178.

provided by family papers, legal documents, and letters is overwhelming. Moreover, the system was accepted, for the most part, by the young for whom the matches were made, as well as by the parents who did the match-making. Wallace Notestein, who has probably read as much of the relevant material as anyone, tells us in his charming essay "The English Woman, 1580-1650" that the parents

were bound by community opinion to busy themselves about the marriages of their sons and daughters. Those who failed to make good matches for their progeny, or who left a daughter unbestowed, were censured by their neighbours and indeed by the children themselves.[10]

It must be added also that this way of going about things did not work too badly, at least when the two persons most intimately involved in it were young and healthy. The much quoted proverb, "Marry first and Love will come after" (Tilley, L534) was not without its validity. Furthermore, merely to be married meant much when marriage was seen as woman's proper and often sole objective in life. The prospect of leading children into heaven was far more attractive than that of leading apes into hell, the proverbial fate that awaited the spinster.

But the system was, of course, peculiarly open to abuse; and at this point I want to turn back for a short time to the marriage of Lady Hatton and Sir Edward Coke in 1597 and some of its consequences. According to the scandalous Aubrey, its beginnings were not exactly auspicious. He writes:

His [Coke's] second wife, Elizabeth, the relickt of Sir William Hatton, was with Child when he married her: laying his hand on her belly (when he came to bed) and finding a Child to stirre, What, sayd he, Flesh in the Pott. Yea, quoth she, or els I would not have maried a Cooke.[11]

The story is too good to be true, in the literal sense; but in another sense, it is so good that it must be true; and it is. In the question and the answer Aubrey has captured, in a dozen words or so, the essential characters of two people. Coke's crude, brutal query is absolutely typical of him. It was by his use of language such as this

10. In J. H. Plumb (ed.), *Studies in Social History* (London, 1955), pp. 86-7.
11. *Brief Lives*, ed. Dick, p. 162.

that he had made himself the most feared prosecutor in England, one who brow-beat the accused and any witness in favour of the accused. Equally Lady Hatton's answer is typical of her; she was high-spirited, indomitable, and witty. Their marriage took the course implicit in that story; it consisted of violent conflicts, punctuated by periods of armed neutrality. Coke had married his wife for her wealth and her powerful connections—she was a Cecil, a grand-daughter of Lord Burghley—and no sooner were they married than he sought to get her possessions into his own hands. She retorted by refusing to take the name of Coke, preferring to be known as Lady Hatton, and by fighting him every inch of the way. Nevertheless, she took her wifely responsibilities seriously enough to bear him two daughters.

In 1616, Frances, the younger of the two, was a very beautiful girl of fifteen, attracting much attention at the court of James I, including that of Sir John Villiers, the elder and decidedly dim-witted brother of James's favourite, George Villiers, soon to be made Earl of Buckingham. Now it was in this same year that Coke, largely as a consequence of some skilful manoeuvres by his old rival Bacon, was first suspended and then dismissed from the office of Lord Chief Justice. In the interval between his suspension and his dismissal, Lady Compton, the mother of Sir John Villiers, relying on the fact that Coke would be eager to secure the alliance of Buckingham as a means of recovering the King's favour, opened negotiations with him for a match between Frances and her son Sir John. Being a grasping old woman, however, eager to establish the fortunes of her family, she proposed higher terms than Coke, who was also an inveterate money-grubber, was willing to pay. She wanted him to give his daughter a portion of £10,000, together with a life allowance of £1,000 a year. Coke offered two-thirds of the sum, but would go no further. The negotiations were broken off, and Coke was finally dismissed from his post. But the loss of office rankled sorely with him, and in an effort to win it back he eventually told Lady Compton he was ready to comply with her terms. It was only at this stage that he told his wife what had been going on. She was furious, and with good reason. Frances was her daughter as well as Coke's; she feared, and was right to fear, that Coke intended most if not all the money he was laying out to come from her estate, not his; and there was the further fact that Frances did not like Sir John Villiers. She therefore carried Frances off and hid her at a house in the country, alleging that the girl was plighted to the Earl of Oxford, who was conveniently away in Italy at the time.

The Villiers family applied to Bacon, on behalf of Coke, for a warrant ordering the girl to be returned to her father. But Bacon, not knowing what was going on, refused it. A warrant was, however, obtained from another source; and, armed with it, Coke, who had now learned where his daughter was, set off with a band of relatives and retainers, including his son "fighting Clem", who was something of a pugilist. When they arrived at the house where Lady Hatton and Frances were, they were refused entrance. Thereupon the ex-Lord Chief Justice picked up a large log which was lying handy and, with the help of his men, battered in the door, dragged out the wretched girl, and hurried her into a coach where old Lady Compton was waiting for her.

Justifiably enraged by these proceedings, Lady Hatton drove up to London, to demand of Bacon that her daughter be restored to her. When she eventually arrived at the Lord Keeper's house—the journey had been an arduous one since her coach had overturned on the way—she was told that the Lord Keeper was unwell and resting. She then insisted on being allowed to wait in the room next to his bedroom, so that she could see him as soon as he emerged. After a time she could bear the suspense no longer and, in her agitation, began "bouncing" against his door. The noise awoke Bacon, as it was intended to, and he called his servants in alarm. The moment they opened the door Lady Hatton pushed past them, asking to be excused on the plea that "she was like a cow that had lost her calf." At first Bacon did what he could to help her, until he learned that both Buckingham and the King were in favour of the match, after which he did all he could to forward it. On September 28, 1617, Coke was restored to his place at the council table—he had ceased to be a Privy Councillor on being suspended as Lord Chief Justice—and on the following day his daughter's wedding to Sir John Villiers took place at Hampton Court. Lady Hatton was not present at it.

The marriage was a disaster. Sir John Villiers, soon promoted to the title of Viscount Purbeck, became subject to periodic fits of insanity; and his wife, the victim of an enforced match, left him to live in adultery with Sir Robert Howard. At the instance of the Villiers family, she was arraigned before the Court of High Commission, and was ordered to do public penance by being exposed, dressed in a white sheet, to the gaze of the London mob. Happily, she avoided this miserable fate not once but twice, and she did it by the same means as the heroines of many a romantic comedy had used and were using to get themselves out of awkward situations. In 1627, when the house where she was clandestinely living was surrounded by constables and officers of the court, a coach drove up, a young lady with fair hair climbed into it, and was hurried off at great speed, hotly pursued by the minions of the law. No sooner were they gone than a young man came out of the house next door, got into another coach that had been waiting unobtrusively by, and was also driven away. The girl with fair hair, who was eventually captured, proved to be a pageboy in disguise. The boy who escaped unmolested was, of course, Frances herself.

For the next five years Frances lived with Sir Robert Howard in great seclusion somewhere in Shropshire; but when her father fell seriously ill in 1632 she went to see him and to look after him. Very soon after his death in 1634, however, she was arrested again on the charge of not having performed the penance, and confined in the Gatehouse prison in Westminster. The sentence of 1627 was confirmed; but a friend of Sir Robert's bribed one of the gaolers, provided her with a male disguise once more, and managed to convey her to France. There she was converted to Roman Catholicism, and, for a time, lived in a nunnery, although without taking vows. Then, sometime about 1640, she was pardoned by Charles I and permitted to return to England.[12]

Material of the kind I have just been describing is evidently full of dramatic possibilities; but though Shakespeare makes, I think, some indirect comments on the system, he does not, as I remarked earlier go very far in dramatizing Elizabethan marriage as it was. For that we must turn to other playwrights, and especially to Thomas Middleton. Born and bred in London, Middleton was fascinated by the trickery that the arranged marriage so readily lent itself to; by the legal chicanery which surrounded it, since lawyers were not only employed to draw up the contracts that preceded marriage, but also did very well out of the financial arrangements that had to be made if it broke down; and, above all, by the issues which arose when men and women married, as they were increasingly tending to do in the early seventeenth century, out of their own class, as Bacon had done in marrying Alice Barnham. In fact, class relationships and tensions,

12. See S. R. Gardiner, *Prince Charles and the Spanish Match*, Vol. I (London, 1869), pp. 91-104, and *History of England 1603-1642*, Vol. VIII (London, 1884), pp. 144-6; J. G. Crowther, *Francis Bacon* (London, 1960), pp. 282-6; and Laura Norsworthy, *The Lady of Bleeding Heart Yard* (London, 1935).

as they come to a head in marriage, are, it seems to me, the major theme of his comedies, as well as of one of his two great tragedies. The main participants in the comedies are thriving London citizens, who wish to acquire land in the country as a means of moving up the social ladder and who seek to ally their sons and daughters to the gentry or nobility, and, on the other side, members of the gentry, usually in debt, invariably short of ready cash, and prepared to resort to almost any means in order to get hold of it. The gentry despise the citizens for their meanness; the citizens despise the gentry for their foolish prodigality. Each class dislikes the other, yet finds that it cannot manage without the other. As a result, intermarriage between the two classes becomes a game of "catch-as-catch-can".

But the basic assumption underlying much of Middleton's comedy is best stated in his own words. He sets it out in the first scene of *Michaelmas Term*, a play which was written around 1605. There a London woollen-draper and usurer, Quomodo by name, explains to his man Shortyard, who has just asked him what mark he aims at, his intentions in dealing with Master Easy, a gentleman of Essex:

> Why, the fairest to cleave the heir in twain,
> I mean his title; to murder his estate,
> Stifle his right in some detested prison.
> There are means and ways enow to hook in gentry,
> Besides our deadly enmity, which thus stands:
> They're busy 'bout our wives, we 'bout their lands. (I.i.102-7)[13]

Quomodo is much more interested in land than he is in his wife; and, to clinch the point, he is given a soliloquy in which he actually describes Easy's estate, which he intends to win, as though it were a beautiful girl, referring to it as:

> that sweet, neat, comely, delicate parcel of land, like a fine gentlewoman
> i' th' waist, not so great as pretty.... (II.iii.82-3)

I do not intend to say more about *Michaelmas Term*, because there are other plays of Middleton's that are more germane to my theme. But, before I come to them, I should like to quote one passage from his comedy, *A Trick to Catch the Old One*, first published in 1607.

13. Thomas Middleton, *Michaelmas Term*, ed. R. Levin (London, 1967).

In this play Witgood, a young prodigal, dresses up one of his ex-mistresses in fine clothes, gives out that she is a wealthy widow from the country whom he is about to marry, and wins himself credit on the strength of his supposed expectations. She is won from him, with his full connivance and to his great satisfaction, by a wealthy old usurer called Hoard. Thereupon, Witgood asserts that she was precontracted to him and offers to súe Hoard. Thoroughly alarmed, Hoard seeks to buy him off, and eventually, with well assumed reluctance, Witgood agrees. A bond is then drawn up between them; and it is this that I want to cite, because it defines the position of women with great accuracy:

> Be it known to all men, by these presents, that I, Theodorus Witgood, gentleman, sole nephew to Pecunius Lucre, having unjustly made title and claim to one Jane Medler, late widow of Anthony Medler, and now wife to Walkadine Hoard, in consideration of a competent sum of money to discharge my debts, do for ever hereafter disclaim any title, right, estate, or interest in the said widow, late in the occupation of the said Anthony Medler, and now in the occupation of Walkadine Hoard; as also neither to lay claim by virtue of any former contract, grant, promise, or demise, to any of her manors, manor-houses, parks, groves, meadow-grounds, arable lands, barns, stacks, stables, dove-holes, and coney-burrows; together with all her cattle, money, plates, jewels, borders, chains, bracelets, furnitures, hangings, moveables or immoveables. . . . (IV.iv)[14]

You will notice how the supposed widow is regarded there exactly as though she were a piece of land, to be occupied by one man and then transferred to another for a cash payment. The satire is evident and telling.

I now turn to what is, I think, the most thorough-going treatment of the subject I am pursuing in the whole of Elizabethan drama, Middleton's *A Chaste Maid in Cheapside*, first produced in all likelihood in 1613. A fitting sub-title for it might well be *The Anatomy of Matrimony*. The only thing I shall say about the plot of this comedy, which is quite complicated, is that the main line of it is provided by the efforts of two young lovers, Moll Yellowhammer, the daughter of a goldsmith in Cheapside, and Touchwood Junior, a gentleman whose prospects are poor, to marry one another.

14. Thomas Middleton, *Plays*, ed. Havelock Ellis (London, 1887), Vol. I.

Thwarted twice by Moll's parents, who intend her to marry a disgusting but titled individual of their own choice, Sir Walter Whorehound, the lovers ultimately achieve their goal, but only by pretending to die. And their sham deaths are, it seems to me, something more than a mere resort on the part of the author to what was, in the early seventeenth century, a well established theatrical trick. Rather, the sham deaths are Middleton's way of indicating the strength of the forces against which the lovers are doing battle, and the extreme lengths to which they are driven in their efforts to overcome that opposition.

This relationship between the lovers is the focus for a whole series of other relationships that I should like to consider one by one. In the first place—I am taking them in the order of their decency and respectability—there is that which exists between Touchwood Senior, the elder but not the eldest brother of Moll's lover, and his wife. It exposes a feature of Elizabethan marriage that is often forgotten. As a younger son, Touchwood Senior has, as he tells us himself, nothing (II.i.88). Nevertheless, he has married, and, when the play opens, he is facing the consequences of his phenomenal capacity for begetting children. Since they live in a world where contraceptive devices are unknown and unthought of, the only thing he and his wife can do to save themselves and the children they already have from the utter destitution that having yet more mouths to feed would bring with it is to part from each other. Touchwood tells his wife:

> we must give way to need,
> And live awhile asunder; our desires
> Are both too fruitful for our barren fortunes.
> How adverse runs the destiny of some creatures:
> Some only can get riches and no children,
> We only can get children and no riches! (II.i.7-12)[15]

Middleton enlists sympathy for the couple, and paints their situation with understanding, but he is also realistic about it. The relationship between them is not a romantic one. When his wife has expressed her obedience to his will, Touchwood praises her in the

15. Thomas Middleton, *A Chaste Maid in Cheapside*, ed. R. B. Parker (London, 1969).

following terms, which give the conventional view of what a wife ought to be:

> of all creatures
> I hold that wife a most unmatched treasure
> That can unto her fortunes fix her pleasure
> And not unto her blood: this is like wedlock;
> The feast of marriage is not lust but love
> And care of the estate. (II.i.46-51)

Moreover, while Touchwood Senior is fond of his wife after his fashion, he has no intention of forgoing the pleasures of which he is depriving her. He expects his wife to remain chaste during the period of their enforced separation, but looks forward to the opportunity for promiscuous riot among "country wenches" that it will give him. And, no sooner are the words out of his mouth than a Country Wench appears, carrying one of his bastards in her arms. He takes the double standard of morality for granted.

Over against Touchwood Senior and his wife are set Sir Oliver and Lady Kix. A "kix" or "kex" is the dried stalk of the hemlock plant; and Middleton's choice of it, for he is a great master of nomenclature, is significant. The Kixes are in trouble because their marriage, now seven years old, has proved fruitless; and they need an heir badly, since, should they fail to produce one, their estate will pass to the unspeakable Sir Walter Whorehound. The wife blames the husband—rightly, as it proves—for their childless state, and they spend their days in bickering and their money on quack remedies which are of no avail. The solution to their difficulties, and also to his own, is provided by the fertile Touchwood Senior. Posing as a specialist and charging a handsome fee for his services, he treats Sir Oliver by sending him off for a nice long ride in the country to tone up his system, and Lady Kix by ordering her to bed and then joining her there himself. The remedy (need I say it?) works perfectly, of course.

The next couple demanding consideration in Middleton's comprehensive survey of the married state in all its grim variety is the Yellowhammers. Well-to-do, with a son and daughter of marriageable age, this pair are intent on social climbing. They have sent their son Tim to Cambridge, where he is receiving the useless and, to him, totally unintelligible education in Latin and logic, which will, it is supposed, equip him to become a gentleman. Moll, the daughter, meanwhile remains at home, as daughters did. When the play begins, arrangements are already in hand for Moll to be married to Sir Walter Whorehound, a Welsh knight whose main interest in life is conveniently summed up in his name, while, in true aristocratic fashion, the alliance between the two families is to be further cemented by the wedding of Tim, who as yet knows nothing whatever about what is being planned for him, to Sir Walter's landed niece. I say "in true aristocratic fashion" because multiple cross-marriages were a common feature of upper-class life at the time. The most bizarre example I know of is the two subsidiary marriages which served as a prologue to the dynastic marriage in 1568 of George Talbot, Earl of Shrewsbury, himself a widower, to the celebrated Bess of Hardwick who had, by this time, already buried three previous husbands. Bess, who began life as the daughter of a Derbyshire squire, is the great example of how a woman could, with a bit of luck, achieve wealth and power in a man's world. She did it through marriage and through a kind of genius that she had for accepting men whose expectations of life were, roughly speaking, in inverse ratio to the size of their estates. In 1568 she was forty-four and the mother, by her second husband Sir William Cavendish, of three sons and three daughters. She was also the wealthiest woman in England, apart from the Queen. Taking advantage of this, she drove a hard bargain with Talbot. Set on the aggrandizement of the Cavendish family, she would not consent to marry him until he agreed that her eldest son Henry, who was then eighteen, should be wedded to Mary Talbot, the Earl's eldest daughter, and that his second son Gilbert—she could not get her claws into the eldest son, as he was married already—should be united to her youngest daughter Mary, who was then eleven. The double wedding of the two young couples took place early in 1568, and was followed almost immediately by the union of their parents.

To return to Middleton's comedy: Sir Walter Whorehound is exploiting the Yellowhammers' snobbery for his own ends. His desire to wed Moll is nothing more than a desire to lay his hands on her dowry of "two thousand pound in gold", while his "niece",

> A huge heir in Wales at least to nineteen mountains,
> Besides her goods and cattle (III.ii.109-10),

is, in truth, his cast-off mistress, whom he intends to palm off, and does palm off, on the unsuspecting Tim, whose expensive Cambridge education might almost have been designed to insure a total incapacity to see through the cheat.

Finally, to complete the picture of the matrimonial state, there is yet another couple, the Allwits. They, however, are man and wife only in name and in law. Mistress Allwit is Sir Walter's kept mistress, while Allwit, the "wittol" or contented cuckold, is quite happy to serve as a nominal father to the children Sir Walter begets on his wife, because it provides him with a steady income for doing nothing whatever. Immensely satisfied with his easy lot in life, Allwit voices his happiness in a long speech of self-congratulation, after hearing that Sir Walter has come to town. It begins thus:

> The founder's come to town: I am like a man
> Finding a table furnish'd to his hand,
> As mine is still to me, prays for the founder, —
> 'Bless the right worshipful the good founder's life.'
> I thank him, 'has maintain'd my house this ten years,
> Not only keeps my wife, but a keeps me
> And all my family: I am at his table;
> He gets me all my children, and pays the nurse
> Monthly or weekly; puts me to nothing,
> Rent, nor church-duties, not so much as the scavenger:
> The happiest state that ever man was born to! (I.ii.11-21)

Allwit's one anxiety is lest Sir Walter should marry. Discovering that he intends to do so, he goes to Yellowhammer and, under an assumed identity, tells him of Sir Walter's relations with Mistress Allwit. Apparently shaken by this news, Yellowhammer says that he will have no further dealings with Whorehound, but, no sooner has Allwit made his exit, than Yellowhammer's determination to sacrifice his wretched daughter on the altar of social advancement and money reasserts itself as he says:

> The knight is rich, he shall be my son-in-law;
> No matter, so the whore he keeps be wholesome,
> My daughter takes no hurt then; so let them wed:
> I'll have him sweat well ere they go to bed. (IV.i.247-50)

The callousness of the father is matched by the sheer brutality of the mother. When Moll runs away a second time in order to marry her lover, Mistress Yellowhammer hauls her out of the Thames boat in which she is escaping, drags her through the water by the hair of her head, and half-drowns her in the process. The Waterman, shocked by this spectacle, tells Touchwood Junior:

> Half drown'd! She cruelly
> Tugg'd her by the hair, forc'd her disgracefully,
> Not like a mother. (IV.iv.51-3)

Nor is there anything inherently improbable in this conduct. There were rumours that the unfortunate Frances Coke, whom I spoke about earlier, "was tyed to a bedposte and severely whipped" in order to make her consent to the match with Sir John Villiers that her father had arranged for her.[16] Confronted by this harsh sordid world, the lovers seem to stand little chance of realizing their hopes. But they have the poor on their side. The Waterman not only expresses pity for Moll when talking to her lover; he has already done his best to intervene on her behalf with that mother. Speaking to Moll, Mistress Yellowhammer cries:

> I'll tug thee home by the hair.

This is what follows:

> 1 *Waterman* Good mistress, spare her!
> *Maudline* Tend your own business.
> 2 *Waterman* You are a cruel mother. (IV.iv.19-20)

More important than the Watermen, however, is Susan, Moll's chambermaid. "Made of pity" (III.iii.30), Susan is also intelligent, and it is she who devises and executes the plan that eventually brings the lovers together. Furthermore, these representatives of common humanity, Susan and the Watermen, have public opinion with them. In some ways the most interesting speech in the entire play is made by Moll's father near the end of it. Moll has just swooned, and Yellowhammer, thinking she is dead, says to his wife:

> All the whole street will hate us, and the world
> Point me out cruel; it is our best course, wife,
> After we have given order for the funeral,
> To absent ourselves till she be laid in ground. (V.ii.92-5)

16. Lawrence Stone, *The Crisis of the Aristocracy, 1558-1641* (Oxford, 1965), p. 596.

The attitude of the street suggests that something was changing; and indeed it was, for while the arranged marriage was still the normal and approved way of doing things in Shakespeare's England, there was also some criticism of it and even some opposition to it coming from those who spoke to and wrote for the public at large. The moralists and preachers criticized it on two grounds: that it was all too often a manifestation of avarice, and that it led to adultery. But, since these same moralists and preachers still continued to assert that children must obey their parents in all things, they can hardly be regarded as out-and-out champions of freedom. A further factor was the growth of Puritanism, with its insistence on partnership between man and woman as one of the prime essentials in marriage, together with the general tendency of Protestantism at large to exalt the married state over the unmarried state. John Milton, for whom "the apt and cheerful conversation [meaning 'intimacy' in all its senses] of man with woman", rather than the begetting of children, was the true end of marriage, is scathing on the subject of the arranged match and sums up the enforced marriage thus:

> As for the custom that some Parents and Guardians have of forcing Marriages, it will be better to say nothing of such a savage inhumanity, but only thus, that the Law which gives not all freedom of divorce to any creature endued with reason so assassinated is next in cruelty.[17]

In his revolutionary ideas about divorce —and the passage I have just cited comes from his tract *The Doctrine and Discipline of Divorce*, first published in 1643 —Milton was, of course, far ahead of his time, but in his stress on mutual love and compatibility as the foundations of marriage he was at one with many of the Elizabethan dramatists. He, like some of the playwrights, had found delight in the writings of Spenser, where marriage is seen as the proper end and fulfilment of love; and romance, in its various forms, is the other main source from which opposition to the marriage conventions of the time was fed.

It is, perhaps, no accident that the most delightful and informative love letters that we have from the seventeenth century were written by Dorothy Osborne who was a great reader of romances, and especially of French romances. The situation in which she and Sir William Temple found themselves in the years 1652 to 1654 has

17. John Milton, *Milton's Prose*, ed. M. W. Wallace (Oxford, 1925), p. 202.

much in common with that of Romeo and Juliet. Deeply in love with Temple, she could not marry him, because her father, an ardent royalist who had suffered heavy fines after the victory of the parliamentary forces, was strongly opposed to a match between his daughter and the son of a family which had supported the other side in the Civil War. Temple's father was not in favour of the match either, though he had the good sense not to stand in his son's way when it became clear that the young man was determined. There the resemblance to Shakespeare's lovers ends. In 1652, when it all began, Dorothy was twenty-five, not fourteen, and she had more than a little of Jane Austen in her make-up. Temple was twenty-four, and by no means given to "fire-eyed fury". Moreover, all came came right for them in the end, because Dorothy's father died in 1654.

For two years, however, Dorothy had to resist one suitor after another, together with some very heavy pressure from her brother who was constantly urging the claims of these suitors; and the letters she wrote to Temple portray a conflict of loyalties which throws, I think, a most revealing light on the change that was gradually taking place in the general attitude to marriage. On the one hand, she had no faith whatever in the old proverb so often invoked to justify the arranged match: "Marry first and Love will come after" (Tilley, L534).[18] On the other, she was not so taken with the charms of romance as to ignore all prudential considerations, and regarded "a competency", as she puts it, as necessary for a happy marriage (pp. 138-9). Living in a world where, as she tells Temple, "(Almost) all are denyed the sattisfaction of disposeing themselves to their own desyr's" (p. 45), she was nevertheless fully alive to the unfortunate consequences of runaway matches, writing:

> To marry for Love were noe reproachfull thing if wee did not see that of ten thousand couples that doe it, hardly one can be brought for an Example that it may bee done & not repented afterwards. (p. 135)

But it was, above all, her respect for her father's will that held her back from taking any rash step. Attractive though she found the notion of marriage for love, the traditional pieties were even stronger. On July 2, 1653, when things were especially difficult, she wrote to Temple:

18. G. C. Moore Smith (ed.), *The Letters of Dorothy Osborne to William Temple* (Oxford, 1928), pp. 9-10.

sure the whole worlde could never perswade mee (unlesse a Parent commanded it) to marry one that I had noe Esteem for, and where I have any, I am not less scrupulous then your father, for I should never bee brought to do them the injury as to give them a wife whose affections they could never hope for, besydes that I must sacrifice my self int and live a walking missery till the only hope that would then be left mee, were perfected. (p. 62)

As one reads that one realizes that John Ford's Penthea in *The Broken Heart* may not be as remote from the pressures of living in the actual world as, on a first acquaintance with the play, one is inclined to think.

In speaking of Dorothy Osborne and Sir William Temple I mentioned Romeo and Juliet. What, you may well feel like asking on hearing those names, does the greatest dramatist of the age have to tell us about the matters I have been discussing? Were they for him an essential part of the "form and pressure" of "the very age and body of the time", which, according to Hamlet, if not to his creator, it was "the purpose of playing" to present to the audience? It is a good question; and I shall attempt to offer a short answer to it.

Shakespeare knew all about the "facts" that I have been describing. He puts them into the dialogue between Lysander and Hermia that comes immediately after Theseus and the rest have left the stage in the opening scene of *A Midsummer Night's Dream*, a dialogue that runs thus:

> *Lysander* How now, my love! Why is your cheek so pale?
> How chance the roses there do fade so fast?
> *Hermia* Belike for want of rain, which I could well
> Beteem them from the tempest of my eyes.
> *Lysander* Ay me! for aught that I could ever read,
> Could ever hear by tale or history,
> The course of true love never did run smooth;
> But either it was different in blood —
> *Hermia* O cross! too high to be enthrall'd to low.
> *Lysander* Or else misgraffed in respect of years —
> *Hermia* O spite! too old to be engag'd to young.
> *Lysander* Or else it stood upon the choice of friends —
> *Hermia* O hell! to choose love by another's eyes.
> *Lysander* Or if there were a sympathy in choice,
> War, death, or sickness, did lay siege to it,

Making it momentary as a sound,
Swift as a shadow, short as any dream,
Brief as the lightning in the collied night
That, in a spleen, unfolds both heaven and earth,
And ere a man hath power to say 'Behold!'
The jaws of darkness do devour it up;
So quick bright things come to confusion. (I.i.128-49)[19]

In that formalized verse-duet Shakespeare has said everything
that I have said in this paper and more, with this crucial difference:
that he has turned it all into something of quite extraordinary
beauty. And it is for this capacity of his, above all others, I think,
that we value him so highly. There are indeed plays of his which
deal with the matters I have been describing in some detail. In *The
Taming of the Shrew* Petruchio makes no bones about his reason for
coming to Padua:

I come to wive it wealthily in Padua;
If wealthily, then happily in Padua. (I.ii.73-4)

He marries Katherina first and wins her love afterwards. In the
same play we are shown the old father Baptista virtually putting up
his second daughter, Bianca, for auction, and knocking her down to
the higher bidder. In *The Merry Wives of Windsor* Page plans to
marry his daughter to one suitor, while her mother plans to marry
her to another; and the third suitor, Master Fenton, admits candidly
that her father's wealth "Was the first motive that I woo'd thee,
Anne" (III.iv.14). In *All's Well That Ends Well*, where the King of
France exerts his power to make Bertram wed Helena, Shakespeare
dramatizes an enforced marriage. But then, as in *The Taming of the
Shrew*, something unexpected happens: we are not asked to extend
our sympathy to Bertram as a victim; instead, he is presented as
both foolish and callous when he refuses to consummate the match
he has consented to. Moreover, whether we read these plays or see
them, we have the feeling that they are, in some way, outside the
mainstream of Shakespeare's comic writing.

So where does Shakespeare stand on the issues I have been
raising? I think we begin to see the answer if we look for a moment

19. The text used for this and subsequent quotations from the works of Shakespeare is
that of Peter Alexander (ed.), *The Complete Works* (London and Glasgow, 1951).

at one of the happiest of the comedies, *A Midsummer Night's Dream*. At the opening we find Egeus seeking to force his daughter Hermia into a loveless match with Demetrius, despite her avowed love for Lysander. And he receives the support of Duke Theseus, because his action has the sanction of a law, "Which," says Theseus, "by no means we may extenuate" (i.i.20). Yet, when the events of the night are over, and each Jack has found his proper Jill, Theseus does not hesitate to abrogate that law, because it has shown itself an ass. The play asserts the reality and the importance of dreams, of ideals, and among them is the dream of men and women making their own choices in marriage. The same ideal lies behind the other happy comedies, and lead to such trenchant challenges to the status quo as that made by Beatrice in *Much Ado About Nothing*, when, after Antonio has said to Hero "Well, niece, I trust you will be rul'd by your father," she adds:

> Yes, faith; it is my cousin's duty to make curtsy, and say 'Father, as it please you'. But yet for all that, cousin, let him be a handsome fellow, or else make another curtsy and say 'Father, as it please me'. (ii.i.42-7)

I should dearly like to know how the original audience for the play, somewhere about the year 1598, responded to that sally, which must have been at least as delightfully shocking then as Liza Doolittle's "Not bloody likely" would be some three hundred years later.

The comedies we think of as romantic are truly romantic in that, like all romantic art, they shadow forth glorious ideals, some possible of realization, some impossible of realization, but all serving, at least by implication, to bring out the deficiencies, the errors, and the tyranny of that which exists. And this is true also of the great tragedies. Desdemona's "downright violence and storm of fortunes" in order to live with the Moor she loves gives concrete form on the stage to something that has yet to be realized, in any full or convincing fashion, in the world we know and live in.

How far and in what manner art affects life, and especially the quality of life, is a topic I have neither the time nor the ability to take up. What I do want to suggest, in conclusion, is that what Shakespeare has to say about love and marriage touches us at a much deeper level that what Middleton says, though it is Middleton and others like him who tell us far more, in terms of factual detail, about the way these matters were viewed and dealt with in

Shakespeare's England. And what Shakespeare says touches us at this deeper level because it comes to us through the ideal figures he creates and through the heightened language he gives them. *Romeo and Juliet* is an integral part of the consciousness of the modern world. Composers in particular have been drawn to it time after time; but who can imagine a Berlioz or a Tchaikovsky writing a Touchstone Junior and Moll Yellowhammer overture? The thing is unthinkable; the very names forbid it; and so does the play, for these two are precisely the characters in it who never come to life. Middleton is a master of dissection, but he does not know how to breathe life into a dream. Shakespeare does; and into no other idea did he breathe more life than that of love as an absolute value. When a character we are clearly meant to approve of, and the poet himself, speak with one voice, what they say carries unusual weight and authority. In the first scene of *King Lear*, the King of France turns to his rival the Duke of Burgundy and asks him, referring to the dowerless Cordelia:

> What say you to the lady? Love's not love
> When it is mingled with regards that stands
> Aloof from th'entire point. Will you have her?
> She is herself a dowry. (I.i. 238-41)

And whenever I hear those words, which are a complete rejection of Elizabethan marriage as I described it earlier, my mind leaps spontaneously to the opening of Sonnet 116:

> Let me not to the marriage of true minds
> Admit impediments. Love is not love
> Which alters when it alteration finds....

However Shakespeare the man may have acted and behaved in his private life, the faith of Shakepeare the artist seems clear enough.

The Contributors

WILLIAM BABULA, Professor of English, University of Miami. Author of articles on Shakespeare, Elizabethan Drama and Modern Drama.

M. C. BRADBROOK, Mistress of Girton College and Professor of English, University of Cambridge. Author of *Themes and Conventions of Elizabethan Tragedy, Ibsen the Norwegian, Conrad: England's Polish Genius, The Growth and Structure of Elizabethan Comedy, Shakespeare and Elizabethan Poetry, The Rise of the Common Player*, other books and numerous articles.

NEIL CARSON, Professor of English, University of Guelph. Author of articles on Shakespeare, Elizabethan Drama and Modern Drama.

R. A. FOAKES, Professor of English, University of Kent, Canterbury. Author of *The Romantic Assertion, Shakespeare: The Dark Comedies and the Last Plays;* editor (with R. T. Rickert) of *Henslowe's Diary, The Revenger's Tragedy,* etc.; and author of numerous articles.

W. R. GAIR, Professor of English, University of New Brunswick. Editor of *Antonio's Revenge,* and author of articles on Elizabethan Theatre, Elizabethan Drama and Milton.

G. R. HIBBARD, Professor of English, University of Waterloo. Author of *Thomas Nashe: A Critical Introduction* and numerous articles; editor of several volumes in the New Penguin Shakespeare and of *Bartholomew Fair* in the New Mermaids.

RICHARD HOSLEY, Professor of English, University of Arizona. Author of the section on Playhouses in *The Revels History of Drama in English,* Volume III, and of numerous articles; editor of *Essays on Shakespeare and Elizabethan Drama in Honor of Hardin Craig, Shakespeare's Holinshed,* etc.

STANLEY WELLS, Reader in English and Fellow of the Shakespeare Institute, University of Birmingham. Author of *Literature and Drama: with Special Reference to Shakespeare and his Contemporaries,* and of numerous articles. Associate Editor of the New Penguin Shakespeare, for which he had edited several volumes.

Index